Love

Lies

&

Fight

By Terri D and Julie Bellatrix

ISBN 978-0-9831887-6-6

Prologue

My name is Joy Dickerson. I am a Licensed Professional Counselor. I have been in this field since graduating from college over 15 years ago. I wanted to become a counselor ever since I was a teenager. My mom died when I was sixteen and my older brother Darien and his wife Toni took me in while struggling to deal with my mother's sudden death, which I felt somewhat responsible for. I never knew my father, so it was a difficult time for me. I found myself in the middle of major adult drama between my brother Darien, his wife Toni, and their circle of friends. There were a lot of secrets, lies and half-truths amongst them all. Ultimately my brother Darien lost his life by being in the wrong place at the wrong time as a direct result of the drama between their friends. After my experience as a teenager I vowed to help others by becoming a counselor.

This story is not about me though. This is a story about one of my clients named Valerie. Valerie's story is shared with her permission, names and other details being changed to protect the privacy of those involved. I have worked with many clients over the years, but Valerie is different. Once you read her story you will understand why. The title sums up her journey. She experienced love, she was betrayed by the lies she had been told, and then she fought to regain her strength and confidence to move forward.

Chapter 1

After spending many years working as a counselor at an addiction clinic just outside of Richmond, I decided to join the virtual counseling movement for some extra cash. I signed up with Empowerment Insights to work with clients via video sessions and through email chats. I was more old school and preferred to interact with my clients face to face, but I was willing to give this a try. My first few clients were the usual relationship issues or young women trying to figure out their purpose in life. It was hard not to see some of my younger self in these women.

I had come a long way over the years, but even the best counselors need someone they can talk to from time to time. I still connected with my favorite therapist, Robin, at least once a month. At first it was a therapist-client relationship, but over the years it seemed like we both needed each other to vent to and since then we have become great friends. Robin is the one who encouraged me to branch out and try video counseling. She felt I might be stuck in a bit of a rut dealing with the addiction clients. At first, I was extremely passionate about my work in the addiction field. My passion was fueled by the loss of a close friend's partner. The pain she endured while the addiction was active and the suffering after he overdosed was hard to watch. I was on a mission to do as much as I could to help as many addicts and their families as possible.

About two years ago the clinic where I have been working was bought by a new company and things have not been the same. We have shifted from dealing with true drug addicts, you know the ones, without private insurance to gambling and sex addicts. These were the 'high end' clients with great insurance or wealthy families to foot the bill. They were mostly men and over time the clinic began to look more and more like a country club than an actual clinic. Just a little while longer and I could leave and retain some benefits. That was the only thing good about the sale of the company, the employees got to keep their tenure and rich benefits package.

I hurried home to prepare for my evening video clients. My time with Empowerment Insights was my own. I was an independent contractor. I set my own hours and decided how many clients I would take on. I retired to my office to review the files of the clients I had for the day while nibbling on my turkey sandwich. When I first read the summary for Valerie, my first thought was that she probably was a typical middle-aged woman suffering from empty nest syndrome. I had no idea she would be the client that would forever change my life.

I logged into the video session a few minutes early and waited for Valerie to join. She joined right on time. I wasn't sure what to expect but the woman who appeared on the screen looked tired, no, not just tired; her eyes looked vacant, void of emotion or feeling. She was a middle-aged Caucasian woman with shoulder length curly brown hair. I found myself wondering if those were natural curls. Either way the style suited her.

"Hello Valerie, my name is Joy. How are you today?" She hesitated for a moment before responding. I waited patiently while thinking this might be a little harder than I thought.

"Hi Joy. Um, I'm okay I guess." She said while trying to sound a little less annoyed than she really was. I could tell that Valerie really didn't want to be doing this right now.

"Okay, well, let us just jump right in. Tell me why you're meeting with me today?"

"I was told this was a requirement for my release from the hospital." Her voice sounding very monotone.

I nodded and said, "How long have you been home?"

"It's been about a week."

I looked down briefly to make a note, then continued. "How have things been going since you have been back home?"

"Things have been going okay, I guess. I did manage to make it to church on Sunday by myself."

"That is great you were able to do that Valerie. Let me get some additional information. Are you currently taking any medications?" I asked while making a note about church being important to her.

"Yes, but I don't have that information with me right now."

"It's okay you can just email me the names of the medications and their dosage when we get off this call." She nodded but did not respond.

"Are you seeing any other doctors at this time?" Valerie seemed a little uncomfortable, but I did not understand why.

She sat up a little and asked, "Why do you need to know that? Are you going to contact them and talk about me?"

I shook my head while jotting down another quick note, potential trust issues. "No, Valerie, absolutely not, I just like to have an idea of everything that's going on with my clients, but if you're not comfortable sharing, it's fine. Let us move on, okay?" She relaxed a bit and I continued. "Can you tell me a little bit about your hospital stay?"

"I was in the psychiatric ward for two weeks over at the Medical Center."

"I see and did you check yourself in for treatment?" I sensed by her body language my question had struck a nerve. Her body tensed up and she hesitated for a moment, took a deep breath, and said softly but with clenched teeth, "Absolutely not. I was taken there under false pretenses."

"By whom and do you know why this person felt you needed to be committed?"

She began to shake her head. "I still don't have all of the facts but what I do know is my next-door neighbor, Paula, told me we were going to a psychologist appointment for my youngest son."

"How old is your son?"

"I have two boys, the oldest, Scott is a sophomore in college at UVA, he's twenty and my youngest, David, is a senior in high school and he's seventeen." Talking about her children seemed to perk her up a bit.

"Okay, why would your neighbor think you would believe your son would need to see a psychologist?"

Valerie let out a heavy sigh. "Because he was home with me when everything happened." I could see Valerie tensing up again. She closed her eyes tight as if she were trying to block out a painful memory.

I let her go for a minute or so and then said, "Valerie, are you still with me?"

She opened her eyes. "Ah, yes I'm sorry, the medications make me a little groggy and it's hard to focus sometimes."

"Yes, I completely understand. I asked you what happened prior to your hospital stay that led you to believe your son needed to see a psychologist?"

"Oh gosh, there's just so much. I'm not exactly sure where to start." She put her head down and covered her face as she shook her head.

"I understand, but just tell me what you think is the most important thing for me to know right now in order to understand why you would feel your son needed to see a psychologist."

She nodded to indicate she understood my request, took a deep breath, lifted her head and then responded, "My youngest son, David, was at home the night, um, my husband Seth came home and told me he was being accused of drugging and raping someone he worked with." Her voice trailed off and she closed her eyes as if she were trying to erase the painful memory.

Her matter of fact tone and lack of emotion surprised me. I thought to myself that I would be hysterically crying if I had to explain this to someone. "Oh, I see, so how did David react?" Valerie's eyes were still closed, but I knew she heard me and was preparing to answer because I noticed her body tensing up again.

"When Seth was explaining everything to me in the living room, David was right upstairs and could hear everything. I wanted to make sure David understood the situation, so Seth called for David to come down. Seth told David about the allegations and he attempted to minimize it by saying he had friends that had similar legal problems before, and everything turned out okay."

"Yes, I agree, that is a lot for a child to deal with. Okay now tell me how you reacted when you first heard the news?"

Valerie slowly reached for a bottle of water and took a sip before responding. "I am, I mean I was angry and very emotional. I had just had a hysterectomy a few days before this all happened. I was devastated but I knew I had to try and be strong for my kids. Seth left after talking to David and headed to our house in Charlottesville. David and I thought we would hear from Seth when he met up with Scott a few hours later, but we never heard anything that night or most of the next day. We both were not able to sleep much. I tried to hold things together the best I could for him, but it was hard especially once it hit the news later that week. That is why I thought it would be good for him to talk with someone about the whole situation."

"I see so I think it might be helpful if you gave me a little bit more information about your marriage."

She sighed and responded. "My husband, Seth, whom I've been with for the past twenty-five years, came home a few weeks ago to tell me he was being accused of this heinous crime. He assured me he had not done what he was being accused of. He also told me he expected it to hit the news within the next few days and at the advice of his criminal attorney he needed to leave the house. He advised me to unplug the house phone to avoid phone calls from the media."

"Okay, hold on Valerie. I am missing some key information here. What does your husband do for a living?"

"He's a member of the State Senate. We live in Chatham, but he stays at the house we bought in Richmond quite a bit due to his work there."

"I see and how long has he been in politics?"

"It's been about fifteen years."

"That's a long time. Do you feel things have gotten worse since he's been involved in politics?"

"I think that was a part of it, but that wasn't the only thing."

"Okay at this point he's come home and told you about these charges, but he's claiming to be innocent?"

"Yes, that's correct."

"Has he ever cheated before?"

"No, I mean yes, well that night he did admit to cheating on me in the past, which he had previously denied in marriage counseling. I let him know right then and there I would be filing for divorce."

"He tells you he's being accused of drugging and raping a woman; he denies it but then admits he has cheated with other women in the past and just not this woman?"

She nodded and explained further. "He told me the night of the incident he had attended several work receptions, so he had a few drinks which was normal for him to do. While telling me this, he admitted he knew his drinking was a problem and he planned to address it. I had absolutely no faith that he would follow through on that promise. His issue with drinking had been evident for years, but he never wanted to admit there was a problem. He said when he woke up the next morning there was a woman in his bed, but he did not think or remember doing anything with her. I asked him if this type of thing had happened before. He said yes it had, and that is when he finally admitted to being unfaithful to me. He admitted to cheating on me with other women, saying while it went on for years, he was not emotionally attached to anyone as if that made it all better."

"No judgment here at all, but why did you immediately jump to divorce?"

"He and I already had a lot of issues with our marriage and this was the final straw. I saw this was finally my way out."

"Okay, Valerie, we've covered a lot, and our time is almost up. I think this is a good place to stop."

"Yes, I'm feeling very tired and could use a nap."

"Okay, I understand. So how about this? Email me your list of medications. You can email me anytime you want, and I will respond as soon as possible. When you are ready you can schedule our next session.'"

"Yes, that would be fine. I'll email you the information."

"Great and I look forward to hearing from you again soon."

I had a short break before my next client. I made myself a few more notes about my conversation with Valerie. I really needed to know what medications she was taking because her overall mood did not match the things she shared with me. I expected to see a lot more emotion than I was seeing. I got up to stretch my legs a bit. I walked into the kitchen to grab a bottle of water. I found myself wondering what Valerie thought about me, a younger African American woman, being her therapist. Maybe she felt as if I couldn't relate to her situation and in some ways; maybe I couldn't. I stood in the kitchen and thought about how after being with her husband for over twenty-five years, Valerie was more than eager to throw in the towel. I knew there was much more to this story, but I wondered if she felt like it was worth it or not?

I had given up on love over fifteen years ago. I loved a man once; I fell for him hard. We made plans for a wonderful future together. He broke me and I never looked back, never felt I really missed out on anything. Seeing the pain and disappointment in Valerie's eyes made me wonder. Is love worth the pain?

Chapter 2

A few days passed with no word from Valerie. I had taken on a few other new clients, but my mind continued to drift back to my session with Valerie. Robin and I had plans to talk later tonight and I wanted to discuss how I have been feeling with her. As I drove home, I turned on the smooth jazz station and enjoyed the music while thinking about what I wanted to share with Robin later. When I pulled up to my house, I sat in the car for a few minutes just staring at the house. I remember how proud I was when I bought this house, a cozy Cape Cod. I remember the realtor saying these were perfect for small families or first-time home buyers. I'm still proud, but I'm realizing that the expression a house doesn't make a home is very true. I grabbed my bags and headed into the house with heavy thoughts on my mind.

My client session was uneventful. A young college girl who is processing how to handle her newfound freedom and how to handle her parents' divorce. Parents who hold on until the kids are grown to get divorced do not understand they keep counselors in business. Children are resilient. Divorce is difficult, but they can survive it. For young adults it comes at the worst time for them. They are already struggling to find themselves and when their normal is also blown up, it is often times too much for them to handle. They are curious and exploring and unfortunately many make poor choices and end up as my addiction clients.

As I made dinner and prepared to talk to Robin. I checked the time and my phone rang; Robin is always punctual.

I answered, "Hey Robin, how are you?"

"I'm great and you?"

"I'm good, I can't complain. Well I guess I could but what good would it do?"

She laughed. "Yeah, you are right. Does no good to complain. I'm eager to hear what you think about the online counseling."

"It's interesting, I think I'm getting the hang of it."

"How many clients did you take?"

"I initially just accepted three, but I just added two more this week."

"Okay five is a good start."

"Yeah, but I think I might be down to four again."

"Oh, why is that?"

"My one client hasn't gotten back to me yet."

"How long has it been?"

"Today is the fourth day."

"That isn't too terribly long. How did you leave things with them?"

"Well, I expected her to send me an email with the list of her medications and I reminded her she can email me whenever she wants, but I have not heard anything from her at all."

"You could email her and remind her about the medications and see if you can start the conversation again that way."

"Yeah, I thought about that, but there's something else that's bothering me a little bit."

"Like what?"

"I am not sure. I have not been able to stop thinking about her story since we spoke, and I feel like I've been so emotional since then also. It's interesting because during our session she displayed very little emotion and based on the things she shared with me there should have been a lot."

"Hmm, that is interesting."

"I knew you would say that."

"So you know what I'm going to ask you next right?"

"Yes, I do Robin."

"So, what is it?"

"I see a woman who is a little older than me, but our lives took quite different paths. She's married with children."

"Okay, I see. Her situation is making you question your choices?"

"No, I am not questioning my choices not consciously, but I find myself wondering if she is questioning hers or feeling any regret."

"Of course, I do not know all of the details, but it is not your place to ask those questions, at least not directly to her, not this early in your relationship with her."

"You are right, but I really am concerned about her lack of emotion. I need to find out what medications she is on in order to get a better sense of why there's a bit of a disconnect between her story and her emotions or lack thereof. I'm going to just send her an email to check in and leave it at that."

Robin and I continued to chat for another half hour or so. As soon as we hung up, I went into my office to check my email messages. Nothing from Valerie yet so I sent her the following message.

Valerie,

Just touching base with you because it has been a few days since our session. I was expecting to hear from you by now, at least the medication list. I hope all is well and please let me know you are okay even if you have decided not to continue counseling services with me.

Joy

I did have a few emails from my other clients, so I read through them and responded accordingly. Just as I was finishing up for the night and about to log off, I received a response from Valerie.

Joy,

I apologize for the delay in responding to you. Things have been hectic here the past few days. I went to Charlottesville to visit Scott. I also have had so many appointments. I had my first session with my psychiatrist which I am required to do to keep from ending up back in the hospital. I also met with my attorney to get things moving on my divorce. Prior to that I visited Seth at the clinic because I knew he was going through a rough time and I wanted to be supportive. You might think that is silly of me to want to be supportive of him after all that has happened, but I felt good about it. I am still not taking him back even though he seemed extremely remorseful in the letters he sent me.

The medication is still making me very groggy, so I have not been able to find the time to email you until now. I am currently taking Zyprexa 30 mg in the morning and Lithium 300 mg twice a day. I also wanted to give you a little bit more information about my situation before our next video session which I scheduled for the day after tomorrow.

Anyway, Seth and I had problems in our marriage for many years. I had ignored advice from others to get out because I really did not know how to make that happen although I thought about it a lot. In the past when we were having problems, I felt with Seth's political connections he would have the best attorneys if I tried to file for divorce so it would be quite a battle. At one point when I no longer felt Seth was there for me or the kids, I had trial separation paperwork written up. He was furious I had taken this step. If he agreed to go to counseling, I would not take further action. We did start going to therapy, so I contacted the attorney and let him know we had reconciled but I kept his contact information.

With everything that has taken place I have decided it is time for a fresh start. Things had already seemed to be getting much worse over the past several months. The night Seth told me what was going on I immediately sent an email to the attorney I had dealt with before and let him know I had an urgent situation to address. He responded and gave me an outline of exactly what to do.

Anyway, it's late, and I am tired so I will close for now. We can talk further during my next session.

Valerie

My suspicions were confirmed. Valerie was on an extremely high dose of medication. That explains her emotionless demeanor. Even though she said no response was necessary I decided to send one.

Valerie,

Thanks for sharing the additional information with me about your marriage. I look forward to talking to you tomorrow and since our time is so short, I would like to tell you what my questions are, so you have time to think about them before our session.

I would like for you to tell me why you felt things had gotten worse over the past few months leading up to your husband's confession?

You mentioned you previously went to marriage counseling together. How long did that last and did things improve?

I think that will be enough for us to cover during our next session. I will talk to you then.

Joy

Chapter 3

I had a restless night, I tossed and turned for a while before drifting off to sleep and then I awoke around 4 am and could not get back to sleep. I do not typically have trouble sleeping, this only happens to me when I am not dealing with something. Finally, around 5 am, I gave up on sleep and got up to start my day; albeit much earlier than usual. I showered and stood staring at my clothes for at least five minutes. Although it was chilly outside which was appropriate for February, the office was always very warm. Once I decided on an outfit, black slacks and a sheer long-sleeved teal colored shirt, I got dressed for work and went down to my office to review my calendar for the day.

I logged on and read the email from Valerie again. Even though we were scheduled to talk the next day I decided to respond to her email.

I checked my schedule and it looked like a light day, which I was grateful for since I did not sleep well. I also only had one video session tonight after work at the clinic. I could catch up on my sleep tonight. I grabbed my bags and headed out the door to work. The brisk air hit me as I stepped outside which caused me to rethink my decision to wear this blouse. I hurried to my car and cranked up the heat. I switched the radio to my favorite morning talk show and started my commute.

I arrived at work a little early and decided to drink my morning tea in the breakroom and catch up on my social media before going to my office to start my day. I noticed a few other counselors were in the corner chatting amongst themselves while sipping their coffee. I was instantly reminded why I rarely came into the breakroom; the smell of coffee turns my stomach. I found a small table as far away from the coffee as possible and settled in. A few other therapists walked in, filled up their coffee mugs and walked over to the table where the other therapists were sitting. They began talking about their lives, boyfriends, husbands, and kids. I thought to myself, I have absolutely nothing to add to that conversation. I immediately began to feel a little sad. I should at least have a boyfriend to chit chat about. I checked the time and was almost time for my first appointment of the day. I gathered up my things and walked down the hall to my office. Something is still floating around in my subconscious which has me a little off-kilter. I shake it off, sit down at my desk, and pull the file for my first client of the day. It is Martha, she is one of my favorite clients. Honestly, she has been in and out of this clinic for a couple of years now. Every time she comes back, she asks for me. I challenged her after the third time. I said, 'Clearly I am not doing a good job if you keep coming back.' Martha laughed and said, 'You are looking at it all wrong my dear. Maybe I am coming back just to see you.' She winked and strutted over to her favorite chair. She was a spunky old lady with silver hair that reminds me of my grandmother. She had a terrible gambling addiction that has plagued her for most of her adult life, but in spite of all of that she felt as if she had lived a very fulfilling life and she did not apologize for it.

Martha arrives and gently taps on the doorframe. I look up from my desk, smile and welcome her into my office.

"Good morning Martha, how are you feeling today?"

"I'm feeling pretty good Joy, and you?" I resisted the urge to tell her that I did not sleep well last night because Martha had a habit of deflecting the attention from herself to others.

"I am well, thanks for asking." I moved from behind my desk to the chair next to Martha's and continued, "So, Martha did you do your homework?" She looked away for a moment then turned back to me.

"Well, not all of it."

I sighed. "Martha, do you want to get out of here?" She began to rock back and forth in her chair wringing her hands which is something she did when she was trying to avoid conflict. I asked again, "Martha, you need to answer me. Do you want to leave here?" She continued to rock back and forth, and she was looking down at her hands. I decided to wait it out, let the silence become uncomfortable until she spoke up.

Finally, after about five minutes of silence Martha raised her head up, looked at me and said, "Joy, I'm afraid to leave here."

"Afraid? Why is that Martha? I have known you for several years now and I have never heard you use the word afraid or express fear." She paused for a minute and said in a soft voice just above a whisper,

"I am afraid of dying alone."

"Oh, Martha why are you worried about dying? You are in better shape than most people much younger than you."

She chuckled. "Yes, that is true, but I am still an old lady. I have outlived three husbands and all but one of my children. My grandchildren no longer want me in their lives, I do not blame them though. I have burned so many bridges with my family over the years."

"You have had some rough times that is for sure, but I never got the impression that your family had given up on you."

She nodded her head. "This last time was pretty bad for everyone."

"Tell me what happened Martha? Why are you back here again after only being gone for less than two months?"

"Well Joy when I first got home, I tried really hard to stay away from the casino but after a few weeks I just could not help myself. At first, I just drove there and sat in my car. I did not go in. One time I sat there in my car for so long the security guard stopped and asked if I was okay. After that I left and went home but a few days later I returned. I went inside and did not leave for a few days. That is why I am back here."

My session with Martha went a few minutes over which caused everything to run late for the remainder of the day. Thankfully, Martha's was the most difficult, but I do think we made some great progress and I might be finally getting to the root of her issues. When she mentioned about being afraid of dying alone, I really felt her emotion because I too worry that I may always be alone.

Finally finished up with my last client of the day, made some minor adjustments to my schedule for the next day to fit another session in with Martha and I was on my way out the door. Right before I reached the door my supervisor Bill stopped me, "Joy, glad I caught you. Do you have a minute or are you in a hurry?"

I really wanted to get home, I was exhausted but instead I said, "Sure, Bill I have a few minutes." I turned and followed him to his office. He held the door for me and closed it behind him. I took a seat by his desk and waited for him to sit down.

"Joy, I've been thinking about making some changes and I wanted to run a few things past you about how I see your role."

I was intrigued and said, "I'm all ears Bill. Tell me more."

"I've been thinking about having you work more with me on policies and procedures, maybe look at starting that mentoring program again that we used to have."

Although I was very interested, I wondered what this meant from a time perspective. I already had taken on online counseling, so I was not interested in having to be here at the clinic more. I asked, "How do you see this impacting my client schedule and general work hours?"

"I think we could reduce your client hours a bit and it would mean that you and I would be spending more time together as you work in a more administrative role."

I leaned back a little in my chair as I thought about his proposal. It sounded very intriguing, but I couldn't help but think there was a little more to this then he was letting on. I noticed he emphasized that he and I would be spending more time together. "Okay this sounds like something I may be interested in, but can I have some time to think about it?"

"I know how you feel about your clients and I respect your position, however, I could really use your help on this one Joy. You are one of my most senior therapists and this is a great opportunity."

I nodded my head in agreement. "Ok Bill, I'll give it some more thought and get back to you."

He stood up and reached out his hand, I stood and shook his hand.

"Thanks, so much Joy, I really appreciate you giving this idea some consideration."

As I drove home, I felt excited about the possibility of being in the role of mentor again. It had been awhile since I had been in that role. The thought of being able to work with Bill to develop policies and procedures was also very appealing to me. Maybe this challenge was exactly what I needed to get myself out of this rut I have been in for the past few days. Even though it seemed like a wonderful opportunity, I couldn't shake the feeling that Bill might be trying to get closer to me on a more personal level and that was not something I was interested in at all.

*****

At work the next day I felt excited and motivated. My conversation with Bill had given me a fresh outlook on how I could affect some positive changes. I wasn't quite ready to share my excitement with him, but I was fairly certain I would accept his proposal.

I logged in and checked my emails and was surprised when I saw one from Bill. It was a meeting invitation to discuss my new role. I shook my head in disbelief. I hadn't even accepted yet. I decided to respond as tentative and I continued to review my other emails and then decided to review my schedule to see if Martha had made another appointment and she had, I would see her again later this morning.

I was still annoyed by Bill's meeting invite, but I decided to focus on Martha. I pulled her file and reviewed my notes from our last session, and I went into my archives files to pull her older files to review them as well.

About an hour later, I was sitting on my sofa reading through Martha's files when I heard a knock on my door. I looked up and saw Bill standing in my doorway. I stood up.

"Hello, Bill I saw your invitation and responded."

He stepped inside my office and closed the door. "Yes, I know, that is why I am here. I decided to talk to you in person versus sending emails back and forth." His tone concerned me greatly. He motioned for me to sit down, so I backed up and sat back on the sofa. He sat in the chair I usually sit in while talking to my clients. "I'll start with the easy part first." I nodded and he continued, "The conversation we had yesterday, I really wasn't 100% up front with you. It really wasn't just a suggestion Joy. It's something that is going to happen."

"Okay, why do I feel like that is just the tip of the iceberg?"

He nervously chuckled. "Well, Joy I have always liked your intuitiveness, you are absolutely correct in your assessment of this situation."

I sat up a little in my chair to give Bill my full attention. After a brief pause, he stood up and began pacing back and forth. He began to tell me how corporate was making changes and since I was one of the more senior therapists I had been flagged as someone to work on the project. I really did not have a choice. They wanted me to reduce my client hours to half of what they are now and for me to spend the other time working with Bill.

"Bill, I have to be honest with you. I left here last night very excited about the opportunity and all the possibilities. With that said I became a therapist because I like helping people. I never saw myself in an administrative role and certainly am not interested in a management position."

He laughed. "Joy I know you very well and I knew that you would have concerns about being taken away from your clients. I promise you that we can ease into this transition. You will keep everyone you already have, and we will determine how any new ones are assigned to you. I promise you will still get to work with clients."

"Okay Bill, I trust you and yes, since you and I have worked together so long, you do know how much I enjoy the work that I do. Any idea on the timing of this transition in my schedule?"

"Actually, I think we should plan on making this adjustment immediately. Why don't you review your clients and where they are in their treatment today? Get back to me tomorrow with a summary of where they are and how much more time you think you will need to work with them. How does that sound?"

"That's fine Bill, but please promise that you will allow me to finish with everyone that I am already working with and if Martha returns again, she will be assigned to me also."

He nodded and said, "Yes, Joy, I promise." He got up and said, "Thanks Joy, I really appreciate you." As he walked to the door and opened it and left.

I glanced at the clock and realized Martha would be arriving shortly. I gathered up her files that were all over the sofa and table and threw them on my desk and quickly went to the restroom.

When I returned Martha was waiting for me, but she was not her usual self. She looked worn, almost as if she had aged since yesterday.

We jumped right into the session picking up where we left off yesterday.

Martha shared with me she did not sleep well the night before. She thought a lot about the things we discussed, and she told me she felt very unsettled all night. It was the question I asked her about why she felt she continued to come back here, repeatedly. After a little prodding she finally opened up and shared with me what she thought about that.

Previously Martha had always told me she loved to go to the casinos because she would go there with her late husband and it reminded her of him. Martha had been married three times but as the saying goes the third time was the charm for her. She absolutely adored her third husband. I remember her telling me he made her wish her life started the day she met him. That is saying a lot because she had children with the other husbands. Martha has lived a very full life. All her husbands were wealthy which made the whole gambling thing hard for me to understand. If you already have millions of dollars, why risk losing it that way?

Today Martha told me although the casinos did remind her of her late husband, she knows she has a gambling problem and she wants to stop. She comes here and gets treatment and then she leaves. When she goes home, she is all alone. Her relationship with her children had deteriorated over the years since she married the last time. Her only surviving child, a daughter, does not come to visit or even call. She told me the casino is always open, and it is a safe place for her to go because everyone knows her there. She said she hardly ever gambles anymore when she goes, she just does not want to be home alone. Coming here is also an escape for her. I can see a heavy weight had been lifted from Martha as she spoke the truth to me. I asked if she felt like she could repair her relationship with her daughter or not. She asked for some time to think about it and we decided to discuss it some more in our next session.

Between my conversation with Bill and my session with Martha I was whipped, and it was just lunch time. Thankfully, I had a light afternoon schedule today so that I could begin going through all my files to provide Bill with the information he requested.

Chapter 4

I arrived home about 45 minutes before my scheduled session with Valerie. I had just enough time to grab a quick bite to eat and check my messages to see if she responded to my email. I walked into my office to turn my laptop on. I straightened up my desk and opened my file drawer and pulled Valerie's file and set it on my desk.

I sat at the kitchen table scrolling through my social media feeds while enjoying my vegetable lasagna. I finished dinner and logged in about ten minutes ahead of schedule. I checked my inbox and I did not see a response from Valerie. I opened her file and reviewed the email I sent her to refresh my memory. While reading through my notes I received a notification Valerie was connected, and I joined the video chat.

"Hello Valerie, how are you?" I noticed that she looked a little less tired today than before although her eyes still showed very little emotion.

"Hi Joy, I am okay." She said and sounded a lot more interested than our first encounter.

"That is great. Did you have a chance to read my last email?"

"Yes, I did, but I decided to wait for our session to answer your questions."

"That is fine. Let us jump right in."

"You asked me to explain a little more about why I felt things had gotten worse between Seth and I recently. I had to think about where to start because if I am being honest with myself many of our issues were always there.

"Okay Valerie, can I stop you for a minute and ask: what were the issues? Just give me words, the first things that come to your mind."

She thought for a minute and finally said, "Ah let me see, controlling, selfish, insensitive. Those are the first three that come to mind."

"Okay, great. Now you can continue."

"I think I began to realize things were not getting better towards the end of last year."

I interrupted again, "Was there a specific event that occurred which brought you to that realization?"

"The first incident I recall is when I took a girl's trip to South Carolina in October. Seth had promised that he would make sure David was up for his early morning track practice in my absence. I really could never count on Seth and deep down I knew that he would not come through for me this time. I had trouble sleeping that night worried about if he would actually handle everything that I needed him to do. I was surprised late one night when I received a notification about activity in my driveway. I checked my security camera app on my phone and saw Seth leaving the house with a few guys. I was furious when I saw this and called him right away. When he answered the phone, he put on an act that he had been sleeping and was giving me a hard time for waking him up. My blood pressure must have been sky high as I yelled at him. He immediately hung up on me, ignored my calls, and later when he got home he turned off the cameras since I mentioned seeing him earlier. This is really the first time I caught him lying to me and it was even more embarrassing because my friends were aware since I was with them at the time it all happened."

Valerie paused for a moment to take a sip of water and I could see how angry she was getting, her hand appeared to be trembling as she raised the water bottle she continued, "I remember when I first began to realize exactly how controlling Seth was. I am a part of a book club and when it was my turn to host, Seth insisted on selecting the book and cooking dinner for the group. When all the women were busy chatting before we sat down to discuss the book, one of the women complimented me on my boots. I thanked her and proudly stated that my husband bought them and that he bought all my clothes since he liked to do that. Her response stunned me when she said it seemed his behavior was very controlling. I started thinking about her comment and some of the other things Seth did. He always packed my clothes for me when I would take trips. If I attempted to take something he had not picked out he would become incredibly angry. Then he would say I was grown woman and it was ridiculous I could not do this for myself. He constantly berated me and made me feel like I was incapable of doing simple things such as shopping or cooking that I did before I met him. I also stopped offering my opinion when making any types of decisions because things had to be his way or he would get really upset."

"I am sorry you had to go through that. No one deserves to be treated that way." I could not imagine how Valerie must have felt to be treated that way. I could see reliving these memories was upsetting, but she seemed open to sharing what she experienced recently so I let her keep talking.

"During the holidays, things got really rough and I guess looking back on it his behavior was odd. The first weekend of December we went to a political event in DC. During one of the receptions he made comments about wanting to do something else besides being a senator. He had just won an election and had not even been sworn in yet, so it seemed to be a strange thing to say. I ended up having an allergic reaction, so I missed going out to dinner and stayed at the hotel. Seth left and was out partying most of that night since he did not want to miss anything."

"Did Seth express concern for you during this time? Was he concerned or worried about your allergic reaction?" I asked.

"Seth knew my family lived close by and thought I could reach out to them if I needed anything. I did not want to hear about how awful it was he was not there for me, so I did not call anyone. It would have been nice to have some company instead of ordering room service for myself."

"It sounds like you were slowly moving towards acceptance during this time."

"Yes, I believe so, even though I was not consciously aware, I do believe that is what was happening. Shall I continue?'

"Oh, yes, of course." I continued to be a little concerned about the lack of emotion from Valerie. He voice and overall demeanor were void of real emotion. I was very worried that she may be over medicated.

"We had a trip scheduled to go to Myrtle Beach, just the two of us, the week before Christmas. We were scheduled to get back in time for our annual Eve of the Eve party."

"Eve of the Eve party? Tell me a little more about this."

"It was held at our house the past few years. We would have a large turnout including kids since we knew so many people in town. Seth would tell everyone as he saw them not to forget about our party."

"It sounds like these were happy times for you."

"Well, sometimes, but not always. I mostly went along with things to keep the peace with Seth. We also had parties just about every holiday weekend so there were rarely times for us to make plans to visit my family. There were several times I headed to Charlottesville before our parties. I would get fed up with things at home, but always came back in time for the parties since I did not want people to know there were issues."

"Okay I see, well finish telling me about your trip with Seth to Myrtle Beach."

"When we arrived, we were met by contractors that were working on all the condos and my prior concerns I raised to Seth were confirmed. There were major foundation issues and we were advised not to allow anyone to stay there until they were addressed. We had seasonal renters coming and I insisted we let them know about the problems right then. Seth refused until I threatened to get an Uber and leave. He told me if I left our marriage was over. I was very unhappy, but I felt I needed to hang in because of the kids."

I interrupted, "Did you feel being in this situation for the kids was better than them seeing you go through a divorce?" Valerie hesitated for a moment as if she was reflecting.

I thought to myself that I knew divorce was probably the best option, but it was so close to the holidays and I didn't want to ruin that time for the kids. I also knew that any hint of family problems would be bad for Seth's career. I just felt stuck. I finally responded, "I had seen so many families go through divorces and heard about it from my kids on what their friends went through including not having a relationship with one parent or the other anymore. Since Seth was not around much, I figured I would try my best to stay. From what I knew he had not cheated, and I would just think of our relationship as a lot of ups and downs. I had a hard time even thinking about divorce as an option due to my faith." Her voice cracked and she paused briefly to regain her composure then continued, "You know the more I think about it, I believe Seth knew about this investigation long before he told me about it."

"Oh really, why do you think that?"

Seth would not miss work for anything. Previously when I had any medical procedures, I could never count on him to be there for me. I always had to ask a friend. When my hysterectomy surgery came up and he said he would be around to take me to the hospital, it just seemed odd. I guess I wanted to believe that he was changing and wanted to be there for me and the kids. Now I realize he was probably just trying to avoid going to work because of the ongoing investigation."

I could see the tears start flowing and Valerie grabbed a tissue. I am sure this is all extremely hard for her, especially if she thought things were going to take a more positive turn and did not. "Okay. I believe I have a better idea of what you were dealing with prior to finding out about the accusations and him admitting to cheating on you. We are almost out of time, and I want to get to the other question

I asked you about in my email about you and Seth going to marriage counseling."

"We had gone to counseling on two separate occasions. Honestly though it was just a waste of time. Seth was never very interested in going to counseling to actually improve our marriage. He just like to go there and put on show. He liked to hear himself talk and it was brutal for me to sit there and listen to all his excuses. He was so self-centered, and really thought that he was so important and that everyone else should cater to his wants and needs. He really believed that his job was the most important thing and he should not be expected to be there for me and the kids. It was extremely difficult for me to accept that. I knew that me and my kids deserved better, but I truly felt stuck."

Hearing all of this made me feel very angry for Valerie. There were so many things that I wanted to say to her, but it really wasn't my place to do so. I managed to hold back all of my other thoughts and comments and simply said, "Our time is up for this session. Next time I would like for you to walk me through the days immediately after Seth confessed to you and before the hospital admission."

Valerie wiped tears from her eyes, nodded and then said, "Okay, yes that will be good. I will check your schedule against mine and get another session scheduled as soon as possible."

"That would be great, and remember you have unlimited emails on your plan, so feel free to email me any time." I was shocked and happy to see her finally showing some emotion about her situation. Of course, I don't want to see anyone hurting or in pain, but the tears she shed were absolutely understandable based on what she is currently dealing with.

"Yes, I might do that, sometimes it is easier to type my thoughts and review them. I am still not adjusting well to this medication."

I made a note about the comment about her medication and said, "You might want to follow up with the psychiatrist if your symptoms do not improve. Have a good night, Valerie, I look forward to hearing from you soon."

After my session with Valerie I made some tea and sat in the living and thought about my day. I felt my conversation with Martha was applicable to both of us. I had some decisions to make about my family relationships also. I was not quite ready yet, but it is getting increasingly harder to counsel people about their family relationships when I had so much I need to work on. Sometimes I feel like God sends me clients that have issues I also need to work through. Counselors do not have all the answers, we have just been trained to ask the right questions to help our clients find their way to the answers.

Before going up to bed, I stopped in my office to check for any last-minute online appointments. I agreed to accept appointments on Saturday mornings and needed to see if I could sleep in or not.

I was pleased to see no appointments scheduled but was surprised to find an email from Valerie since we had just ended our session a little over an hour ago. I was curious so I settled in my chair and opened the email.

Joy,

After our session I felt like I needed to give you a little bit more information. I know we covered a lot but there is more. First, I failed to mention to you previously: this is not my first time doing online therapy. When I got home from the hospital, the therapist I was seeing was not showing available for the amount of time I needed so I matched up with you to move forward.

Anyway, I started online therapy back in December because I was at such a point of frustration. I did not let my family know I had reached out for help. Seth would often say I was depressed and had issues but really what I had a problem with was our relationship.

During the holidays, when the problems between Seth and I caused my son Scott to leave and go back to college early, I had reached my breaking point. Scott is on the autism spectrum and does at times struggle with handling his emotions, but Seth makes things so much worse. I mentioned to you that Seth has a drinking problem, but I did not tell you that he is an angry drunk. Of course, he blamed me because everything was always my fault. We argued and I told him to leave and he did. I really felt as if he was leaving for good. I felt free and liberated but also a little anxious and nervous. He did return a few days later and I was hopeful that things were going to improve. My thoughts of him changing were short lived. He always wanted everything to be on his terms. He ruined New Years by insisting that we leave our friends party way before the ball dropped. This was after I had to give up on even thinking about planning a trip to the UVA bowl game which was actually being held not too far from our vacation home in South Carolina. Seth had made me feel guilty because he said we always rang in New Years together.

Seth went on a guy's trip to Myrtle Beach the day after his swearing in. He booked flights in and out of different airports, so he needed me to drive him to the ceremony. I ended up dropping him off at the capitol and went to our house in Charlottesville. After the game was over, I called Seth to touch base. He was already drinking and was annoyed that I was bothering him. I don't know why I was surprised by his response; I had gotten used to this behavior from him. I took comfort in having a break from him being around physically since things could be worse if he were at home. As each day passed, I began to realize that I was truly alone. My kids were older and did not need me as much. My prior therapist asked if I even wanted Seth around more. It was a great question and I began to realize that things were better for me when he wasn't around.

Well, that is all for now. I just wanted to share this with you before I forgot about it. I will check my schedule for next week and book a time for us to chat. Meanwhile if you have any questions about any of this, feel free to email me your questions.

Valerie

Chapter 5

After reading Valerie's email last night I did not respond. I decided to read it again with fresh eyes and thoughts this morning before sending a response. I was happy to have been able to sleep in a little longer than usual this morning. I leisurely got out of bed and made my way downstairs to make myself some tea and some granola to nibble on.

After about an hour of scrolling through my social media and catching up on the latest gossip and news, I decided to read the email again and I really did not have questions I should be asking as her therapist. I had a million questions I wanted to ask, but I was happy she was opening up to me. I also felt as though I was finally beginning to see how things really were for her during this time. I sent a quick response to her email.

Valerie,

Thanks so much for sharing this additional information with me. It does help me understand your relationship better and your state of mind. It seems as if even though you and Seth were still together you had already grown so far apart. Please feel free to correct me if I am wrong on that.

Joy

It was a beautiful day, a little warmer than usual for February, so I decided to get dressed and go for a walk to the park. My clients were stirring up things inside of me I needed to deal with. Walking and writing have always been therapeutic for me. I have not written in a while. I used to journal all the time. I quickly shook my head to erase those thoughts and gathered my keys and walked out the door.

As I approached the park, I noticed a family near the playground. A mother, father, and two small children. The father was pushing the little girl on the swing and the mother appeared to be consoling the little boy. I slowed my pace to observe more. It was the picture I had always imagined for myself, married to a man I adored, and a couple of kids enjoying our lives together. My thoughts shifted to Valerie and I wondered if there were ever any Saturday morning trips to the park like this for her family.

There were not many people at the park yet, so I decided to continue walking along the path. I was enjoying the warm sun on my face, the gentle breeze and the leaves swirling around and crackling under my feet. Further down the path I saw a couple sitting on a bench, holding hands and laughing. Robin once asked me why I had not allowed myself to open my heart again.

My answer was after my third heartbreak, I was simply done. I remember the first time I told her that. She asked, 'Tell me about your heartbreaks, one by one'. I told her my very first heartbreak was my father. I really did not know much about him. My mother spoke little about him. She simply said things did not work out for them and he had moved on. When I told Robin this the first time, she had a hard time understanding how he broke my heart since he was not around. I simply said a little girl's first love is supposed to be her father. If she is raised and nurtured properly, she will seek to find a man that reminds her of her father, because she felt safe and secure with him and every woman wants to feel that same sense of security throughout their life.

Robin was speechless and later she told me she had been inspired by my explanation.

My second heartbreak was the day my older brother died. Obviously, he did not consciously abandon me like my father did but losing him was even more devastating. Darien was 13 years older than me. Darien did all that he could to help my mother raise me. After my mother died, I went to live with Darien and his wife Toni.

I met Miles, heartbreak number 3, during my freshman year at Penn State Harrisburg. We were both psychology majors and we shared many of the same friends. Miles stood out in our crowd. He was tall, 6'3, and built like a football player. I was surprised he didn't play sports because he had such a muscular build. His best feature was his smile. He has the most beautiful bright smile. He was from New York originally, but had attended a private school in Hershey and ended up getting a scholarship to attend Penn State Harrisburg. Miles was always very closed mouthed about his childhood and family, but I figured it just was not something that was easy for him to share. I decided to focus on our time together, which started off very innocently as friends, but by the end of our sophomore year we became a couple. We were both hard workers, we studied together, and we also both had jobs outside of school. I never questioned the weekends he was unavailable because I was also busy with schoolwork, my job, and spending time helping Toni with the kids. Maybe I should have paid closer attention, especially during our senior year when our time together seemed to dwindle even more. I really thought it was because of the intensity of schoolwork, but as it turned out it was so much more.

I did like to hang with my friends and have a good time, but sex was not something I was interested in while I was in high school. After my mom died and I went to live with Darien and Toni, we started attending church on a regular basis and it was my goal to wait for marriage. I wish I had waited, but Miles talked me into it but only because I genuinely believed he was going to be the one I would marry.

On graduation day, I saw him once before the ceremony and he seemed okay, maybe a little preoccupied and standoffish, but still no alarms went off for me. I remember thinking to myself how handsome he looked in his cap and gown. I was so accustomed to seeing him dressed in casual attire. After the ceremony I searched for him and just as I found him and began walking towards him another young girl walked up to him and gave him a hug and a kiss. Not just a quick congratulations kiss, but what appeared to be a real kiss. She stepped back a bit and I noticed an infant in her arms, and she said, 'We are both so proud of you'. Just as I began to back away, I heard Toni calling my name. Miles heard it also and he turned and saw me standing nearby. His smile briefly left his face as he saw me, our eyes locked for a moment and just as I began to turn away to acknowledge Toni, he mouthed the words, 'I am sorry'.

Toni witnessed the entire thing and she was there to wipe my tears for the weeks that followed. I was hurt and angry that I had allowed myself to be taken advantage of. Miles did attempt to contact me many times. He called, emailed, and sent text messages. I eventually changed my phone number and email address just to avoid him and to erase the hurt and disappointment.

My plan was to start graduate school in the fall, and I was more determined than ever to stick to my plans and not allow myself to get caught up in my hurt. I wanted to grow from this heartbreak. Just as I was pulling myself out of the slump I was hit with another blow. During my routine annual gynecology visit, my doctor noticed a lesion during my internal exam. She asked if I had noticed any others previously. I did recall a time when I had what I thought was a boil on the outside of my vagina but maybe it was something else. The doctor informed me it appeared to be a herpes blister, but a blood test would confirm for sure. She knew I had only had one sexual partner and she advised me to contact him to let him know he should be tested as well. I shared with her I had recently discovered he was having sex with someone else. She decided to do a full STD panel just to make sure there was nothing else to be concerned about.

A week later I was back at her office to go over the results. I had been unable to sleep much over the past week and did all the online research I could on herpes and every other STD I could find. She sat down behind her desk and gave me the news. Both good and bad. Good news is everything else came back negative but unfortunately, I did have genital herpes. I was relieved but devastated. Yes, I was thankful I did not have HIV, but herpes stays with you for life. It could cause problems during childbirth also. I felt as though I was being punished for having sex before marriage. I fell back into a deep depression. I was not able to start my classes on time and fell behind quickly. This is how I ended up meeting Robin. Robin helped me get back on track emotionally and I was able to get caught up with school. It seemed as if I had accepted it and moved on. Now over fifteen years later, I wonder if I did really deal with it all. That is what I intended to discuss with Robin this week.

I needed to be honest with myself about why I had not been in any serious relationships since Miles. I really was not close to anyone. The person I felt the closest to besides Toni was Robin. All the friendships I developed while in school faded away over time. When I decided to leave Pennsylvania, I no longer kept in touch with many of my friends from there. When I first moved to Virginia, I was still finishing up my master's degree and I had little time to socialize. Between working full time and online classes, I was terribly busy. Months turned into years and I loved my job, so that is what I poured my heart and soul into. An occasional dinner with coworkers and my weekly talks with Toni and Robin are what has kept me sane. My sessions with Valerie have me questioning if there is something more out there for me? Did I give up on love too soon?

I remembered how difficult things were for me right after the death of my mother. I felt responsible for her death. The night before my brother came to the house and found my mother unresponsive, she and I had a big fight. I wanted to go hang out with one of my friends she did not like. We argued and I left the house that night and stayed out all night. When I returned in the morning, I found my brother hunched over my mothers' lifeless body. I was deeply depressed for a while afterwards and moving in with my brother and his wife was one of the best things that happened to me during this time. Although my mother raised me in church, I had not been led to accept Christ as my savior until I was living with Darien and Toni. My sister in law Toni introduced me to journaling which has been such a useful self-care tool in my life.

As I recalled these memories the tears began to roll down my cheeks. I looked around to make sure I was not drawing any attention to myself as I reached into my pocket for a tissue. As I wiped my face, I began to take deep breaths to control my emotions After a few minutes of deep focused breathing I was able to compose myself. I checked the time and decided I better head back home. It was almost time for my weekly touch base call with Toni.

Toni and I kept in contact each week even after all these years. Even though we were not related by blood, she and my nephew and niece were all the family I had left. I try to visit her at least once a year. Returning to Pennsylvania is still extremely hard for me, all my heartbreaks happened there, but I make the sacrifice for Toni.

As I walked in the door my cell phone rang. I answered and spent the next hour chatting on the phone with Toni just like we did most Saturdays. She filled me in on what was going on with my niece and nephew and she always asked me a million questions about my love life. I did fill her in on my newest venture, online counseling and she was very intrigued by the concept. I had missed visiting for the holidays and she begged me to make plans to visit them soon.

I would love to see Darien Jr and Denise, but I am sort of in a weird place right now emotionally and going there is always a trigger for me. I decided to discuss it with Robin and then I would let Toni know. After ending my call with Toni, I sat in my living room drinking my tea and looking out the window reflecting on my life.

My thoughts were interrupted by a notification on my phone of an email. When I picked up my phone, I noticed it was from Valerie. I got up to go into my office to read her message on my laptop.

Joy,

Even with taking the medicine I do sometimes I wake up in the middle of the night and struggle to fall back to sleep. I see flashbacks of the victim that accused Seth of sexual assault and can picture in my mind what I think happened that night based on what she reported in her sworn testimony. I can see her walk up the narrow stairway to the bedroom and hit her head on the low ceiling. I feel her fear when she kissed him goodbye since she did not want to upset him when she refused his advances in the morning. I don't want to believe anything terrible happened, but I cannot imagine anyone would make up such a horrific story.

I also think about my time in the hospital and what it was like there. Last night I could not shake the feeling of wondering whether I had upset another patient. We shared a birthday which was posted on the message board in the lunchroom since it was coming up. He was diagnosed bipolar and had been in the hospital many times before. He seemed pretty agitated the night before I was discharged, and he tried to leave when the visitors were being escorted out. The nurse was knocked down to the floor and rushed into surgery almost immediately. He is now facing assault charges related to the incident. When I had my meetings with my treatment team, we had discussed trying to get me home in time for my birthday. I don't know if I talked about it to other patients and if it could have contributed to what happened. It is so hard to remember everything but at the same time I wish I could forget that I was ever put in the hospital.

Valerie

I felt so bad for Valerie. She was really struggling, and she really did need help and a good support system. I had to carefully craft my response to not push her away, but to maintain the appropriate therapist client relationship.

Valerie,

I am so sorry that you are having trouble sleeping and having these nightmares. I know it may not seem like it, but I think you are trying to process everything which is good. As memories came back to you it is okay to feel whatever emotion comes with the memory. I do want to caution you about putting too much of your past experiences or fears into the information you read from the different articles. You will cause yourself grief that you do not need right now. The same applies to you feeling responsible for the man's breakdown in the hospital. You can only be responsible for your actions not those of others. Remember that. Why don't you schedule another session for us soon so we can talk? You can still always email me whenever you need to.

  Joy

Chapter 6

On Sunday after church I decided to check in on my clients and did not have any emails from anyone except Valerie. I settled in with my cup of tea and began to read her message.

Joy,

I scheduled a video session for us on Tuesday evening. In advance of that you asked me to tell you more about what happened after Seth told me about the allegations.

As soon as he left the house that night, I contacted my parents first and then my sister and brother. It was hard to call my family and tell them what had happened even though I knew they would be supportive. Over the years I had tried to keep our problems from my parents, but they could see how controlling he was with me and the kids. I had reached out to my sister Fran in the past also when we had problems. She had given me advice to leave but since I felt I could not do that I stopped reaching out to her. Once my family knew what Seth had done there would be no turning back to work things out and I could feel my world crumbling apart.

I reached out to my friend Jill and she came over and brought me food. We had been friends since our sons were in the baby room together in daycare. Our husbands also became friends and Seth was always up for vacations, so we did a lot of traveling together. She became one of my closest friends to confide in when there were issues at home. I also

*sent a message to Celeste to let her know there was
something going on and I would be in touch with her later
since she worked in the evenings. She was always someone I
could turn to and get advice from on what to do.*

*The next day after Seth told me the news it was not
even a week after my surgery, but I had things that had to be
taken care of. My attorney sent me a list of things to do as
soon as possible. I handled as many of them as I could but
still felt a little worried about doing anything to upset Seth. I
received a call later in the day from Seth's criminal attorney
to discuss next steps including Seth checking himself into an
addiction clinic. I made it clear that it was my firm intention
still to file for divorce, but I would help anyway I could.*

I stopped to re-read Valerie's email. Addiction
clinic? Oh my, there were only a couple of clinics in this
area and I certainly hoped her husband was not in the one
where I worked. I got up from my desk and paced back and
forth for a minute, thinking about the situation. Talking to
myself. Was it even an issue? Why would it be? If he was
there, he was not one of my clients. So, it should not be a
problem. I had to casually bring it up to Valerie without
causing her any alarm to confirm where Seth was for his
treatment. I sat back down at my desk and made a note
before continuing to read the rest of her email.

*I was really getting worried when I did not hear from
Seth not only the night he left for Charlottesville, but almost
the entire next day had gone by. He seemed distraught while
explaining everything to me. I had never seen him that way
before. I remember thinking that he seemed like he was
having a nervous breakdown. Even with all of our issues Seth
and I were always in touch many times throughout the day
and I had never gone that long without hearing from him. I
thought about contacting the police since maybe he had been*

in an accident, but I also worried about upsetting him since he would think I was overreacting. What if he was in a ditch somewhere and I had not done anything? He had our dog with him so I did not think he would hurt himself, but I was panicking as I thought about all of the possibilities. The lack of sleep I had was kicking in.

When I reached out to Scott, he would not tell me whether he had seen his dad or not. I felt terrible even having to involve him in this whole situation. I could tell how upset Scott was and it seemed he was keeping something from me. I was really starting to get pretty emotional as the day went on. I decided to call a neighbor to see if he could determine if Seth was in fact there. I tried to calmly say my husband had gone up the night before and maybe his phone died because I had not heard from him. Seth got on the phone and he acted like nothing was wrong. He said he had already spent time with Scott and would be seeing him again after his class. He told me I would hear from him the next day after he met with his attorney. I could not sleep again that night since things still seemed off. Seth was behaving like nothing had happened. I was annoyed yet concerned about his behavior.

I am getting tired, so I am going to close for now. If you have any questions before our scheduled session, please feel free to email me. I am finding that emailing you is great way for me to revisit some of these experiences since I can take time to process what I am sending you.

Valerie

I read the email several times before I began writing notes of things I wanted to address. There was so much, I had so many questions. One thing that struck me was how in such a short period of time Valerie had been able to come to certain conclusions about her relationship on her own. Maybe it was she always knew, or she has known for a while, but the most recent events have solidified her feelings.

. I often wondered if my clients realized I also had a therapist and what they might think about that if they did know. I do believe I have made some progress. The toughest hurdle has been my college sweetheart, Miles.

I feel as though I have made peace with everything that happened, but I guess what I am still struggling with is how I have not moved past it. Fifteen years later and I have not been in a serious relationship. After talking to Toni this weekend, I really feel as though my lack of interest in a serious relationship has more to do with what she and Darien went through than what happened with Miles and me. I walked back over to my desk to make myself a note to discuss all of this with Robin the next time we talked.

I sat down and started an email to Valerie to ask a few follow up questions from her email. Once I looked over all my notes, I decided not to email my questions but to hold them until our session. I sent a short message letting her know I received her email and we would discuss everything on Tuesday

Valerie,

Thank you so much for your email. I do have a few questions, but I would prefer to wait until our session on Tuesday.

Joy

After emailing Valerie, I decided to send Robin and email to see when she and I can touch base again. She must have been sitting right by her computer because within minutes she responded, and we exchanged messages until we settled on catching up on Wednesday evening. That would give me some time to think about things.

After doing some chores around the house, making dinner, and binge watching a few episodes of my shows from the past week I came back into my office to check my emails once more before heading up to my room for the night. I had a few emails from my online clients, confirming scheduled appointments. Nothing that required a response, so I shut down my laptop and headed upstairs to bed.

*****

Things at work the next day were uneventful. I wanted to broach the subject with Bill about Valerie's husband possibly being a patient here at the clinic, but since I had not confirmed exactly where he was, I decided to wait until I spoke with Valerie to confirm.

Tuesday came quickly and before I knew it, I was on my way home to prepare for my session with Valerie. Things had been slow this week at work, so I brought her file with me to review everything again during my lunch break to be prepared. I had printed out the emails, highlighted and made notes along the margins.

Traffic was a little heavier than usual, so I did not make it home in time to grab anything to eat before my session with Valerie. I did take the time to change into more comfortable pants, sweats of course, and my slippers. She could only see my shirt, so it did not matter. I had my notes spread out on my desk and I logged in right on time for our session. As soon as Valerie connected, I greeted her, "Hello Valerie, how are you?" With each session she was looking better and better, more alert, and much more expression in her face.

She smiled. "I am well, all things considered."

"I am glad to hear that. Well we have a lot to discuss tonight so let us jump right in okay?"

"Sure, no problem."

"I printed out your email and made some notes, so if you do not mind, I would like to go through my questions in the order you wrote the email."

"Yeah, sure, that is fine with me."

"Okay, well first I am curious about how your parents and siblings reacted to hearing the news about Seth and the allegations?"

"Although I tried my best to pull myself together before calling them, I began crying as soon as my mom answered the phone. My father had a stroke about 10 years ago and since then any emotional stress could cause him to have seizures. I had to let my parents know what was happening without giving them too much information in order to avoid causing my dad to get too upset. I think overall they felt bad for me and I know they were incredibly angry with Seth."

"I understand completely and what about your siblings? You have a brother and sister correct?"

"Yes, when I talked to my brother I remember him mentioning it was a good thing our dad could not travel due to his health or he would have gotten himself into trouble since he would have wanted to come beat the shit out of Seth for what did."

I interrupted. "Yes, I think most fathers would react that way, and your sister? How did she react?"

"Fran was not fond of Seth and was not surprised by his actions."

"Okay, let us move on. Can you tell me a little bit more about your relationship with Celeste? How did you meet and why do you consider her someone you can go to for advice?"

"My schedule was always hectic trying to balance work, kids, properties, and politics. There were times both Seth and I were out of town and Celeste would stay at our house. She would take care of everything while we were away. I turned to her since she knew about all I was balancing more than anyone else. Celeste started helping me with the boys when her son started junior high. I met her through working with her husband."

"I see so she was definitely someone you knew you could trust and confide in?"

"Absolutely. Since I do not live close to family Celeste has been the one there for me including being temporary guardian for David while I was in the hospital." Her voice trailed off as she said the word hospital.

I could tell that the hospital was an extremely difficult subject for Valerie. She could barely say the word without it causing her so much pain. I cannot even imagine how it would feel to go through what she endured. Valerie grabbed a tissue and wiped away her tears.

I decided to move on and change the subject. "You mentioned Seth went to an addiction clinic. Where was he and what for?"

"Seth decided to check himself in a clinic close to Scott's school since we had a house close by. His attorney advised him to go there due to the ongoing investigation of the sexual assault allegations. Seth told me he did not know exactly what he was addicted to but wanted to figure that out."

"Close to your son's school in Charlottesville?"

"Yes, that is correct."

"Is he still there now?"

"No, he left a few days ago. He has been staying out of the public eye since he is getting pressure to resign from office, so he is at our house near Scott."

"Let us switch gears a bit. I would like to ask you more about your son, Scott. When was he diagnosed? Was Seth involved in the process?"

"Scott was not diagnosed on the autism spectrum until fourth grade. Since there were calls from several concerned teachers, I reached out to our family doctor who referred Scott to be evaluated. When we had school meetings about help for Scott to address any issues Seth would usually work it into his schedule to attend even if it were by phone. He liked his presence to be known since he was an elected official, although he rarely knew what was really going on. I would provide all the information and work with the teachers and administrators on what accommodations may be needed for Scott."

I could sense just talking about Seth invoked so many emotions for Valerie. I sensed hurt and anger of course, but still there seemed to be so much more.

"I am sure this was also a very hectic and stressful time for you."

"Yes, it really was."

"Do you feel as though that may have also been a factor in things breaking down in your marriage?"

"No, not really. We had problems before Scott was diagnosed."

"I do not recall if we have ever discussed how you and Seth met. Can you share that with me?"

"I was headed out for what I thought was going to be a girl's night with one of my friends. She said that first we were going to stop at a place to eat on the way. Little did I know she had set me up on a blind date without telling me. I was somewhat annoyed but figured I would be polite. Seth was not necessarily the type of guy I usually fell for in the past, but I did find him attractive. He was a little taller than me and I really liked his blue eyes. I tended to go for guys with darker hair and Seth's was more on the blonde side. We started talking about sports and seemed to really hit it off right away. He seemed pretty charming and we started spending a lot of time together. We got engaged after dating about a year and a half. He wanted to move back to his hometown of Lynchburg, and I thought it would be nice to be close to his family. After a few years we moved not too far away to Chatham, Virginia. When Seth decided to run for Senate we worked together on his campaign. I wanted to help him achieve his dreams in life."

"I see, I might come back to that later, but I want to move on for now. In your email you also mentioned you had trouble sleeping after Seth told you about the investigation. You were still healing physically from your surgery and then had all this added emotional stress."

"I went back to work the next morning since I planned to start half days a week after my surgery."

"Wow, Valerie, that is pretty impressive. I mean with everything else going on you still decided to return to work. What do you do for a living?"

"I do project planning mostly from home. Yeah, I really felt it was best to stay busy, and I knew I needed my job since Seth and I were divorcing."

"Yes, I get it. What about your younger son, David? Did he stop going to school during this time or was he still going?"

"It was hard for him, but he did make it most days. There were also several college interviews he had since he was considering several Ivy leagues and options for full scholarships."

"That is great. You must be so proud of him."

"I really am. He was also in a lot of activities including winter track at the time. He was doing his best to get there even though he was very tired as well. He especially did not want to miss school the day of the Rib Fest. It was at our neighbors house after practice and our family was to co-host the event."

"Were you able to help given the fact you had surgery?"

"Seth was the one who had agreed to help, but he was gone. It was tough to admit since I just had surgery and he should have been home. I had to call our neighbor Paula to let her know we would not be able to help. I felt horrible about leaving her without any support, so I immediately sent a text to another parent that lived close by and got someone to fill in. I did tell Paula there was news coming out soon about Seth and tried not to share too much information. I wanted to let her know David may need support since he could be at school with her foreign exchange student when the news hit."

"Oh, I see, even though you had so much going on you still seemed to be on top of everything Valerie. That can be both good and bad. It is also especially important to pay attention and take care of yourself. Let us move on. Did you hear from Seth after he met with his attorney that day?"

"Seth did call and let me know he would be checking into an addiction clinic the next day."

I simply nodded and continued, "How did everything go after getting some sleep?"

"It felt great to get back to some normalcy. I started back to work, and David was excited about his track meet. I usually went to all of them, but knew I was not going to be able to make this one which was a little disappointing since I was still recovering from my surgery. There was another one at his school in a few days so I hoped I would be able to make it to that one. I skimmed through emails that morning and focused on getting caught up after being off for a week. I called into my team meeting since I thought it would be announced my mentor Lila would be moving onto another team and wanted to make sure she got recognized for her hard work. I really enjoyed interacting with my co-workers and I looked forward to seeing them soon at our upcoming planning session."

"How did the rest of the day go after you worked that morning?"

"I was working with my attorney's office to gather information for my divorce filing and was reaching out to people regarding our rental properties. I knew I would need some help with our dog due to my surgery, so I had gotten in contact with someone I thought would be perfect for the job. Haley was my friend Tina's niece and she has a passion for taking care of animals. She set up her own business while also taking college classes. Even though I was juggling a lot at the time when she arrived, I focused my full attention on her since she is on the autism spectrum like my son. I knew how important that would be to make her feel comfortable. During our meeting I could see my phone starting to blow up and that is when the story started to hit the news."

"How about you send me an email about what happened when the news hit so we can discuss that next time? Our time is about up for this session. I wanted to follow up and ask if you are sleeping any better now? Still having those nightmares?"

Valerie dabbed her eyes to wipe away the tears. "Yes, I am still waking up occasionally but not as often."

"Well that's good, and hopefully with time they will go away completely."

"I do hope so. This whole situation can be a little overwhelming at times. I am a little surprised at how talking through this and emailing you is helping me to deal with it all."

"You have been through a lot, but it seems you are handling it all pretty well considering."

"Thanks. I appreciate that and will get that email to you soon."

After ending the call with Valerie her comment about talking through things being a big help stuck with me. After I saw Miles with that other woman, I shut him out of my life. I never accepted his calls or read his emails. I literally shut the door and proceeded as if he never existed. Although

Valerie is making some progress, she does not appear to be as numb as before. I still have concerns with her nightmares and her imagining what the victim experienced. I think she is trying so hard to resume her normal life and activities too soon. She is not really taking the time to heal.

Chapter 7

The next few days at work seemed calmer than I expected them to be. After I gave Bill my client summaries, he hasn't scheduled any time with me yet, so I have just continued to meet with my clients.

Martha was doing well. She seemed to have made peace with everything and had decided to contact her daughter. I worked with her during our session on how to prepare for the conversation and how to handle things if she was rejected again.

My other clients were all doing well including my online clients. I felt as if I was making a difference in their lives and that is the part I enjoyed. Even Valerie seems to be doing well. I received an email from her.

Joy,

I have to say there are times I feel bad about what Celeste had to go through when I was in the hospital. She had helped me for years with my kids and as they got older it gave her the time she needed for herself. She takes care of her elderly aunt and also works a lot of hours. We have maintained a strong friendship and she is always there for me without question. Fran had come into town when I was hospitalized and since she needed to get back home Celeste stepped in as temporary guardian for David. It was his senior year which should be the best time of his life and instead he was dealing with both his parents being in facilities. Celeste came to visit me almost every day and when I finally got discharged she was there. The day after I got out of the hospital she went with me to my divorce attorney's office and let me drive. I was a little nervous since I had not driven in a while because of my surgery and I was still on a lot of heavy medicine. I was so happy to hear that she thought I was doing ok although I am sure it was still not back to the way I was before the hospital. She also went with me to my psychiatrist appointment and sat out in the car reading a book on her Kindle. It meant the world to me to have her support and I am so appreciative of her friendship.

Valerie

I am so happy to hear that she has someone close to her to help and support her. I have been worried that she is attempting to carry this heavy burden on her own.

Valerie,
I am so happy to hear that you have Celeste to help you and she seems like a really good friend. I know you feel bad for leaning on her so much but remember your true friends will be there for you no matter what. She knows that you need her now. Just make sure that she knows how much you appreciate her friendship and sacrifice.
Joy

.   Wednesday was here and I was prepared for my chat with Robin. When she called, I had papers spread out all over the kitchen table. Over the past several days I made notes in my journal and everywhere else I could as things came to my mind.

"Hello Robin."

"Hi, Joy. How are you doing?"

"I'm good, just have a lot on my mind."

"I know and that is why I cleared my schedule for the evening to give you my full attention."

I laughed. "Okay, I really appreciate that."

"I know you do. Well where should we start?"

I scanned the papers lying in front of me and then when I found the list of questions and picked it up, I began. "I would like to start with asking you some questions."

"Oh, I see so this is about me not you?" She asked sounding a little perplexed.

"No, it is about me, but I need to ask you a couple of things." I persisted.

"Okay, go ahead and ask away."

"Before I ask the questions let me explain why I feel compelled to ask them."

"Okay." She said and I continued, "Over the past week or so I have been evaluating my clients and how well I feel they are responding to therapy. Which led me to my first question which is do you feel I have made progress and moved past my issues?" There was a brief silence and then I heard a faint sigh.

"First of all, you realize you are no longer officially my client, right?"

I thought for a moment before I responded but finally, I said, "Well, I guess I was not sure."

Robin continued, "Joy, I stopped billing your insurance for our talks years ago. I consider you a close friend, yes, I am still a therapist. I know that is how we met, but now when we talk, it is just a talk amongst friends."

I smiled. "I appreciate you telling me this and I consider you a good friend as well, but as a therapist can you answer my question?"

Robin laughed. "I will not answer your question as a therapist, but as your friend here is what I think. I believe you have made a lot of progress since our first conversation all those years ago. Look at you now. You are a successful therapist, helping others to address their issues and move forward with their lives. Do you still have some stuff to work through? Yes, and please understand when I say that it is from a place of love and everyone has something to work on." Robin paused and let her words linger for a minute.

I closed my eyes for a moment and processed her response.   "Yes, I understand exactly what you are saying, but I still have questions."

She sighed. "Okay ask your questions and I will see if I am able to answer them for you or not."

Again, I scanned the papers strewn all over my table and grabbed one I recall scribbling notes on at work yesterday. I quickly scanned it. "Are you able to share with me your thoughts on what stuff of mine still needs work?"

She laughed. "You do realize we are both therapists, right? So, I know how to ask the same question differently too."

Now it was my turn to sigh. "Okay how about I just talk, and you can interject whenever you have something to add or maybe if you want to ask me a question. Does that work?"

"Yes, that should be fine."

I took a sip of water and collected my thoughts. "Recently I recalled a time when you asked me to explain my three heartbreaks to you. As I thought about them, I realized you had been very instrumental in helping me to work through those."

She interrupted, "Actually Joy, you have to take credit for that. You did the hard work."

I nodded my head in agreement even though she could not see me. "Yes, that is correct, however the more I thought about everything I realized although I had worked through the issues on the surface there are still some layers underneath the surface that have not been addressed." I paused to wait for a moment for a reaction from Robin.

She said, "I am very intrigued, so please, continue." I decided to try again to ask Robin a question that has been on my mind.

"May I ask what you feel was the most traumatic thing for me about my relationship with Miles?" Robin sighed again. I braced for her nonresponse and I was surprised when she said, "You know Joy, if I am being honest with you I have always felt as though there was much more to that then you shared with me, but to answer your question I believe it was he left you with a lifelong reminder of him, genital herpes." As soon as the words left her lips and hit my ears the tears that had been welling up in my eyes made their way down my cheeks. I could not speak right away, I needed to let myself feel these emotions. Robin understood and she remained silent for a few minutes. Finally, she broke the silence on the phone line. "Joy, are you okay dear?"

I took a deep breath, wiped my eyes and nose, and said weakly, "Yes, I will be, just give me a minute to clean myself up." I got up and went to the powder room to blow my nose and splash some water on my face. I needed to get through this conversation. I wanted and needed to feel these emotions, but I also needed to make it through everything I needed to say. As I looked at myself in the mirror, I thought about Valerie for a brief moment. I really felt that if she let herself really feel everything and just had one good cry; she might feel so much better. The more I talk to her I feel that some of it is her attempting to be so strong. I made my way back to the kitchen table and resumed my conversation with Robin, "Okay I am back now, and I am ready to continue."

"Are you sure you are going to be okay to continue this?"

"Yes, I may cry, but I absolutely have to get through this Robin. Please bear with me. I think some of this has been bottled up for so long, that is why it is so difficult."

"I understand, dear, and I am here for you as long as you need me to be. If at any point something is just too difficult just let me know and we can take a break."

I smiled. "Thanks Robin, I really appreciate that, but I will be fine. I have been preparing for this conversation for several days now."

"Okay then so I answered your question, but you have not told me if I was correct or not."

"I cannot say you are wrong about that, because for a long time I too felt that was the worst part. As you know, I decided many years ago not to have children. I always thought that decision was about me having herpes. I had done all the research about it potentially causing blindness among other health issues for the child. It can be serious."

"Yes, I recall us talking through all of the pros and cons. So, tell me why now you feel there is more to this?"

"I believe even though at the time I somewhat downplayed it; I believe the deception was the worst part. Miles and I were only in a relationship for three and a half years and that is nothing compared to what my client Valerie has been through. She had been with her husband for over 25 years."

"Okay, hold on Joy. You really have to be careful to not compare yourself and your situation to your clients."

"I know Robin, but I need to explain everything, and it is impossible not to notice the similarities and the differences. I mean yes people are quite different, but honestly, there are a finite number of situations, right?"

Robin nervously chuckled. "Yes, I guess that is true. Okay please continue, no judgment. Go ahead and tell me why you feel your client's situation has sparked these new feelings about your life and situation."

I thought for a few moments before I responded. "I know it is still incredibly early in Valerie's therapy, but I see a woman who has endured years of emotional abuse. She is now dealing with the fact she was constantly being lied to about many things for an awfully long time."

"So, you see that being similar to what Miles did with you?"

"Yes, but I realize there really is no comparison because it was only a few years, and honestly, I am assuming he was lying to me the entire time, but I do not really know if that is true."

"That is exactly what I was about to say to you. The reality is you do not know at what point Miles began to lie to you. It could have been from the very beginning or it could have only been for a short period of time. You will never know since you refused to take any of his calls." I thought for a moment.

"Do you think I was wrong?"

"Wrong about what Joy?"

"Not taking his calls?"

"Oh, honey I cannot answer that for you. Everyone is different. Me, I need to know everything." She laughed and I said, "At the time, I think I was just so young and hurt and it was easier for me to imagine what happened than risk finding out the truth and being hurt even more."

"Yes, I can certainly understand that."

"But now I think it is really more than that."

"What do you mean Joy?"

"The last time I went to the park, I saw some families and I began to reminisce about my life, my childhood and my brother Darien. Then I came home and had my weekly talk with Toni. As I thought about things that day, it hit me that my relationship issues, or trust issues have more to do with Darien and Toni than they do with Miles."

"Okay now I am very intrigued. Please continue to explain."

I sipped on some water, then continued, "As you know my brother Darien and Toni went through some terrible things themselves and with their friends. I was an impressionable teenager during that time, and I am not sure either of them realized I heard things and knew a lot more about everything that was going on than I should have."

"I see, well did they ever talk to you about it at all?"

"No, not really. I mean I guess they tried, but again, they really did not know how much I knew or understood. Anyway, there was a lot of secrets and lies and half-truths in their circle. I believe when Miles hurt me it brought up all the repressed trauma I had been around, and I built a wall that has yet to be penetrated by anyone."

"That is not true. You trust me, right?"

I smiled. "Of course I do, but I am not in an intimate relationship with you either."

Robin laughed. "Good point. So, speaking of intimate relationships, that is not something you are interested in, even now?"

I thought for a minute. "Honestly, it has been so long I am not sure I even know what that means." We both laughed. Finally I said, "Seriously, I had not thought about it until Valerie. I still cannot put my finger on exactly what it is about her but there is something about her tenacity and her will to break through this trauma and get to the other side that inspires me."

"May I suggest something to you?"

"Of course."

"Not saying this as your therapist, but as a therapist I do think it would be good for you to write your feelings out and eventually you need to talk to Toni about everything. I am sure you will feel better and since she probably has no idea it might be good for you both to talk about it."

I thought for a minute before I responded, "Yes, I agree writing will be good, and I have actually been writing in my journal more about these feelings recently. Toni has been asking me to come visit. It has been awhile."

"That sounds good. Spend some more time writing things out and next time you and I chat if you feel up to it, I would love to hear some of what you wrote. I must be honest. I was really surprised to hear there were other things you felt were the cause of you losing your desire to open your heart to anyone else since Miles. It makes sense though. Please do not be offended by this next comment. Ultimately you might need to seek out another therapist to really work through all of those feelings."

"I am not surprised you are saying that, and I actually thought about it. I am open to it but first I just want to try to get the feelings out and on paper."

"That is a great start."

"Robin, I really appreciate you and your friendship. I owe you so much."

"No, you do not owe me anything, I appreciate your friendship as well."

Robin and I continued talking for at least another hour. She filled me in on her life, her kids, and grandkids. Robin had been married but divorced about ten years ago. She never talked to me about the details of what happened, but I could tell it affected her. I was not certain if she was dating again until tonight. She shared with me she finally felt ready and had been on a few dinner dates.

Chapter 8

After my talk with Robin I logged on to check my messages and my schedule for the next few days. I really wanted to take some time while the emotions were fresh to capture everything as Robin suggested in my journals. I checked my online client schedule and nothing new had been added. I decided to block myself out the rest of the week. I double checked to make sure Valerie had grabbed a slot for Monday, and she had so we were all set.

As I looked through my emails, I saw one from Valerie.

Joy,

As promised here is the email that gives you the details about the day the news broke. I was meeting with Haley and feeling so grateful that I had finally found someone that would be able to give our dog the attention he deserved. I felt so helpless since my surgery because it was still difficult for me to move around. I knew it would take time for me to heal, but I never liked having to rely on anyone else. My phone was on vibrate and it started going off several times. I glanced down quickly and saw there was a text from Fran as well as an email notification from my attorney. I was relieved that my meeting with Haley had just wrapped up so I could then focus on what was coming across my phone. I started up my laptop so I could bring up the emails full screen although I was extremely nervous to read the articles. Up to this point I only knew what Seth had shared which was not all that much.

I found myself looking at all the details in the stories multiple times because it just did not seem real. I began thinking about all I had gone through over the years of being with Seth. I felt afraid thinking that the man that I've been married to could have done such horrible things. Included in one of the articles was a picture of our Richmond house where the victim stated that he had taken her to after they were at a work reception together. I felt bad for her since she made it clear before that night she was not interested in him. I still could not believe what I was seeing in front of me in print. What would people think of me since I have been with him for so long? I reluctantly called Fran back since in her text it was clear she wanted to talk about what she was seeing. I was not in the mood to hear I told you so right now. I got off the phone with her as quickly as I could since I was struggling to hold back my tears.

I knew I needed to get in touch with my boys and was relieved to be able to speak to them before they saw or heard anything about the allegations. I was also happy neither of them were interested in reading any of the articles themselves. It was a lot to absorb and process for all of us. The big unknown was how this would all play out and the impact it would have on our lives.

That evening the phone calls and texts messages began streaming in from friends and family which started to be a little overwhelming. Jill called me several times so I figured she might need something besides just reaching out to me since the news hit. She was very distraught and let me know her son got expelled from school. For some reason we always seemed to have things happen to each other at the same time and we always were able to help each other *through. I gave her some ideas on how to start addressing her situation and also reached out to her later that night. I was very thankful to have her to turn to and knew she appreciated me helping her as well.*

Maybe we can pick up in our next session on how things were the next day when the news really started to spread across social media. I had hoped to work that day since I had just started back the day before, but after I logged in my phone started blowing up again with messages, so I figured it was best to take the day off. I also really did not want to face people from work reaching out to me about what they might be seeing. I will schedule our next session for early next week.

Valerie

I'm finally starting to see more emotion from Valerie. Maybe she's getting more comfortable with me and letting her guard down, but I am now beginning to see how things were affecting her. Based on this email it also seems that Jill is someone she can count on.

Valerie,

I wanted to let you know I received your email. I think it will be good for us to talk through my questions during our next session. I see you are scheduled for Monday. I am going to be taking a couple days off to handle some personal business. Feel free to email me if you want or need to. I will try to check in daily in case something comes up you need immediate support for.

Joy

At work the next day I moved my clients around so I could take the day off on Friday. I felt like I rushed through my day to get home to start my personal intensive therapy session. Once I was home I decided I was going to spend my therapy time in the living room. It was close to the kitchen to refuel on food and drink, it was also close to the bathroom. It had a great view of my yard for gazing and thinking, comfortable seating options, several chairs, and a nice sofa for naps. I had my journal, a blank legal pad, sticky notes, pens, pencils, and highlighters. I was ready to start, but as I sat there absolutely nothing came to mind.

I decided to read some of my entries from the past couple of weeks to see if that sparked anything. Still nothing. I decided to document the highlights of my conversation with Robin last night. That was a great exercise, I felt the emotions begin to flow and I was off to the races. The words flowed and pages were filled in my journal. I took breaks for food and water, but I stayed in there all-night writing, reminiscing, and listening to music. Music is one way I can get my emotions flowing.

I ended up spending almost the entire day Friday and through Sunday early afternoon in my living room working through my emotions. When I was finally ready, I sent Robin an email. After writing dozens of pages in my journal, I reread everything and made an outline of the items that were things I needed to address with Toni. That is what I sent Robin first. Next, I had made up a list of items I should have addressed with Miles but did not. Those were on the shelf. I would deal with those after I handled things with Toni.

In my email to Robin I asked her to call me later Sunday evening to discuss what I sent her. I then busied myself with my weekly chores around the house. I started with cleaning up the mess I had managed to make in the living room. I moved my self-therapy supplies into my office. I had been snacking on too much junk food for the past several days, so I decided to make a nice dinner.

Just as I sat down at the table to eat dinner Robin called. She was in tears.

"Joy, this is amazing. Have you considered becoming a writer?"

I laughed. "No, I have not and will not."

"I am telling you the way you write is very good and I am certain you could have a successful career."

"Thanks, but I think I will stick to therapy."

She pressed further, "What about a therapy book?"

I raised my eyebrow as I considered it. "Hmm now that is an idea. I'll consider that but for now tell me your thoughts on the email."

"I think it is excellent. You should send it to Toni and plan a trip to come visit."

I smiled but then quickly thought about how emotionally difficult returning to Pennsylvania is for me. "Do you think I should just send Toni the email or should I call her and tell her that it's coming? She did call me yesterday afternoon and I have not called her back yet."

"I think you should definitely return her call, or she might think something is wrong. You talk weekly right?"

"Yes, we typically do but there have been times where we missed a week."

"I think you should, do whatever you feel comfortable with, go with your gut."

"My gut is telling me not to call."

"Why is that?"

"I feel as though it will become a discussion and I want her to read everything before we talk."

"Yes, I understand that. So why don't you just send her the email tonight? Do you think you will be able to drive up this weekend?"

"I'm not sure about this weekend, but I will see if I am able to. I need to see where my clients are since I took this past weekend off. But I will send her the email tonight before bed."

I promised to follow up with Robin the following day after Toni got the email. Our talk was brief since we were both eating dinner. I wanted to prepare for work tomorrow and check on my clients since I had been disconnected for the past three days.

After ending my call with Robin, I sat and thought more about our conversation and about the email to Toni. I decided I still was not ready to send it yet but since I had missed her call over the weekend, I decided to just send her a brief email letting her know I was okay.

I went into my office and started my email.

Dear Toni,

I am so sorry I missed your call. I was busy all weekend working on a project. I hope all is well with you and the kids. I talked to Robin earlier and she is trying to get me to drive up this weekend. I still need to make sure I can swing it from a work perspective, but I wanted to make sure you were also going to be around if I decide to drive up. Let me know. I would love to see Darien and Denise also if they are going to be around. I will confirm by Wednesday if I am going to be able to come.

> *Love,*

> *Your Joy*

I read my email again and smiled at my signature. I had grown very fond of it over the years. At first, I found it to be a bit corny and somewhat annoying, but I think everything is corny and annoying to teenagers. The older I got the more I began to realize how special it was and now I fully embraced Toni's term of endearment for me.

I decided to read the email I had shared with Robin I wrote for Toni again.

> *Toni,*

> *I have had so much to say to you for so long. Before I begin, I want to first thank you for all you did for me following the death of my mother. You welcomed me into your home without hesitation. I want to also thank you for loving my brother the way you did. Darien deserved a love like yours and although your time together was brief I know he was incredibly happy with you. Last, but certainly not least, I appreciate you continuing to welcome me into your home even after Darien died. I was not your responsibility, but you took me on without hesitation. I am the woman I am today because of your love, nurturing, and encouragement.*

> *With all of that said, I am also a broken woman. It is by no means your fault, but there are things I have never shared with you maybe I should have before now. I am not sure you are fully aware of how much I knew about everything you and Darien went through. There was so much going on back then and I know you and Darien were working extremely hard to work through your issues to save*

your marriage. Talking to me was not in the forefront of either of your minds. Since I do not have children, I cannot say with any certainty talking through things with me would have helped, but I can tell you I feel it did impact me greatly. Again, please do not feel this is a personal attack on you, it really is not. This is just me, a woman who is attempting to work through her issues and to speak her truth.

I have never fully understood how you and Darien met, or more importantly, how it was possible you had a child with his best friend Vince. That was very confusing to me as a teenager, and the tension this issue put on my brother and his relationship with Vince was very evident to me.

When I first met you, I admired your relationship with Jada and hoped I would grow up to have a best friend like her. When things got bad between the two of you, it was hard for me to imagine how and why it happened. In time I came to understand there were a couple of issues which caused the rift between the two of you, but they were all centered around lies and ultimately a loss of trust. I am not sure you realize this, but I still do not have any close friends. I have been unable to form bonds with women and men because I have been afraid to become vulnerable. You are probably thinking I should have worked this out a long time ago and you are right, however, until recently I did not realize these things were a problem. That is the thing about emotions and feelings, sometimes when you bury them deep enough they seem to disappear and then when you least expect it, they can rear their ugly heads again and catch you off guard.

There is another thing I need to apologize to you for. I believe I made you feel guilty for taking Darien off life support. Deep down I feel you have not moved on and started a relationship with anyone else because of that guilt or because you were unsure how I would react. Toni I am terribly sorry if I made you feel that way. I know Darien was gone long before the machines were disconnected. I know you had no other choice and I know you loved my brother deeply. I also know if he could he would tell you it is okay for you to move on with your life.

Bottom line Toni is you and I have impacted each other lives both positively and negatively and we have only dealt with the issues on the surface. There are layers beyond the surface that still need to heal and the only way to do that is to be honest with each other and talk about everything. Before responding, I ask you take some time and think about what I've shared and if you like we can talk about it when I visit you.

Love Always,

Your Joy

Reading my words again invoked so many emotions for me. I could only imagine how reading this would impact Toni. There was no way I could send this email before I was certain I would be able to visit her this weekend. Thinking about old times made me feel happy, but then the sadness soon followed. I imagined Valerie also felt this same type of conflict with her emotions as she works through the healing process.

*****

My lack of sleep over the weekend caught up with me and I ended up oversleeping a bit. I was not late to work, but I did not have time to follow up with Robin before work as I planned. We rarely communicated during the workday, but I decided I would reach out to her during my lunch break.

I was pleased things had been quiet over the long weekend and my schedule was typical for a Monday. As I scrolled through my emails and sipped on my tea making notes about things to follow up on, I heard a light knock on my door. I looked up and saw Bill standing in my doorway. I put my pen down and stood up.

"Hey Bill, how are you?"

He stepped inside my office and smiled. "I am fine and how are you feeling today? Did you enjoy your long weekend?"

I walked around my desk. "Yes, it was wonderful. Thank you so much for allowing me to take the day off on such short notice. I really appreciate it." He motioned for me to sit down.

"It was no problem Joy; you hardly ever take anytime off so when you need a day or week for that matter just let me know."

I made a mental note of his comment since I might need that favor again for my planned trip this coming weekend. I sat down. "So, what is going on Bill?"

He chuckled and asked, "Am I not allowed to just stop by and check on you?"

I laughed. "Yes of course you are, however, after working for you for over ten years it would be something new."

He nodded. "Well, of course you are correct." He sat down and continued, "I just wanted to follow up with you on your new role and schedule."

"Ah, yes, I was wondering what was happening, but I figured you would let me know if you needed anything from me."

"There isn't anything I need from you except some time. You and I need to start meeting on a regular basis to start putting our heads together about how to move forward.

"Okay Bill, I should be able to carve out a few hours in between clients for you, but you really didn't need to come down here for that. You have access to my schedule and can put meetings on my calendar." I felt that my comment may have been a bit too harsh and I waited to his response.

He smiled then said. "Joy, you are truly an amazing woman and therapist."

I felt like he added the therapist part as an afterthought. I felt myself blush. "Thanks Bill, I appreciate you saying that."

"Seriously Joy, I see something in you that is rare. You are truly passionate about your work and genuinely want to help people. You have always looked for ways to improve things, never settling for status quo."

"Thank you again for saying that. May I share something else with you?" I decided I needed to mention my outside affiliation with Bill since I did not want him to be surprised if it came up.

"Yes of course Joy. What is it?"

"You remember that I started as an independent consultant with the online therapy group last month?"

"Yes, I do recall that. How is that going?"

I smiled. "It is going well. I only have a handful of clients and I work with them evening and weekends of course." I hesitated for a moment calculating the potential damage from sharing too much information versus not saying anything and having it come out later. Finally, I continued, "Bill, I am almost certain that one of my online clients is related to one of our clients."

Bill raised his eyebrows, but he did not say anything right away. I saw him thinking and processing what I had shared with him He sat forward in his seat and said, "I don't think there's an issue with that. As long as you are not treating the client directly. In regard to your schedule, I am sure that we will be able to work things out Joy. I am willing to be very flexible with you on this."

Although I was pleased that he wasn't concerned about their being a conflict, I also felt a little uneasy. There seemed to be some hidden meaning in his words. He put emphasis on certain words, and I was beginning to think that Bill might be interested in me. I had never sensed this from him before and I did not want to jump to any conclusions or accuse him of anything. I simply said, "Great, thanks Bill for your understanding."

Bill stood up and said, "Yeah, I am certain that there is nothing for us to be concerned about, but I do appreciate you mentioning it to me."

I also stood up. "Of course. If there is anything I can do before we meet to prepare just let me know."

As he moved closer to the door he said, "Yes, I will be in touch. Oh, Joy, a couple more things while I am here. Great work with Martha." I felt as though I was missing something, and I made a face.

"Oh, you have not gotten through your emails yet?"

I looked over to my desk. "No, I was just starting to read them when you stopped by."

He smiled and said, "Well, there is a nice email in there for you from her daughter. She came and picked her mom up on Saturday and she wanted to thank you personally for convincing her mother to contact her."

I smiled and responded, "Oh really? I am so happy. Martha was genuinely concerned about being rejected again."

Bill smiled and said, "And the other email is that we had to assign you another client in Martha's place because we had another therapist quit over the weekend."

"Oh, okay, no problem Bill. You know I am willing to pitch in and help anyway I can."

Bill simply smiled and nodded as he walked out the door. I walked over to my desk, sat down, and looked for the email about Martha. When I found it, I read Bill's comments first then scrolled down to the personal note from Martha's daughter. It was very heartfelt and brought me to tears. I was incredibly pleased with Martha's progress over the past two weeks and it was clients like her that made this job worthwhile.

Chapter 9

During lunch I attempted to reach Robin, but I got her voice mail. I decided not to leave her any details. I just asked her to call me this evening before my scheduled session with Valerie.

My afternoon was uneventful. My new client, Kara was a pleasant young woman, but I sensed she was a little guarded. She did not trust me or the process. I could tell she was going to be tough to reach, but I was up to the challenge. After my session with Valerie tonight I would go over my notes and come up with a strategy to reach Kara.

Robin called during my ride home. "Did you send the email? What did she say?"

I rolled my eyes. "Robin, give me a minute to explain."

"So that means you did not send it." She sighed and continued, "Why, Joy?"

I laughed. "Why are you being so dramatic today?"

Now she laughed. "It has been one of those days. My clients were all in rare form today." We both laughed together, and I began to explain. Ultimately Robin said she understood, and she felt waiting until later in the week once I confirmed I could make the trip would probably be best. We decided to touch base again on Thursday. We continued to chat for the remainder of my commute. She shared the highlights of her challenging day with me, without sharing her client's names of course.

****

I logged onto my session a few minutes early and waited for Valerie to join while I skimmed through her email and my notes again. When I heard the notification she had joined I looked up from my notes and greeted her. "Hello Valerie. How are you?"

She smiled. "I am doing pretty well."

I smiled back. "I am happy to hear that. Let us get started, we have a lot to cover. I went through your email you sent detailing when the story hit the news. I was curious where was the story being reported?"

"It started out in a few newspapers locally and then was in several across the state. Then there was a national story and I had heard it was also on television. I began thinking about what Seth had said to me when he left and disconnected our home phone for me to not talk with reporters. I worried about who was coming and going from my house, so I watched the security cameras from an app on my cell phone."

"That must have been extremely difficult to deal with. You mentioned you were getting a lot of messages on your phone from friends and family also."

"I was and I wanted to acknowledge everyone that offered their support. I saw a text from a friend who had gone through a divorce with similar circumstances, her ex also had a drinking problem. I responded to her and asked if she was able to come over and she arrived around lunchtime. Not only did she provide much needed emotional support, but she also ironed clothes for David since he had an interview that day for the college that was top on his list."

"That was really nice of her. How was David doing given everything that was going on?"

"He had decided to stay home from school and went to the gym. I was concerned about media showing up to my house, so I checked the security cameras each time before David left. I was expecting Haley to arrive right around the same time that afternoon when he left for his interview. When I saw someone with brown hair headed towards the front door, I decided to open it thinking it was her."

"So, who was it?"

Valerie began sobbing uncontrollably. I let her take her time since this was obviously hard for her.

"It is okay, just take your time."

She nodded to acknowledge she heard me. Once she regained her composure, she continued, "It was a reporter asking me questions and a camera guy shining bright lights in my eyes. I immediately closed the door and locked it. I was mortified because I was still in my pajamas. Very soon after that I got a text from Fran letting me know she had seen me on the news. How she was seeing everything first I had no idea although she seemed to want to make sure I knew everything going on."

"Oh my. I am sure that was traumatic. I am curious though, had you gotten used to being in the public eye since that was a big part of Seth's job?"

"While I did not mind socializing with people, I was still a pretty private person. We were in a small community, so I would get approached frequently. It was important to show support for Seth so he could continue getting re-elected and keep his job which depended on him being well liked. It took time to adjust to the political lifestyle and it was not something I was entirely comfortable with. I hated the idea of speaking in public and found myself having to sometimes do this for Seth if he was at another event."

"Did Haley eventually get to your house after you closed the door on the reporter?"

"She did get there shortly after and my friend that helped David get ready for his interview was still there talking with me. I started to feel overwhelmed with everything going on and had a full-fledged panic attack. I really did not know what was going on because that had never happened to me before. It seemed everything hit me like a ton of bricks all at once. One of the news articles had a follow up story that stated additional security measures were being put in place for the capitol as a result of the investigation which made me realize just how serious the allegations were. The tone of the articles had gotten a lot harsher from the day before and now Seth was being told to resign and focus on being there for his family."

"You were being hit with a lot Valerie, but It seems like you were doing well considering everything. How did David's interview go?"

"It went really well, and he was in such a great mood afterwards. He stopped home later and it was nice to see him happy and around friends given the tough week we endured. We were both very thankful it was Friday."

"How was the weekend? Did you still feel as if you had a lot of support? Did you have some more friends stop by?"

"The weekend was good. My friends continued to show their support by bringing food, cleaning my house, and keeping me company. Sunday morning when I woke up I was starting to have a sense of peace with what was happening and believed God was looking out for me."

"That is good you were starting to feel a little better with everything. I know there were many people stopping by and helping you out but were you sharing your feelings with anyone?"

"My parents offered any support I needed and were being very understanding. I also had several friends I was in touch with."

"It sounds like there were a lot of people concerned about you. I imagine it was hard to keep in touch with everyone." I could sense Valerie seemed a little overwhelmed which was understandable. There was a lot that happened, and she was trying to give me the whole picture, so I let her continue.

"It was and since Fran lived in DC it was hard for her to understand I had grown close to people I lived near and they were there to help me. Fran insisted I get in touch with a grief counselor immediately even though I was working with a therapist."

"Did you follow Fran's advice? Did she have someone in mind for you to talk to?"

"My friend Tina suggested meeting with her mom who specializes in helping clients through the loss of a loved one or in my case getting a divorce. Tina and I had known each other since our boys played little league together. She was someone I had reached out to on many occasions when I needed to talk. I mentioned this to Fran, and she reached out to Tina directly."

"So how did the session go?"

"The session ended up being too much for me at the time and would have probably been better to deal with later. I ended up canceling with the therapist I was already working with that day to accommodate the appointment which was the day before I ended up at the hospital."

"Okay I think we are in a good place to stop for today. Are you ready to move on to talking more about when you were admitted to the hospital? You can send me an email and we can go through any questions I have on that next time."

"Sure. I can do that. I really am finding it helpful to go through this with you Joy. Thank you for your help."

"You are welcome, and I think it seems to be getting a little easier for you to express how you were feeling as you recount what happened. I can see you are also processing things now and getting a better understanding. You are making great progress."

"Thanks. Since it is early in the week should I schedule something towards the end of this week or wait until the beginning of next week?"

"Why don't you schedule something for early next week. Work on the email and we can play it by ear. If I feel we need to talk sooner maybe we can move your next video session up. I recently lost a client so I should have some free time later in the week."

"That sounds good. I will send the email within the next day or so. Thanks again Joy."

"Take care Valerie."

I made some notes after ending my session with Valerie. In general, I felt she was handling things very well. I did sense we were about to enter some difficult memories for her. Although Valerie felt she had a lot of support around her I am not sure everyone is working for her benefit. Sometimes less is more. Hindsight is 20/20 but based on my recent revelations about things I never properly addressed I am going to do everything I can to help Valerie. The key is to pace yourself and allow the feelings and emotions to happen as they naturally unfold. Sometimes your emotions and reactions are not logical and do not happen in the same order the trauma did. I am going to mention this to Valerie the next time we talk. I want her to understand she has twenty-five years to process and it will take time.

I checked my emails and saw Toni had responded.

Joy,

I am elated you are considering coming up for a visit. We will be around all weekend so whenever you can come visit will be fine. Just let me know once you can confirm your plans.

Toni

I thought about how long it had been since I visited. I really did want to see everyone. I just know how visiting Pennsylvania affects me for at least a week afterwards. I had clients counting on me for their mental health. I could not afford to be going through my own crisis while trying to help them.

Valerie was the only one I was concerned about now, but she is doing very well. I thought for a moment and decided if I could make headway with Kara in the next day or two then I would go for the weekend and return on Monday. I could just go for the weekend, but I felt as though Toni and I would need some time to talk and process our emotions. Staying the extra day was going to be best.

I decided to take a break and review Kara's file after dinner and my workout. I loved to walk but it is always dark when I get home from work, so I typically try to find a quick workout routine on YouTube at least a few times a week. I decided to only schedule one online client per evening when possible.

After dinner and a light workout, I retrieved my planner from my office. I sat in the living room and thought about Kara and how best to get her to trust me enough to honestly talk to me about her problems. Kara is in her late twenties; she has one child and has struggled with addiction issues since she was a teenager. She was clean for almost two years before her most recent relapse. What I need to get her to talk about is what led to that and I also sense there is more than addiction in Kara's history. I believe she may need additional services, but I need to get her to share more to get that information.

*****

At work the following day I was incredibly pleased with my session with Kara. She seemed to be in much better spirits and was much more talkative. She is genuinely concerned about losing her son. He is currently staying with someone on his fathers' side of the family. Before I could ask Kara shared with me why she felt she turned back to drugs again. Her son's father was killed in a car accident before he was born. She did not seem to be terribly upset about losing him. When I asked about it, she stated they were young and just having a good time. She did not feel there was real love between them. Her sadness about it was more focused on the fact her son would never know his father. She had a rough pregnancy with some complications along the way and felt she did not have any real support from her family. She then suffered from postpartum depression.

A year after she had her son, she started using again after reconnecting with some old friends from high school. She got into another relationship which she felt was more serious, at least from her perspective. As her son got older, she felt pressure to get clean and she did. However, her partner did not follow suit and it became an issue in their relationship. Her partner did not support her sobriety and often attempted to entice her to use again. Kara says she did not use drugs, however, somehow there were drugs in her system when she went for her monthly drug screening which was a requirement for her job and her ongoing outpatient therapy. She believes her partner somehow gave her drugs in her food or drink.

As an addiction therapist we often hear stories from clients about someone else being responsible for giving them drugs or without their knowledge. I felt Kara was sincere. I also still believe Kara has some other underlying issues that should be addressed. She mentioned postpartum depression, but I do not believe she has ever sought professional help for it. We covered a lot in our session, and I asked her to schedule a follow up for the next day. I felt we are making great progress and I do not want to slow our momentum. I also decided to join her group sessions so I can observe her with the other clients. I sense she has some social issues not being able to connect with others but once I observe her I will have a better idea.

By Thursday I had completed my assessment of Kara and had prepared my recommendation for some additional wrap around services for her. Kara clearly had some social awkwardness issues and I decided to request a full evaluation which includes mental health, psychiatric and cognitive development. I also had decided to request Monday off so I could travel to Pennsylvania for the weekend. My plan was to drive up tomorrow after work. During my lunch earlier today I sent both Robin and Toni emails letting them know I would be visiting this weekend. They were both incredibly happy and excited about seeing me. Although I was a little anxious about the aftermath of my visit, I was looking forward to seeing them both.

I decided to send the email to Toni first thing tomorrow morning and I was planning to add a note asking her not to respond via email. I wanted us to talk about it while I was there. Robin thought that was a good idea also.

My next major decision was going to be where to stay while I was there. Usually I stayed with Toni, however there had been times when I stayed with Robin. I had not committed to either one of them. I thought it best to decide once I was there and see how things went with Toni.

On my way home from work on Thursday Robin called and asked where I was planning to stay. I told her I was not sure yet but to prepare her guest room just in case. She did not press me either way. I just knew she was going to be happy to see me.

I had so much to get done tonight to prepare for my trip. I was no good at packing. It was nearly impossible for me to decide what I planned to wear two days from now. I was known for over-packing, no matter if it was a weekend trip or a weeklong vacation. It seemed I always required at least three bags. Although I vowed to try to only carry two bags, by the time I had finished packing there were three and an exceptionally large purse.

I had a scheduled session with one of my online clients tonight, my youngest client. Her parents divorcing had totally caught her off guard during her freshman year of college. She was finally entering into the acceptance stage of her grieving and hinted she was considering cutting back on our sessions. She suggested moving from weekly to bi-weekly and I agreed.

Just as I was ending my session, I received an email notification from Valerie. It had been a few days since our session. I had checked earlier to confirm she had booked our next appointment for Tuesday evening. I began to read the email but quickly decided to stop. I knew this was going to require more brain power than I had now. I decided to send her a quick reply, acknowledging receipt and we could discuss everything during the session next week.

I opened my email for Toni. I read it again and added my note at the end about not responding by email. I saved the draft so in the morning before leaving for work I could send the email.

I put my bags by the front door, all except for my toiletries bag and went upstairs to prepare for bed. I changed into my night clothes and climbed into bed with my journal in hand. I wanted to reread some of my thoughts from the weekend. After that I decided to make a list of all the places I wanted to visit and things to accomplish while I was there.

The very first item on my list was a visit to the cemetery to put flowers on my mother's grave and I also had to visit Darien's grave. At least once I wanted to take a walk along the riverfront. Maybe even walk over to City Island. I may even stop by the market on Saturday morning to see if my favorite food stands are still there.

I was not feeling the sense of dread I typically felt before leaving for Pennsylvania. I was hopeful talking to Toni would help ease some of my anxiety. Next up would be to deal with my Miles unresolved issues.

Chapter 10

I set my alarm for a half hour earlier than usual. I wanted to have time to send the email to Toni before I left for work. I also wanted to make sure I had everything I needed for my trip.

Forty-five minutes later, the email was sent, and the car was packed. I walked through the house checking the windows and doors to make sure everything was locked, and I left for work. Upon arriving I ran into Bill and he told me one of my clients was taken to the emergency room early this morning. They suspect appendicitis. That meant I could possibly shift my schedule around and leave a little earlier to beat some of the Friday afternoon traffic.

I breezed through all my client sessions and was in my car by 2:30. I sent Robin a text letting her know I was headed North. I purposely did not contact Toni. I felt sure she had received my email and I did not want to talk to her about it right now. I filled my tank at the gas station near my job, purchased my travel snacks and I was on my way.

Traffic was light on 29 North. I listened to my music, sang along, and enjoyed the scenery. Traffic picked up slightly once I got to 64 but I was still making great time. I was still feeling good. Once I got on 81 North my anxiety level picked up a little. The closer I got to the Pennsylvania line the heavier I felt. It is strange to have both a sense of joy and dread all at the same time. That is how my relationship is with Robin. I cherish her friendship, but it is a blessing and a curse to be close friends with a therapist. She can never just let me feel what I feel. We eventually must work through everything, even though it is no longer a formal process with her as my therapist. Even for myself it is somewhat exhausting. Once you learn the tools to process emotions and work through issues it is difficult to turn that off.

Once I get to Carlisle, I know I am almost home. As I rode across the George Wade bridge I smiled, and voice dialed Robin. She answered before I even heard the phone ring,

"Are you here?"

I laughed and said, "I just came across the bridge."

"You made great time."

"Yeah I know, there was not a lot of traffic today."

"That is good. Are you coming here?"

"Yeah, I think so. I would like to decompress for a little with you before going to Toni's house."

"That sounds great. I'll see you when you get here."

As I drove along the familiar streets, I was amazed at the changes that had occurred in such a short period of time. It had been 6 months since I had been back to visit. I pulled up to Robin's house and I saw her standing in the doorway looking for me. In that moment it felt good to be missed by someone. I guess I was so wrapped up in my own feelings that it never occurred to me how my presence affects others. Basically, it is not always about me and my feelings. I must do better about those I care about. As I approached her, I made a mental note about how Robin really has not changed much over the 15 years that I have known her. Maybe a few more gray hairs but that's it. She's an average height, about 5'6 and has worn her hair in natural styles for as long as I have known her. Everything about her has an earthy or natural theme. Her clothes we usually warm tones and she did not wear much makeup, but when she did you could barely tell since everything blended together.

Once inside Robin gave me a nice hug and began taking my bags and walking towards the guest room. I looked around and thought about how inviting her home was. It reminded me of my mom's house.

"Have you heard from Toni yet?" Robin asked.

"No, I have not. I think I am going to call her now to let her know I am in town."

"Yeah, that is probably a good idea." Robin responded sounding a little winded from going back and forth with my heavy bags. When she returned, she plopped down on the sofa and let out a heavy sigh.

"Girl, what in the world did you pack in those bags?"

I laughed as I reached in my purse for my cell phone. "You know I cannot pack light. I have to bring everything I might consider wearing at some point in the future." We both laughed and as I dialed Toni's number, I put my finger to my mouth to tell Robin to be quiet.

Toni answered, "Hello."

"Hi Toni, I am here at Robin's house."

"Oh," she said sounding disappointed. "I thought you were coming here."

"Yes, I am coming over to visit, but I decided to stop here first to see Robin."

"Oh, okay because I made dinner for you and the kids are here waiting for you." Robin was distracting me by making gestures and mouthing words I could not understand.

"I just arrived, so I'll shower and be right over."

"Okay, I'll see you when you get here." As soon as I hung up the phone Robin said,

"What did she say? Did she read the email?" I put my hand up.

"Stop, take a breath. She seemed disappointed I was here. She made dinner so I have to go over there now."

"Did she mention the email?"

As I stood up to go into the room to get ready, I said, "No she did not. I am certain she had to have read it by now."

"Hmm maybe she has not read it yet. She could have been busy all day getting the house ready for you to visit."

"Yes, I guess that could be true. Well let me get showered and changed so I can go over there and see."

*****

As I pulled up to Toni's house and parked the memories came to my mind, full force. I had to close my eyes and practice my breathing exercises to calm myself down. I slowly walked up to the door and right before I could ring the doorbell, the door flew open and Denise ran right into my arms.

"Auntie Joy, it is so nice to see you. I missed you so much." I smiled and hugged her tight. Once I pulled away, I held onto her shoulders and just looked her up and down while saying, "Where is my little niece? Girl, you have gotten so tall. You better stop growing up on me." She laughed and as I stepped inside, I saw Darien Jr. walking towards the door to greet me. When he smiled my heart melted. He had my brothers smile, in fact it looked as if he had my brothers entire face. There it was again, that joyful and painful feeling all wrapped up together. Toni emerged from the kitchen and welcomed me with a tight hug. It felt as if she never wanted to let go. Her smell, that I've been in kitchen cooking all day smell reminded me of my mom. It felt good to be home. Toni looked the same as always, maybe a little more gray hair showing than before, but otherwise not much has changed.

"It is so good to see you, my Joy." We both smiled.

"It feels good to be here. I did not realize how much I missed you all until I was in the car headed in this direction."

"Well we are glad you are here, and the food is ready so let us go get started. We can all catch up around the dinner table."

"That sounds great, let me use the restroom quick and I will be right in there." I took my phone with me so I could text Robin. I simply wrote, 'I am here now'. Do not think she read the email yet. Robin responded with a simple 'ok'.

Dinner was great. Darien and Denise both caught me up on their lives. Darien is a college senior and Denise is a freshman in college. It was hard to believe how much time has passed since my brother died. During dinner while Denise or Darien were talking, I caught Toni staring at me which made me wonder if she had in fact read my message.

After dinner, Denise insisted she and I have a private conversation which I agreed we would have later, after we all helped Toni clear the table and clean up the kitchen. I really had a great time. We were almost finished, and Darien and Denise had already left. Toni came over to me and said,

"What is going on, my Joy?"

I was not sure what to say. "What do you mean?" She wiped her hands on her apron and motioned for me to sit down on one of the barstools. I grabbed a paper towel and wiped my hands and then sat. Toni looked at me for a few moments before saying anything.

"I know I came into your life when you were a teenager, but I still know you very well. As soon as you walked through that door tonight, I could tell something is weighing very heavy on you my dear." As she spoke, I evaluated each word and when she finished it was clear to me she had not seen my email yet. I reached for her hand and looked at her.

"Yes, Toni, you are correct. You and I need to have a conversation that should have happened many years ago." She frowned a little and I raised my hand.

"Hear me out please. Toni, I love you and appreciate everything you have done for me over the years. I sent you an email earlier this morning which you obviously have not seen yet." She began shaking her head.

"No, I was so busy cleaning and preparing for your visit, I did not even turn my computer on today." As if she read my thoughts she continued, "And I rarely look at emails on my phone because they are too hard for me to read."

"I understand, but here is what I need you to do. After I leave and you have some quiet time, I want you to read my email. I am going to stay with Robin tonight. Her and I have some catching up to do also. I will come back over here tomorrow afternoon or early evening. You call or text me tomorrow to let me know what time to be here. After you read my email, I would like for the two of us to sit down and have an adult conversation, just you and I." Once I finished, she sat in silence nodding her head, but she did not say anything initially. She stood up and walked over to the sink. With her back turned to me she finally said, "Joy, are you sick?"

"Oh, no Toni it is not anything like that." She turned around and I could see the tears in her eyes. I stood up and went to give her a hug. While hugging her I said, "I am fine Toni physically, do not worry about that."

She leaned back to look me in my eyes. "You promise?"

I smiled and raised my hand. "Scouts honor."

Then she smiled. "Okay, then. Go ahead and visit with Denise so you can leave, and I can read this email of yours. You know I am a little impatient."

I laughed. "Yes, I do know that about you and I thought you would have already seen the email." I got up and headed upstairs.

I spent about an hour with Denise. She and I talked about everything. She seems to be adjusting to college life fairly well. She is still living at home for now but wanted to get my opinion on her living on campus next year. She seemed to be a very well-rounded young lady. As she talked, I looked at her and realized just how much she reminded me of myself at her age. although she was much more focused than I was. I knew Darien would be proud of both of his children. It was getting late and I was tired from the drive. Robin had sent me a text a half hour ago asking if I was coming back to her place tonight. I responded yes and I would be there soon. I went back downstairs and said my goodbyes.

When I arrived at Robin's house, she had a bottle of wine waiting. I walked in and before she could ask, I said, "She has not read the email yet."

Robin scrunched up her face. "Why not?"

I sat down and grabbed a glass. "You called it, my dear. She was too busy preparing for my visit all day. She did not check her emails." Robin and I both busted up laughing. The wine was great, but after only one glass I was ready for bed. Robin understood I was tired, and she had clients to see in the morning. She expected me to be with Toni all day, but we planned to spend tomorrow evening talking about our stuff as she put it.

When I awoke the following morning Robin was already gone. I found a note on the kitchen table telling me there was fruit and yogurt in the fridge and to make myself at home. She also left me a key in case I decided to venture out. Since I had some time to kill, I decided to get my laptop and read my emails. I was especially interested to see if Toni had responded and I wanted to read Valerie's email also.

I quickly scanned my new emails and I did see one from Toni. I opened it and it simply said,

My Joy,

We should talk over lunch today. I will text you later a time and place for us to meet.

Toni

I reached for my phone and texted Robin that Toni read the email and we are meeting for lunch. I knew she was with clients but would check her messages when she could.

I still had several hours before lunch, so I decided to dive into Valerie's email. First, I made myself a bowl of fruit and yogurt and grabbed a bottle of water.

Joy,

I wanted to give you some more information leading up to when I ended up in the hospital before our next session.

I needed to talk through how I was feeling with someone since I was feeling overwhelmed and shocked by everything. I continued to ask myself how could Seth have done this to me? I still could not believe he just walked in and told me what he was accused of and then took off. I thought about what he must be going through at the clinic since he seemed to have an issue with alcohol, and I felt bad for him. Did he realize what I had to deal with on my own? How would it be once I began to go out in public? Would people say things to me or just give me looks of pity? It was a small town and most people already knew our family. This was not going away anytime soon so I had to start processing my emotions now with someone.

Although I had started online counseling with a therapist a few weeks prior to my surgery, the grief counseling session I went through was very intense. The therapist and I went step by step through what happened the night Seth told me what was going on. When he said he needed to talk to me about something and sat down on the couch across from me I knew it had to be something serious. As I was recalling this with the grief counselor I realized I got so worried because the last time I saw him like this was when he told me his best friend from college had been killed by a drunk driver. I knew whatever he was about to tell me what going to be devastating.

Directly after my grief counseling session finished is when Paula was picking me up to go to David's track meet. It would have been better for me to stay home and continue to process what I had been through and rest, but I was also excited about going since I had missed a few meets because of my hysterectomy. When I got in the car Paula was talking about how my focus needed to be on getting David the help he needed right now. Because Paula's brother works at the hospital he was able to get an appointment for David with a top psychologist the very next day. However, I was not sure David would be ready to go so soon.

Paula rarely went to the track meets so we left about halfway through and she dropped me off at my house. I called Jill and we were on the phone for hours talking about all the trips we took together. She was over the night Seth had told me what he was accused of and left so I asked her questions to try to remember everything he had told me. I felt like I needed to put all the pieces together now that I had seen the news stories.

Next thing I knew the sun was shining and Jill told me to take a call from Paula. I remember seeing her name come through on my phone, but I think I may have started hallucinating due to lack of sleep. I did recognize Paula when she came in my house and she told me she was taking me to David's appointment. I went upstairs to tell David I would meet him there, but he was sleeping so I whispered goodbye.

My world changed when I got into the car with Paula that day since I was lied to and committed to the psych ward at the hospital making trusting anyone extremely difficult.

Maybe we can talk about that further in our next session. I am fine waiting to touch base until our video session next Tuesday.

Valerie

I read through her email twice before I began to jot a few notes down. My initial thought was, 'Wow!'. She certainly had a lot going on. It is no wonder she ended up in the hospital although I do not have all the details leading up to her being committed. I am not so sure it was her behavior that landed her in the hospital. It is interesting to me that the Valerie I know is extraordinarily strong and outspoken. The woman I read about in these emails appears to have been being controlled by everyone around her. She was surrounded by so many people who cared for her, but not everyone who cares about you is good for you or has your best interest at heart. I also had extremely negative vibes about the neighbor, but it was not my place to make those observations. Although I had my own issues to work through, I was very eager to discuss this email with Valerie and to learn more about the hospital stay during our next session.

After finishing up my notes for my next session with Valerie I decided to get dressed and to run over to the Broad Street Market. Within the hour I was headed out the door. As I approached the market, I was instantly reminded about why I hated coming here on Saturday mornings. There was never anywhere to park. I ended up circling the block three and a half times before I found someone leaving and took their spot. Since it had been so long, I decided to start at one end and slowly work my way through to see all the stands and vendors.

I noticed several new vendors and was pleased to see some of my favorites were still there. Even though I was having lunch with Toni later I could not come to the market and not get an order of my favorite breaded potato wedges. They were the best. I usually got those with chicken but today I just wanted the potatoes. The line was awfully long and even though it typically moved quickly I decided to come back for those after I got everything else I wanted.

I found my favorite Amish family's stand and purchased the honey sesame sticks I loved as well as some cheese dip and fruit. I decided to treat myself to some cookies and a cupcake from my favorite bakery also. My hands were getting full, but my final stop was for my potatoes. The line was much shorter and within five minutes I was on my way back to my car.

Just as I was walking through the door to exit the market, I heard someone call my name. I could not imagine who it could be, and my hands were full. I continued out the door and towards my car. Once outside I heard my name again and turned my head slightly and saw a man walking towards me, but I still did not think he was coming to talk to me. I was happy to have reached my parking spot. I unlocked my car and began putting my bags inside. Just as I finished and opened the driver's door to enter my vehicle the man who had been calling my name appeared. At first, I was not sure who he was but when he smiled, I immediately knew. It was Curtis. He was a good friend of Miles's from college. We were all friends, I suppose, but he was a year ahead of us. After he graduated, I lost touch with him.

"Hey Joy, I thought that was you. How have you been?"

"Hey Curtis. I am doing well and you?"

"I am well myself. I thought you had moved away years ago." I was surprised he would know that.

"Yes, I am here visiting my family for the weekend." He looked at my hand as if he were looking for a ring.

"Are you here alone?" He seemed to be looking around for evidence of someone else in my car or approaching from nearby.

"Yes, I am but I am on my way to meet my sister in law. It was really nice seeing you, but I need to get going."

"Okay, yeah sure I understand. Are you on Facebook or Instagram? I would like to connect with you sometime and catch up."

"I have accounts, but I really do not use social media very often." He reached into his pocket and pulled out a card and handed it to me.

"Well here is my information. If you get a chance sometime, contact me. I would really like to catch up with you." As I walked back to my car I smiled, I couldn't believe that I ran into Joy after all these years and she still looked as fine as she did back in college. Miles is a fool if he let her go. I remember him telling me that he felt she was the total package, smart, sexy, and beautiful. She was perfect, not skinny but also not too big, but curves in all the right places. I felt ashamed for a moment because of the thoughts going through my head right now. Damn I should have insisted on getting her number. What did I leave the ball in her court?

I managed to smile. "Yeah sure that would be great." He turned and walked away, and I sat in my car for a minute and watched him. Curtis was the exact opposite of Miles. He was average height; maybe 5'10 and had a very slim build. The only thing that really stood out about him was his smile. I wondered if he was still in contact with Miles. I imagined that they were and maybe he even knew about Miles being unfaithful to me all those years ago. My first instinct was to pitch his card, but I decided to keep it just in case.

I took the scenic route through town back to Robin's house to see as much as I could. I thought about stopping by the cemetery but decided to wait until I could have more time. Just as I pulled up to Robin's house Toni called. She wanted us to meet in an hour at Piazza Sorrento in Hershey. That was one of our favorite places. Toni and I had gone there on many occasions after Darien died. It was our special occasion spot.

I put my purchases away and sampled just a few of the potatoes before getting dressed to meet Toni. I left a note for Robin on the table to help herself to any of the food in the fridge from the market.

Chapter 11

As I drove down 322 East towards the restaurant to meet Toni, I recalled some of the other times she and I had come to this restaurant. I tried to remember exactly how we found this place. It was in such an interesting location, hidden between a convenience store and a Subway. Over the years, this has been our place to celebrate special occasions, birthdays, graduations, new jobs etc. As I pulled into the parking lot, I noticed Toni's car already parked. I found a space close to hers and hurried into the restaurant. I was a few minutes late since I had underestimated my travel time.

As I walked in, I was immediately greeted by the smell of garlic and my mouth began to water in anticipation of the wonderful bread they served here. As I approached the hostess station, out of the corner of my eye I noticed Toni waving her arms. I turned to my right and quickly assessed Toni's mood as best I could. She had on sunglasses, but she did smile a little when she noticed me approaching her. She stood up and reached for a hug and said, "My Joy, I am so glad you and I are able to have some time together, just the two of us. You have no idea how happy I am right now." She held onto me a little longer than usual. I closed my eyes and remembered some of the happy occasions we celebrated here in the past. Once she released me, she still clung to my shoulders and looked at me and smiled. Finally, she let me go and motioned for me to sit across from her.

As I sat down, I said, "I'm happy that we are able to get together and talk, and you know this is one of my favorite places."

"Of course, I know that Joy, that is why we are here."

I pushed my menu away. "No need for that. I already know what I am ordering."

Toni chuckled. "Yes, I already know what I am going to be tasting from your plate, crab tortellini." She smiled and then continued, "My Joy, I have so much I want and need to say to you. I am not sure where to start." I opened my mouth to respond but she put her hand up to stop me and continued, "First I would like to say you are an amazing woman Joy. Please do not ever say you are broken to me or anyone else again."

Tears began to form in my eyes. "Toni, please you have to understand that my brokenness is not just because of the things I put in that email." Just as Toni was about to respond our waitress came over to take our order. Since Toni and I both knew what we wanted we gave her our orders quickly and were able to resume our conversation.

Toni began, "Joy, I understand that, and I am no therapist but when you use the word broken it seems as if you are accepting that with no possibility of healing."

I nodded my head. "I can understand how you can see it that way however it is extremely healthy for me to recognize where I am now to begin the healing process. It is like an addict who must first admit they have a problem with drugs or drinking for their healing process to begin."

"Yes, I can understand that. I suppose it is just difficult for me to hear you refer to yourself that way because when I look at you, I do not see a broken woman at all."

I smiled. "I appreciate that Toni and it means a lot to me but you need to understand that in order for me to be healthy how I feel or view myself is the most important thing and that is what I have to focus on." Toni was beaming with pride.

"You see Joy, that is why I feel that you are such an amazing woman. When you talk to me with such an understanding of yourself and what you need it makes me realize what a wonderful therapist you are." I smiled and she continued, "About your email. First, I need to say that you are correct. I did not know you were aware of everything that was going on as you alluded to in your email. It was troubling for me to read that because Darien and I tried so hard to protect you and Darien Jr. from everything that was going on. I know that Darien Jr. does not recall or remember much since he was so young, but when I think about how you must have felt my heart breaks for you my dear." She paused and I reached for her hand.

"I know it was not intentional, but you are right it was difficult."

"For that all I can say is that I am deeply sorry. As for everything else, oh my Joy, there were so many things happening back then, many of them outside of my or Darien's control."

"Yes, I understand, and I truly do not want to make you relive painful memories."

She nodded. "Oh yes these are some difficult memories that is for sure."

"Maybe it would help if I just asked you some questions? Obviously, you are not obligated to answer anything, but it might be helpful for both of us to at least put the questions out there. What do you think?"

"Uh, yeah sure, why not? Ask away."

Right before I got started the waitress appeared with our salads. Toni and I blessed our food and then we both began picking at our salads. I let a few minutes of silence hang in the air between us before I asked my first question. Partly because I wanted to allow us both time to eat a little bit, but I also wanted to collect my thoughts. I decided to start with what I considered to be an easy question.

"So, Toni tell me how you and Darien met."

She smiled, put her fork down and took a sip of water. "I would love to tell you that story, but I have to warn you, it really is not much of a story."

I shrugged my shoulders. "Try me. I might think it is a lot more of a story than you."

"I guess that could be true. Well, Darien and I both worked for the same company. I was in the marketing department and he was in accounting. Darien transferred to the Harrisburg office from Pittsburgh where he did his internship. My understanding is that he moved back to Harrisburg to be closer to you and your mom."

I smiled. "Yes, that is correct. Apparently, I was a real handful." I rolled my eyes and Toni laughed.

"Yeah, well all teenagers are handfuls at some point."

"I guess maybe that is true, but please continue."

"Shortly after he transferred to Harrisburg, I ran into him in the lunchroom, almost literally. I was not paying attention to where I was walking and almost walked right into him. Darien was very handsome, and all the single ladies and a few married ones were very smitten with him. He smiled at me first. We played this smiling game with each other for a couple of weeks until he worked up the nerve to ask me to lunch." She stopped and I sat in anticipation for about a minute. Finally, she smiled and said, "Oh, hell Joy you are grown, so here is the truth. Darien and I hooked up over lunch."

I almost spit my food out. "Wait, what? You are telling me that my brother did not take you out on a date?"

"Well, he eventually did, but initially we just hooked up during lunch and had sex."

"Wow, Toni I have to admit that is a real shocker for me."

"Yeah, I can imagine but things turned out okay."

"Yes, they did for the most part." I felt a somber mood creeping over me, but I subconsciously pushed it away. "Okay so what else can you tell me?"

She thought for a minute. "Darien and I were both very attracted to each other, but at the time neither of us were interested in a serious relationship. So, like I said we hooked up several times before we had a real date. Our first date was amazing though, and I am fairly certain that is when I got pregnant with Darien Jr."

"Where did you go?"

"He took me to a hibachi restaurant, then down to the riverfront for a nice walk."

I smiled. "That does sound nice. I think I know some of the rest of how you two ended up getting married. He proposed at Vince and Gina's wedding correct?"

"Yes, that is correct." She paused while the waitress placed our entrees on the table. We both looked over our plates to make sure everything was as expected and then we did what we always did. We split our meals and shared. Toni ordered steak gorgonzola pasta and I ordered crab tortellini. Once we had both placed some of our entrée on the others plate she continued, "Now, let me explain about how I know Vince."

"Oh, yes please, this part is so confusing to me."

She laughed. "Yes, it is. Anyway, I met Vinnie aka Vince when I was in college. I went to Penn State and our paths crossed at a college party. Obviously, he and I slept together since there was a possibility that he was the father of my baby."

"Okay, I see now. Toni, I must tell you. I had so many other scenarios going through my head about that all these years."

"When Darien and I started dating he talked about his best friend Vince, but I never met him until the day of his wedding. I never once thought that Vinnie from college was Vince. When I saw Vince at the wedding, I recognized him right away."

"What did you do?" This was sounding more and more like a soap opera the more I learned about their story.

"I decided I had to tell Darien right away. By this time, we both knew I was pregnant, and I knew that there was a chance Vince was the father of the baby I gave up for adoption. I could not continue my relationship with Darien without him knowing everything."

"Wow, Toni so even after you told him everything, he still proposed to you that night?"

"Yes, he did. I was shocked but so incredibly happy at the same time."

"My brother was an amazing man."

Toni smiled. "Yes, he truly was."

We both ate our meals in silence for a few minutes. I finally broke the silence and said, "Toni, I want to thank you so much for sharing these things with me. It really means a lot that you were so willing to share these very personal and I am sure painful memories with me."

"You are very welcome Joy. Do you have any other questions for me?"

I thought for a minute. "I do not think so. I want to tell you again how deeply sorry I am that I resented you for taking Darien off life support. I was young and he was the last living relative I had. I knew that him living that way was not really living and I knew that he would not want to live that way. It was just difficult to let him go. Also, I must confess that at the time I felt as if you were letting him go so that you could be with Benjamin."

She did not respond to my comment about Benjamin right away. She raised her eyebrow to acknowledge it but continued to chew her food. I began to get a little nervous with the silence and just as I was about to say something Toni said, "Can I tell you something I have never told anyone else?"

I put my fork down to signal to her that I was giving her my full attention. "Sure, of course."

She put down her fork, took a sip of water and wiped her mouth before she began.

"Joy, I have had more love in my life than most people I know."

I made a face which she saw.

"I am sure that may seem odd to you since it has been so long since Darien died, and I have not remarried or even really dated anyone else."

"I have always felt as though you did not date because of me and not wanting me to feel awkward."

She laughed. "No, my dear, I have not dated anyone else because I knew there was absolutely no way I could hit the love lottery or jackpot again. You see before I met Darien, Benjamin was the love of my life. I had never been loved or felt a love like the love I had with Benjamin before. Yes, we were young, but I always knew it was special. When he vanished into thin air the way he did, I knew that something was not right. When I met Darien from the very beginning, I knew there was something special about him. I remember telling Jada that he was the one. She laughed at me, but he truly was. When I was given a second chance at love with Darien, I knew better than to try my luck a third time."

I chuckled. "Yeah, I guess I understand that, but Toni can I ask you something?"

"Yes, dear of course."

"Don't you ever get lonely?"

"Honestly, not yet." She laughed and continued, "I think once the kids are completely out of the house, maybe loneliness will set in. I have kept myself busy with trying to be the best mother I could be for my children."

"And me too."

She smiled. "Yes, my Joy and you too. You want to know why I press you so hard to get back out there and date again?"

I rolled my eyes. "No, I do not know but I would like to."

She smiled. "It is because once you have been loved the way I was loved by both your brother and Benjamin; you want nothing less for those that you love."

She reached across the table and grabbed my hand. "My Joy, I know that Miles hurt you terribly, but I also know he was not the love of your life. I know there is a love out there for you and I want you to stop hiding from it."

My eyes began to water but I let out a nervous laugh. "I am glad that you feel that way, but honestly I think love has passed me by."

She began shaking her head. "Oh no, my dear. Have you ever heard the expression that good things come to those who wait?"

I rolled my eyes and said, "Of course, I have."

"Okay then well do you believe it?"

"I guess so, but I am almost forty, no kids, and honestly have not had a serious relationship in over fifteen years."

She smiled. "Here is another oldie but goodie for you. Better late than never." I smiled and she laughed.

"Okay Toni, that was a good one. Do you have any real intel on this mystery man that is going to show up and sweep me off my feet?"

She smiled. "No, but I have a feeling he is a lot closer than you realize."

"Hmm, okay, well now I am intrigued."

"Well that is good. Now one last thing and then we need to get to ordering our dessert." I smiled and said,

"Okay, what is it?"

"My relationship with Jada has been extremely complicated. You mentioned in your email that you have not formed lasting relationships. I disagree with your assessment there also. Here is why. You have me and you have Robin correct?"

"Yes, that is correct."

"Well, then who else do you need?" I hunched my shoulders but did not respond and she continued, "Seriously everyone does not need a huge circle around them. Yes, you should probably have a few more friends closer to where you live but there is no minimum friend requirement. What I do feel is missing is the spiritual part of your life."

I nodded. "Yes, you are correct, I do need to get more serious about attending church on a more regular basis."

"Not just attending Joy but being an active participant. There are a whole lot of people who attend church every Sunday, but they are not walking in with the right intentions. Be purposeful with your walk with God. Walking into church every Sunday is not necessarily the answer. Remember Jesus spent his time out visiting the people, not inside the temple."

I nodded. "Yes, Toni I hear you loud and clear."

"Well, good now I am ready for my dessert. Where is that waitress?"

I looked around and motioned for the waitress. When she came over, she said, "You two ladies were having such a wonderful conversation I did not want to interrupt." We both smiled and I said, "Yes, we were but now we need to see that wonderful dessert tray."

"Of course, let me grab that and I will be right back."

She returned and Toni and I had a difficult time choosing our desserts, but we finally decided on two different ones to share. Chocolate mousse cake and lemon cream cake. Both were delicious.

Toni and I enjoyed our desserts and continued to chat about everything for another thirty minutes. We made plans to meet for church on Sunday and after church we were going to go to the cemetery together.

We walked outside and we gave each other the best hugs, the kind where neither of us wanted to be the first to let go. I was so happy that we had a chance to talk about everything. I was also a little bit intrigued by her prediction that my love was close by. I suppose only time would tell on that one.

When I arrived at Robin's house, she was anxiously awaiting my arrival. Of course, she wanted to hear everything. I happily filled her in on the details of my day, starting with running into Curtis at the market and ending with my talk with Toni over lunch. She was particularly interested in my mystery man who is supposedly waiting around the corner for me. We both laughed about that for a while.

Robin and I talked for hours about everything. We ended up warming up the food I bought at the market to snack on later in the evening. We talked about Miles and what my thoughts were how to address those unresolved issues. I was not quite ready to tackle that yet, but I knew it was something that I did need to address sooner rather than later.

Robin suggested that I try to look him up on social media or possibly connect with Curtis to see if he had any contact information for Miles. I was not sure how I was going to handle it, but right now I just wanted to finish processing all that Toni and I had talked about today.

.

Chapter 12

I was awakened by the sound of a notification from my phone that I had an email. I grabbed my phone and saw that it was from Valerie.

Joy,

I had another flashback nightmare from the hospital about not getting to leave. When I woke up in the middle of the night last night, I thought I was going to another facility like one of the other patients. He was kind of quiet, but I had conversations with him in the lunchroom. He did not come to Art because he did not like loud music and seemed afraid to attend. I was not sure, but I thought we received points if we went to different sessions on the schedule, so I thought I might be helping him if I could get him to try it out. I told him not only did we get to pick the songs, but we could adjust the volume and I thought he should try to stop by. I saw him standing in the doorway one day and then reluctantly came in to participate. He then started coming each time we had Art after that. One day he painted a refrigerator magnet bright blue that was the phrase, 'Be Happy', and gave it to me. It was really difficult to watch him leave as he was put on a stretcher and strapped in to get shipped off to a long-term facility. He had told me about his family and I just did not understand how this seemed like the right care for him. It frightened me to think I might not get out of the hospital and end up facing next steps similar to some of the other people I encountered. I tried to express to my treatment team my desire to get home and they kept telling me I wasn't ready. Why did they get to make that decision and not my family? It really shook me to think I did not know where I would end up if it someone decided I was not able to go home.

In spite of this, every night before bed I would say a prayer that the next day I would get to leave. Each morning I would be up before breakfast so I could shower and get my steps in. It did feel good to get sleep, but I really wanted to be home. I would organize the clothes and papers in my dresser with the hopes of finding out it was time to go. I knew I had to reduce the amount of writing I was doing because at first I was doing that to get all my thoughts out and the staff was concerned. I tried to limit it to next steps I need to do now that I was separating from Seth and did word searches mostly instead to pass the time.

When I have trouble sleeping it makes me extremely anxious that I will end up back in the hospital, so that makes the nightmares even more frightening for me. Sometimes I listen to soothing music to try and fall back to sleep. Hopefully this will get better as time passes.

    Valerie

    Valerie was really beginning to open up more and share and it seemed that more and more memories were coming back, and things were going clearer. I wondered if her medications have been adjusted in some way or maybe her body is just adjusting now. Either way she needed to continue to deal with her emotions in a health way in order to heal. As I go up and prepared for church I wondered if Valerie was also continuing to attend on a regular basis. I made a mental note to ask her about that.

*****

I decided to drive to Toni's house and ride with her to church. Even though the church was just around the corner from her house I did not want to worry about parking and then finding her. Toni and I ended up going without Darien

Jr. and Denise. Of course they were both running late. They would meet up with us at church. Denise was assigned to nursery duty today, which she was extremely excited about.

As Toni and I walked into the sanctuary, I was surprised at how different everything looked. The pulpit had been replaced with one that looked much more modern and sleeker. It really opened up the area and allowed you to see the choir stand. The old one was very large and bulky. There were also so many new faces. Toni saw the look on my face and leaned in close to me and said, "There have been a lot of changes."

I nodded and said, "Yes, I can see that." I continued to look around and take as much in as possible while Toni greeted people and continued to her preferred pew, which happened to be awfully close to the front of the church. Toni introduced me to a few ladies who greeted her, and we exchanged pleasantries. I took my seat and continued to survey the crowd to see if there was anyone that I recognized, and sadly, there was not. I did notice that there appeared to be more younger people in attendance than I recalled seeing in the past. The choir came in and the musicians began playing music to signal to everyone that the service was about to start.

Toni finally stopped chit chatting with everyone and sat down next to me. She looked around nervously and said, "I hope the kids make it on time, especially Denise since she is supposed to be in the nursery today." I turned around and looked at the door and just then I noticed Darien Jr. walk in and begin looking in our direction. Toni also noticed him, and she relaxed. Darien Jr. slid into our row and sat beside Toni. Toni leaned over to him and they began whispering, I assumed it was about Denise.

I checked my cell phone to make sure the ringer was off, and I felt Toni reach over and nudge me. I looked up and realized that the pastor had walked in and everyone was standing up. I quickly threw my phone back into my purse and stood up. Toni had mentioned that they recently hired a new pastor. The old pastor retired and moved to Florida. What she did not mention was that the new pastor was much younger and quite handsome. As if Toni could read my mind, she looked over and winked at me. I simply smiled and turned back towards the front of the church and that is when I noticed him. My mouth flew open and Toni nudged me again and mouthed the word 'What'?

We were in the middle of the opening prayer and after the prayer we sang the hymn. During the hymn I whispered to Toni that the armor bearer sitting next to the new pastor was Curtis, Miles's friend who I ran into at the market yesterday. She simply nodded her head indicating she heard me and understood.

When the church welcomed visitors I did not stand since this was my home church. Although I suppose technically, I was a guest. The pastor and his assistants all stood and looked around the church welcoming the visitors. I too looked around and scanned the crowd. Out of the corner of my eye I could sense that someone was looking at me and when I turned slightly back towards the front, I realized Curtis had noticed me. I gave him a nervous grin. He motioned with his head towards the back of the church. When I turned my head towards where he directed me, I saw him. I gasped aloud and Toni jumped in her seat.

She whispered, "Joy, what is wrong?"

I could not respond. I felt as if the room was spinning and I felt sick to my stomach. I closed my eyes and willed myself to pull it together. I silently practiced the breathing exercises that Robin had taught me. Toni realized that something was wrong and nudged me. I opened my eyes to see that she was standing, and she motioned for me to follow her. Thankfully, there was a side door and we did not have to walk to the back of the church past where Miles was sitting.

Once we were outside of the sanctuary there were a few people in the hallway, so Toni and I did not speak until we were behind the closed door of the private restroom that she led me to. She seemed annoyed or maybe it was just concern, I was not sure.

She said, "Joy, what is going on with you?"

I began to cry immediately. "Toni, I am so sorry, but I need to leave."

"Why Joy? What is wrong?" I was crying uncontrollably and gasping for air. I could not respond for a few minutes.

Toni reached in her pocket and grabbed her phone. I had no idea who she was calling but then I heard her say, "Hey Robin, listen I am so sorry to bother you, but I need you to come over to the church right away." She paused for a moment as if she were listening and then she continued, "I am not exactly sure, but I know that Joy saw Curtis initially but then something else happened and she completely broke down."

Just then I blurted out, "Miles is here."

Toni stopped in mid-sentence. "What? Where?" I could hear Robin's voice screaming through the phone,

"Toni, Toni, what is going on?" Toni put the phone back up to her ear.

"Robin, I need you to either come here to the church or meet us back at my house. Joy needs us both right now. Apparently, Miles is here." I heard Robin's voice yell through the phone, "OMG, are you serious? I am on my way."

Toni put her phone back in her pocket and looked at me. "Joy talk to me. Tell me what you need."

I shook my head. I could not speak or at least it felt as if I had no voice. It felt as though the entire three plus years of my relationship with Miles was flashing through my head. The final image which was the most painful was graduation day. Seeing him with the other woman. My emotions were all over the place. I wanted to confront him, however after so much time had passed was it even worth it? I had absolutely no claim to him and honestly, he owed me no explanations. Well maybe an apology, but even that seemed as though it was too late. Here in this moment I realized time does not heal all wounds, especially if you just cover the wound up and do not pay attention to it.

I was angry. Angry with myself for allowing him to have this type of hold on me, so many years later. I turned and looked at myself in the mirror. I looked a mess. I was a therapist who helped other people through their issues in life. Look at me acting like an entire fool over some man who I have not set eyes on in over fifteen years. I briefly thought about my client Valerie, all that she has been through and she is still standing, despite it all. I began shaking my head. I stood up and walked over to the sink, turned the water on and began splashing water on my face.

Toni came over to me and said, "Joy, what are you doing?"

"I am fixing myself up so that we can go back to hear the sermon."

Toni hesitated for a moment. "Oh okay, are you sure?"

I nodded first. "Yes, I am absolutely sure. Miles' hold on me and my emotions ends today."

Toni tried to hide her smile, but I saw it anyway. She looked at me. "Okay then let us go catch the second half of this sermon, Pastor Flee is longwinded."

I smiled and reached in my purse for my phone. I sent Robin a text that said, *Stand down. Headed back in to listen to the sermon. I will talk to you when I get back to the house.*

When we returned, I was disappointed when the pastor said in conclusion.

Toni leaned over and said, "do not be fooled, that is his first of at least a half dozen in conclusions."

I smiled and settled in to listen to Pastor Flee. Although we missed a good portion of his sermon, I was able to capture some key points. He asked us all to consider how we use our time, our talents, and our gifts. I made a mental note to think about those three things more. He also asked us to think about what God is calling you to do. He told the story of a man who wanted to open a store selling clothes. The man put everything he had into planning and opening this business. It seemed that for every plan he made came setbacks. The man was a great problem solver, so as each challenge came, he figured out a way to overcome it. There were zoning issues, problems with the buildings water and heat. Finally, the day before the store was supposed to open one of the apartments upstairs flooded and the man lost his entire inventory. The moral of the story according to Pastor Flee was that opening the store was not the man's calling. Ultimately the man's calling was to work in a position where he could change things for the better. You see, as he worked through all those problems that came up, he was learning and interacting with the city officials. He ended up having a successful career working in the building inspector's office. Pastor Flee surmised that the man was focused on what he wanted, but along the way there were obstacles placed before him that allowed him to learn and hone skills that would be useful for what God was calling him to do. His final remark was that you do not know the day or the hour when your time will be up. He advised us all to live fully each day.

It was a great sermon and I felt as though I had some soul searching to do to figure out what my purpose is. All I knew right then is that I am struggling, I am emotional, but I am also grateful, thankful, and blessed. I had been so engrossed in the sermon that I forgot about Miles being there and as soon as the service was over Toni said, "What is the plan?"

I shrugged my shoulders. "No clue. I have decided not to give it anymore energy unless it is absolutely necessary."

She smiled. "That is my Joy." I noticed Denise weaving her way through the crowd trying to make her way to us. I sat down and took out my cell phone to check for messages from Robin. Of course there were several messages from her asking me what was going on. I sent her a message telling her that service was over and that we were going back to Toni's house briefly before heading over to the cemetery. When I looked up, I saw the Pastor and Curtis walking in our direction. Toni greeted the pastor and introduced herself to Curtis. As Toni and Pastor Flee talked, I noticed Curtis stealing glances at me. Before I allowed myself to become upset again, I reminded myself that I was in control of my emotions and I refused to allow myself to have a meltdown right now. Denise finally made it up to where we were, and she also chatted briefly with the pastor. Finally, Toni motioned for me to move closer.

"Pastor Flee, I would like to introduce you to my sister in law, Joy. She is the therapist I mentioned to you during the last committee meeting."

Pastor Flee extended his hand and gazed into my eyes. "Joy, it is so nice to meet you. I wanted to talk to you about something, but I am a little short on time today. Would it be possible for you to give your contact information to Curtis and I will get in touch with you next week to discuss my ideas with you?" I hesitated for a moment. "Ah, sure, of course."

He smiled. "Great, Curtis please jot down her information and I will meet you in the office. I have to run."

Curtis stepped closer to me. "Of course, Pastor."

The pastor excused himself and Toni and the kids lingered close by while I gave Curtis my email address and phone number.

"Curtis, any idea what the pastor wants to talk to me about?"

He shrugged his shoulders. "Honestly, I have no clue."

I reached back to grab my purse. "Okay then, well, please let him know that I do work during the day so the early evening is probably the best time to call or he can also send me an email."

"Sure, I will let him know." He said as he began to back away from me but then he stopped. "Joy, can I ask you a question?"

"You can always ask, but I cannot promise that I will answer."

"He chucked and said, okay I get it. Well earlier you seemed upset about seeing Miles here."

I rolled my eyes. "Listen Curtis, I do not know what Miles has told you, but things did not end well between us at all."

He looked surprised. "Joy, I really do not know anything. I recently connected with him again since he is back in the area. Since I graduated a year ahead of you, I had no idea that anything happened. As far as I knew you and he were still together. I came back a couple of years ago for another job opportunity and maybe six months ago I ran into Miles at an event."

I shrugged. "You know more than I know and honestly, I am not really interested in reconnecting with Miles at this point."

"Oh, I see is that because you are married or in a relationship?"

I scoffed. "Curtis I am not discussing that with you so that you can run back and tell Miles my business."

He shook his head. "Joy, you have it all wrong. Listen I know Miles and I were cool back then but seriously it has been years since we have talked. I honestly had no idea he was coming here today. He has never been here before."

"How long have you been attending this church?"

"I have been here almost a year. I came in with Pastor Flee. He and I worked together at another church running the youth program."

"That is great, so you have known Pastor Flee for a while then?"

"Yes, it has been about 6 years now. But listen I need to run; we have a meeting. Would it be okay if I used your contact information also?"

I hesitated for a moment. "Joy, I just want to continue catching up with you. There is no hidden agenda here. Clearly things are not what I thought they were with you and Miles."

"Okay Curtis but if you give my information to Miles, I will come find you and it will not be a happy reunion."

He laughed. "Yes ma'am I hear you loud and clear." As he smiled and walked away.

As I watched him walk away, I thought to myself maybe he's not the bad guy here.

Toni, Darien, and Denise were patiently waiting for me. I felt so bad for keeping them waiting. I gathered my things and walked over to them. "Sorry to keep you all waiting."

Toni smiled. "No problem, it seemed as if you and Curtis got along well."

I rolled my eyes. "Trust me there is nothing there."

"Okay if you say so. I know what it looks like when a man is interested in a woman."

"Speaking of that do you have any idea why Pastor Flee wants to talk to me?"

"Yes, I do, and it is sort of my fault."

"Oh no, what did you do Toni?" I asked as we walked towards the exit.

"I may have mentioned that you are a wonderful therapist."

"Okay, so is he looking for one?" I asked.

Toni laughed. "Yes, but not for himself."

"Well for who and why wouldn't you suggest Robin?"

"She is on the list also, but we are looking for a few people. I would rather you speak directly to him about his vision. I do not want to misspeak and ruin everything."

I shook my head. "Okay Toni, but you know I do not like surprises."

"Yes, of course my Joy, I know you very well."

I was surprised that I had not seen Miles again, but I was grateful. The crisis had been averted. Toni and I rode back to her house. She told me again how proud she was of me and how I was able to pull myself back together the way I did. I thanked her for her kind words, but inside I felt embarrassed. I did not know why Miles was there or why I reacted the way I did, but I did know that those feelings must be dealt with sooner rather than later.

For now, I focused on our visit to the cemetery. Once we got back to the house after church both Denise and Darien Jr. decided to let Toni and I visit the cemetery alone today. I was glad they did. Toni and I each took our private time to visit my mom's and Darien's gravesites. Toni knew the emotional strain I was under and I felt extremely comfortable being myself with her. After our visit to the cemetery we returned to her house and I spent a little more time with Toni and the kids before heading back to Robin's house.

After my emotional breakdown earlier I had decided not to drive back home today. I needed to spend more time with Robin talking things through. When I arrived at Robin's house midafternoon, she was waiting for me. When I walked in she did not say anything, she just came over to me and gave me a hug. Once she released me, I plopped down on the sofa and let out a heavy sigh.

"You're staying tonight, right?"

I nodded. "Yeah there is no way I can drive back myself today. I am exhausted."

"Yes, my dear, working through all of those repressed feelings takes a toll on you." I sat in silence replaying the events of the day in my head.

"So tell me exactly what happened." I kicked my shoes off and readjusted myself on the sofa and told Robin everything that happened today. Once I was finished, she began to ask questions just like any good therapist would. "Why do you think that you reacted the way you did today Joy?"

I let out a heavy sigh. "Robin, we both know why. Let us stop dancing around it and just hit it head on."

"Okay, I am all for that, but you go first."

I closed my eyes and thought for a moment on where to begin. "Robin, honestly Miles is not the problem."

She raised her eyebrow. "I'm not sure I am following you but continue."

"Okay, yes Miles was the catalyst, but honestly the issues that I need to resolve are within myself." Robin nodded.

"Miles obviously was not honest with me and yes, that hurt me deeply. I am not the first woman to be lied to or hurt in this manner. Miles's role in this ended the day that I walked away from him and never looked back. It was traumatic, yes, but it is so much worse for me now because I never dealt with it. I simply pushed it aside or hid from it." Robin was still nodding her head, so I knew she was still with me. "I remember when I first started seeing you. You advised me to take his calls or respond to his emails, but I was stubborn, and I did not. I did not feel there was anything he could say to ease my pain. The reality is that my pain began long before that day."

"I hear you, but please elaborate further."

"Even before I realized that Miles was a liar and a cheat, I was in pain Robin. The guilt I felt from the circumstances around my mother's death. I never properly dealt with those feelings. Then when Darien died, that was traumatic event number two that was never properly dealt with. Next was my relationship with Miles. When I got baptized and accepted Jesus as my lord and savior, I also vowed not to have premarital sex. Miles talked me into it by telling me that we were going to be married eventually, so it was okay. I never forgave myself for allowing him to talk me into it. Yes, he was the snake, but I went against my own judgment and allowed it to happen."

"Okay, Joy, I do understand your logic but maybe you are being a little too hard on yourself."

Tears were streaming down my cheeks at this point and I began shaking my head. "No, Robin, I am telling you that I knew I was making a bad decision almost the entire time it was happening. I also think that deep down I knew Miles was lying to me. I believe that after he took my virginity almost immediately things changed between us and I refused to believe it. I was ashamed that I had been fooled. I held onto hope that I was wrong or that he would change."

"Joy, I hear you and maybe you are right, but everyone makes mistakes in life. The key is to learn from them and not make the same mistakes repeatedly."

"Yes, I know and that, is why I am still alone all these years later."

"Is that really the reason, Joy?'

"What else would it be?"

"I have always felt as though you have avoided intimate relationships because of your STD status."

I thought for a minute. "Yes, that is a very big part of it but even with that I am ashamed to admit that I feel as though that was my punishment for disobeying God."

"Come on Joy, you know how I feel about that kind of talk."

"Yes, I know, but I am just being honest with you about how I feel."

"I know you are, but the Bible does not teach us that God punishes us in this manner. It teaches us that he is a forgiving God as long as we repent and ask him for forgiveness."

"I know you are right, but sometimes I have felt responsible."

"Yes Joy, you are responsible for the choices you make, but that does not translate to the consequences being the result of punishment from God."

"Okay Robin, you are right. I need to take responsibility for my actions and the consequences. I still believe it is bigger than that though. The sermon today stirred something within me. The pastor talked about figuring out what you are called to do."

"What do you think that means to you?"

"I have not figured it all out yet, but when I do you will be the first person I discuss it with." She smiled.

"I feel honored and am very confident that you are on the right path Joy."

Robin and I spent the rest of the afternoon and evening chatting about everything but me and my situation, which I appreciated. She shared things with me about her private life which she rarely ever does. She is dating again but nobody special yet and she suggested that I give it a try. She even showed me a few of the dating sites she joined. I played along, but really am not interested in that right now. This weekend showed me I need to address a few things myself.

I went to bed early so I could get up and drive back home. I needed the time to clear my head and I wanted to be ready for my session with Valerie.

Chapter 13

I woke up and was on the road headed back home by 6 am. I slept well and despite everything that happened over the weekend, I felt surprisingly good. I realized that although Robin is a great therapist and my closest friend, I need to seek counseling myself. I need to forgive myself for things I have held onto for too long.

While talking to Robin last night she asked me if I felt that I was able to continue working with my clients. I told her I would think about it but honestly, I do feel that I am able to help my clients. I believe that me being able to help my clients has been what has kept me going. It allows me to focus on someone else so that I do not have to focus on myself.

I made it back home in plenty of time to take care of some personal business plus rest and relax a bit before my session with Valerie. After unpacking the car and putting everything away, I sat at the kitchen table and ate lunch. While eating, I browsed through the EAP brochure from my job. After lunch I made the call and got myself set up with a therapist for the following day.

Feeling satisfied about taking that first step towards healing, I decided to grab my journal and write about the weekend. I chose to sit in the living room on my comfortable sofa which was a little too comfortable because at some point I dozed off. When I awoke a couple of hours later to the sound of my cell phone buzzing, I was surprised at how long I had slept. I grabbed my phone to check the time and realized it was almost time for my session with Valerie. I planned to review her email again before our session. I quickly replied to Robin's text message which is what woke me up. I had not texted her when I got home because I knew she would be with clients. Then I got lost in taking care of things around the house.

I went into my office to grab Valerie's file. I had printed her email out to read it over the weekend. With just a few minutes to spare I grabbed a bottle of water and logged in for my session. Valerie was on time as usual.

"Hello Valerie. How are you?"

"I am doing well and you?"

"I cannot complain and thanks for asking."

"Are you ready to begin?"

"Yes, I am."

"Alright then. I feel we should spend a little time discussing what you shared in your email. I want you to remember it takes time to process everything especially after dealing with what you have for this long. Also healing does not necessarily occur in a linear way. Meaning your trauma occurred in a sequence of events, however your processing and healing from the effects of that trauma may not happen in the same way. Does that make sense?"

"Yes, it does. It makes perfect sense."

"Okay, great. You mentioned you wanted to discuss the issues you are having with trust. Can you explain that a little more?"

Valerie grabbed a tissue and I realized this was an emotional issue for her. I remained silent and let her take the time she needed to cry. It was good to see her get it out and start to deal with the pain. That shows me we are making progress. Tears are often misunderstood as a sign of weakness. They are cleansing and a necessary part of processing pain. After a few minutes, she was able to compose herself and answer my question.

"I think that is something I am going to have a problem with for quite a while. I was still processing Seth's betrayal when I was blindsided by Paula lying to me about an appointment for David. I trusted that Paula was giving me a ride there and instead I ended up in the psych ward. We can talk about my time in the hospital later but what happened put me into a state of shock distrusting everyone."

"That sounds awful and I can understand it would be hard for you to talk about it so we can table that for now. I have been meaning to ask, have you gone back to work yet?"

"Yes, I did start back to work, and it has been pretty difficult for me. At least I do not have to go into the office too much since I mostly work from home. I still find myself getting upset at times and overwhelmed. I am extremely fortunate to have a few people I have gotten close with from work that I turn to when needed. Also, since I had already planned time off for my surgery my projects were covered so I am able to transition back gradually."

"Are you still experiencing issues with your medication?"

"The medicine makes me feel like I am in a fog and it has been hard for me to keep the pace I was used to before. At my last appointment with my psychiatrist I decided to go off all my medication. He gave me a plan on how to do that gradually even though he did not recommend it."

"Okay, I see so how long have you been off the medications now? Do you feel any different?"

"I just started going off them last week so it will take a few weeks until I am off them completely. It still seems that the simplest tasks can be overwhelming to me right now. I do try to just take deep breaths and get up to walk a little when I start to feel anxious. I have also had issues with driving and try to limit going places."

"When did you notice you had problems with driving?"

"The weekend after I got out of the hospital, I went to see Scott. I guess I was just being overly cautious while driving, but he mentioned he felt bad for having me travel. I felt fine driving, but I did not realize that I was behaving differently. We also went to see Seth together at the clinic."

"Just to be clear. You did not feel any different driving, but your son felt you were driving differently?"

"I was not aware I was driving slower until Scott said something. He could tell there was something different and with him telling me that helped me to see that was the case.

"So, you visited Seth right after you were out of the hospital with Scott? How did Seth react to you coming to see him?" I could tell by her body language that this was another rough memory and situation for her.

"He introduced me to everyone and acted like there was nothing wrong with our marriage. I found his behavior extremely irritating. I was also shocked at how nice it was at the facility which was a big difference from the hospital experience I had. I don't think he thought I was serious about ending things and I shared some of the details of his living arrangement when I saw him." I made sure he knew he was not welcome to move back home and his brother had a place for him to live. I planned on giving him some of our furniture to get set it up.

"That seems pretty considerate of you given everything he has put you through. It seems like you have really thought about everything all the way down to what furniture you are willing to part with."

"Yes, I have. Now is my time to make plans for my future."

"That is a great attitude Valerie. Tell me more about your plans."

"I have always wanted a couch that had a built-in recliner. Seth always bought everything, so I did not really have a say in much that we had. Jill and I went furniture shopping and had a blast. I went over to her house first and she asked me if there were any guys from my past I would want to reconnect with. I always had such a great time with Brandon. We casually dated my junior year of college since he was graduating and moving. Jill worked her social media magic and found a picture of him on what I think might have been a department website at UVA. He looked about the same as I remembered but had a beard which is not something I normally found attractive although it looked really good on him. I was surprised that his hair was still dark brown and had very little gray in it. I was not about to reach out to him through work even if that is something I was ready to do."

"When was the last time you saw Brandon?"

"The last time I saw him was when I was traveling for a work conference. It was about six months into my relationship with Seth. I reached out to Brandon since I knew he lived close by. He came over to the hotel where I was staying, and we met for a drink. It was hard for me to resist wanting to be with him, but I was not about to cheat so nothing happened. Maybe when I get more familiar with connecting to people, I will try to see if I can meet up with him somehow since it looks like he might be close to my place in Charlottesville."

I noticed talking about old times seemed to help Valerie relax a bit.

"Have you been able to keep in touch with friends much without being on social media?"

"There are friends I keep in touch with, but I do think getting on Facebook would help me connect more with people. Since I moved away from family and friends to be with Seth when we first got married it has been hard. In college it is not like we had cell phones so there are some people I would really like to find now that I am moving on and restarting my life."

"It sounds like that might be a good thing for you to do then. How has your mood been overall?" I noticed that Valerie shed a few more tears but she was able to continue.

"The one thing that probably bothers me the most is the feeling of being alone. When I was in the hospital my friend Darla from high school was talking about taking a trip to New York City by herself. I could not imagine taking a trip alone, so I made plans to meet her there this past weekend. Seth came over before I headed to the airport early Saturday morning. I am still struggling with being on my own so when he offered to come over to make me breakfast it seemed like a good idea. As he walked in, I got an alert on my phone that my flight was cancelled. Right away he started coming up with Plan B for me to still go. He suggested I re-book leaving from Reagan airport in DC. I was starting to re-think having him in the house because I really didn't like him telling me what I should do but I knew if I did not entertain his suggestions, he would start getting mad."

I noticed that Valerie's body tensed up when she talked about Seth which was probably due to his controlling behavior. It seemed he was still trying to be in control of her decisions.

"How far away was that from where you were supposed to fly out of? I know you were saying earlier you were having some trouble with driving."

"It was probably about an hour and a half longer, but I felt like I needed to go to be there for Darla. I really was looking forward to the trip but the anxiety of getting there was too much. I was not able to relax and my thoughts were all over the place. I was extremely worried about everything including getting around the city and back to an airport that I was not familiar with. I felt bad leaving David at home by himself since I did not know if his dad would stop over and if that was something David was comfortable with or not. Seth did not seem to be taking it seriously that I had filed for divorce since he had not hired an attorney yet, so I didn't know if he would try to take anything from the house."

"How were things when you got back from the weekend? Did you see Seth again?"

"He did stop back over Sunday night and he mentioned he was probably going to resign from office. The news story on that just hit yesterday. He told me it would help protect his pension but still denied he did what he was being accused of."

"How did you feel about his decision?" I could see this was definitely something that upset Valerie as the tears started again.

"If he steps down, he will not be getting any income to help cover bills. I probably would not have spent the money I did on the trip to New York City and the furniture. It also makes it seem there is a reason that he decided to do this on his own without being forced to resign. He tried to justify his decision, but I still don't feel I can trust him, and I don't want him around."

I cannot say that I blamed how Valerie was feeling and understood why she was so upset.

"Hopefully, you can start to move forward with your life. It sounds like it is still a struggle for you to be around him even though you know you want to move on. We are about out of time for our session today. Do you want to continue with weekly sessions for now or do you feel as though we can cut back to every other week or monthly? Remember either way we can still communicate through emails."

"I am not sure right now. With weaning off the medications and getting back into my normal work schedule I may need video sessions weekly. Can I think about it and get back to you?"

"Of course, just schedule a session when you are ready. I should mention my schedule is going to be reduced in the coming weeks. If you have any problems finding a time just email me and we can work something out."

"Okay, that sounds good. I pray everything is okay with you."

"Yes, I am fine Valerie, but thanks for asking. Remember you can continue sending me things in email even if you have not booked a session."

"Okay I will. Take care of yourself Joy and I will schedule another session maybe sometime later next week."

"Sounds good. Take care, Valerie."

After ending my session with Valerie I leaned back in my chair and thought about everything I said to Valerie. I became emotional and began to cry. I knew that everything I said to Valerie about the healing process also applied to me. I recalled the statement I made about healing not occurring in a linear way and I felt every word of that and knew I needed to practice what I had been preaching to Valerie. I also knew being aware and admitting there is a problem is the first step in the process.

I decided to call Robin and talk to her as my friend.

"Hey Joy, I was wondering if you were going to call me tonight. How are you?"

I smiled. "Robin, can I talk to you as my friend?"

She laughed. "Um, haven't we always been friends?"

I shook my head. "No, not really. I think that even after you ended our client/therapist relationship I still saw you as my therapist. Right now I just need my friend to talk to, to listen to me and not ask those therapist questions."

"Okay, Joy I hear you and yes, you can talk to your friend."

I sighed. "Thank you, Robin. Now, I need to let you know I contacted my EAP program and I have an appointment scheduled tomorrow evening."

"That is great Joy. I am really proud of you."

"Thanks Robin, that means a lot coming from you. Also I have decided not to take on any more online clients. I am cutting my schedule back to allow time for me to work on me."

"You continue to amaze me Joy."

"I am feeling very good about everything."

"Joy, I am very happy for you and please know I am here for you no matter what."

"Thanks again Robin. I am going to go to bed a little early tonight. So I will talk to you later."

"Goodnight, Joy."

"Goodnight."

Chapter 14

I purposely set my alarm an hour earlier since I wanted to get to work early to get caught up. I know I only missed one day, but you would be surprised how behind you can get.

Once I arrived in my office, I first checked my schedule for the day and was pleasantly surprised to see that I had a light day. My first session was not until 10 am which gave me plenty of time to read my emails and review client files.

I decided to run back out to Panera to grab a bagel. In my haste to get to work early this morning I left without bringing anything along to eat. I sometimes got something quick from the vending machines or when I was feeling very desperate I might go to the cafeteria but today I was in the mood for a bagel sandwich. As I walked outside, I noticed Bill walking in.

He looked up just as we were about to pass each other and he stopped and said, "Hey, you are going the wrong way."

I laughed. "That all depends on your perspective."

Bill smiled. "Where are you headed?"

"I got here a little early, so I decided to run to Panera to grab a bagel sandwich."

"Hmm, that sounds delicious. Mind if I ride along?"

"Of course not." Bill turned and then said,

"Why don't I drive us?" I shrugged my shoulders.

"That is fine with me. As long as I get my bagel, I will be happy."

We both walked to Bill's car and headed to Panera. As soon as we exited the parking lot Bill said, "You were on my list to touch base with this morning anyway, so running into you like this was perfect."

"Oh, really? Is everything okay?"

"Yes, of course I just wanted to talk to you about Kara."

"Is everything okay? Did something happen while I was away?"

He laughed. "Slow down Joy. Kara is fine. I just wanted to ask you about the evaluation you ordered."

"I feel she has some deeper issues that require some additional services."

"I see, well the problem is corporate is cracking down on ordering these types of evaluations."

"Really? Since when?"

"Honestly, I am not sure. The reality is we are not able to approve your request."

"Are you serious Bill?"

"Yes, I am Joy. It is not me making the rules, but I have to enforce them."

I could not believe my ears. I was fuming inside. I remained silent for a minute doing my best to collect my thoughts and to remain professional.

"Bill, please explain how I am supposed to treat my clients without getting proper evaluations done?"

"Joy, the direction from corporate is we are to treat their addiction issues and that is it."

"Seriously, Bill, you are joking, right?"

"No, Joy I am not."

"Wow, I am not sure what to say."

"I would like for you to say, 'Okay Bill, I understand'."

I sat in my seat staring out the window. We were at Panera now but had not gotten out of the car yet. This conversation made me lose my appetite.

"Joy, Joy, hello."

"Yes Bill, sorry I was deep in thought."

"Yes, I could see that. We are here so are we going in?"

I thought for a moment. "Yes, although I lost my appetite, I do still need to eat."

"Come on Joy, please just work with me on this."

I shook my head. "Bill, you and I go way back, and I have always enjoyed working with you. Obviously, there is nothing I can do if you will not approve my request, but I do not agree with it. The direction this company is going in really has me rethinking my purpose here."

"Wow, Joy, do you really think this young lady needs these other services?"

"Yes, Bill I do. Yes, I can counsel her through this particular addiction crisis, but the reality is if we do not get to the root of their problems they will continue to relapse."

He reached over and put his hand on mine. "Okay Joy, I hear you. Let me try to talk to corporate to see if I can get anything approved for Kara. Meanwhile I need you to continue working with her to resolve the addiction issue."

I moved my hand away from his and for the first time in all the years I had worked with Bill I felt as though he was not being truthful with me. Maybe I was just still emotional from my weekend, but I strongly felt that not getting Kara the evaluation was doing a huge disservice to her.

Bill and I went into Panera and ordered our food. Bill attempted to lighten the mood by offering to buy my sandwich, but I politely declined. All the way back to the clinic he made small talk and I gave him polite shallow responses. I felt a shift in the energy between Bill and me. I knew that he sensed it as well. When we returned to the clinic he said,

"I will touch base with corporate and I will be in touch."

I barely looked at him. "Okay Bill, thanks."

Once back in my office I slowly ate my sandwich while reviewing emails and was still fuming inside about my conversation with Bill. I was no longer motivated to be at the clinic. I asked myself, 'How could I continue to work with my clients if I know that I am not able to give them the best care?' How was I supposed to mentor other counselors or help revise policies that I did not agree with? I thought about the sermon Pastor Flee gave on Sunday and how he challenged us to figure out our purpose. Then it hit me. If I stayed here working at this clinic, I would no longer be able to fulfill my purpose. I remember a sermon before where the pastor told us that when God is ready for you to move, he makes you uncomfortable where you are. Sitting here in this chair in the office right now I am feeling extremely uncomfortable.

I shook the feeling off and continued to go through my emails and prepare for my clients for the day. I decided to focus on what I could do and not what I could not in that moment. I was not scheduled to meet with Kara again until tomorrow. I would formulate my plan tonight or first thing tomorrow on how to handle my session with her in light of my hands being tied.

I made it through the day without any further interaction with Bill and was happy to leave a little early since I came in early this morning. I had been so bothered by my discussion with Bill that I had not taken any time to think about or prepare for my EAP session that was scheduled for this evening.

As I drove home I considered calling Robin, but I decided not to since she was probably still tied up with clients. Just then my phone rang. I did not recognize the number, but it was a Pennsylvania number, so I answered it,

"Hello, this is Joy."

"Hello Joy, this is Curtis."

I rolled my eyes. I was not in the mood for him right now, but I managed to say, "Oh hey Curtis, how are you?"

"I am doing well thanks for asking. I am actually sitting here with Pastor Flee and we thought we would give you a quick call."

"Oh, okay well how can I help you both?"

"Hello Joy." Pastor Flee said.

"Hello Pastor."

"It sounds like you are driving right now." Curtis said.

"Yes, I am on my way home from work."

"Well we will not hold you long. We really just wanted to set a time for us to chat about my idea." Pastor Flee said.

"Normally I get home around 5:30 from work. Some evenings I have some clients that I talk to later in the evening."

"What does your schedule look like tomorrow evening around six?"

"I think I am free but since I am driving, I cannot check my schedule right now. Can I check when I get home and I can text or email you to confirm, whichever you prefer?"

"Yes, that sounds great. We are calling you from Curtis' cell so why don't you text him to confirm and he will contact me."

"Okay, Pastor. I will be in touch with Curtis this evening. Hopefully, we can talk tomorrow at six."

I ended the call and within minutes I was pulling up to my house. I had a couple of hours before my session and decided to grab my journal and write for a little while. I still had so many pent-up emotions about my talk with Bill. I should be focused on my EAP session, but something was stirring inside of me about the new direction of the company and it bothered me.

Before I knew it, the time had come for my EAP session. I went into my office and dialed the number for the call. My assigned therapist was named Sydney. We started off with all of the usual personal information stuff. Then she opened up the floor for me to talk. At first, I was not sure where to start but once I began talking it felt as though I did not stop for the entire hour. Sydney barely had time to ask any questions.

When I did finally take a breath she asked, "Joy, how do you feel right now?"

At first, I thought it was an odd question. "I am feeling surprisingly good."

She chuckled and asked, "Why surprisingly?"

"I guess because I thought I would feel anxious about starting over."

"Staring over?"

"Yes with a new therapist."

"What happened with your old one? If you do not mind me asking."

"We've become friends over the years. I actually had not realized until very recently that our talks were no longer therapy but just friends catching up."

"That is interesting."

Now the therapist in me wondered why. Why is that interesting?"

Sydney laughed. "Okay Joy, remember that I am the therapist here."

"Yes, I know but seriously I want to know why you found that interesting. Am I not allowed to asked questions?"

"Do you allow your clients to ask you questions?"

"Okay, I see your point. This is going to be a bit of a challenge for me."

"Oh so you thought it would be easy because you are a therapist?"

I laughed. "Yeah I guess."

"Well, I can tell you from my personal experience that therapists are the most difficult clients." We both laughed.

"Honestly, it is going to take some getting used to for you, but I feel confident that you will figure it out. I think you are in an incredibly good place Joy. Despite everything you shared with me. You know the areas that you need to heal, and you know why. That is sometimes the hardest part. I think what your experienced today with your boss has really made things a little clearer for you also."

"Yes I agree with you. Obviously, I am going to give everything a lot more thought, but I do think a change is in order."

"Okay Joy, so when do you want to chat again?"

"Can we talk again same time next week?"

"Yes, that works for me. Remember to keep writing in your journal, that is a great tool for you."

"Okay I will. Talk to you next week."

After my EAP session I made a frozen pizza and ate while catching up on my personal email and my emails from online clients. My young client with the parents who were divorcing emailed me that she was ending her services. It seems that her parents decided to reconcile. I shook my head but replied to her that I was happy to hear that and I hope all goes well. I had not heard anything from my other two online clients in over a week. I checked my schedule and there was nothing scheduled for either of them. I sent them both emails checking in. Just as I was about to log off, I received an email from Valerie.

Joy,

It has been difficult to write about getting admitted to the hospital since it was a very upsetting time, but it may also help me move on from this awful experience.

Paula was supposed to be taking me to an appointment for David. While in the car with her she seemed to be driving extremely fast. It really started to frighten me, and I asked her to slow down. She did not seem to hear me, and I became extremely anxious thinking we might get in a car accident. There are medical buildings near the hospital, and I did not notice that we walked in the emergency entrance. Paula had me take a seat in the waiting room and went up to the front desk. I thought she was checking to see if the doctor was ready to meet with me about David. While I waited, I decided to check the security cameras from my phone. When I saw a police car in my driveway panic set in. As any worried parent would, I became more and more distraught thinking about all the possibilities of what could have happened.

Finally a nurse walked over and said they were going to need to get a urine specimen from me as a follow up to my recent surgery. I was confused as to why they were asking questions about my health when that is not what I was there for. Paula reappeared standing beside the nurse and they had me get into a wheelchair. At this point I was crying hysterically since I thought something awful happened to someone in my family due to seeing the police on the camera.

In the observation room everyone started asking me a lot of questions. I felt as though I was on a game show that I was trying to win by providing the right answers. I know it sounds strange but looking back at what happened now realize I may have been starting to have a mental breakdown.

My phone rang but it was not in the bed next to me. Paula answered it and I could hear Fran getting loud on the other end. She was demanding to know what was going on and who did Paula think she was for making decisions on my behalf. Fran was getting on the next flight and they were not to do anything else without her consent.

I remembered about seeing the police at my house earlier, so I wanted to hear Scott's voice to make sure he was ok. I did get my phone back briefly to call him and I frightened him because I was so upset. He had no idea what was going on with me at the time since no one had reached out to him to tell him I was at the hospital. I was brought a tray with a sandwich and some juice since it turns out the staff was told I had not been eating or drinking for days. I did have some of it although I really was not that hungry but figured that would help me go home sooner.

I asked Paula for my phone back and she told me it was dead. I knew that could not be the case since I always had my phone charged. I really wanted to get in touch with Celeste to let her know where I was. Paula was gone and the nurse then told me I was being transferred to the psych floor. I tried to leave the room and could not because there was a security guard at the door. I thought I heard my sister in law Deb's voice in the hall when I was getting blocked from leaving. I gave up and got back on the stretcher and closed my eyes. Maybe I would be lucky and when I woke up this would all have been just be a bad nightmare.

I know that is a lot of information but hopefully it will put into perspective how things were when I went into the hospital and we can possibly discuss this during some of our video sessions.

Valerie

After my EAP session, my disagreement with Bill earlier and reading Valerie's email I was emotionally spent. Just when I thought my issues were insurmountable or at the very least difficult, I am reminded that someone else has a higher mountain to climb. Valerie has endured unimaginable challenges, but she is still moving forward.

I planned to read everything again with a fresh mind and make my notes for our next session, but I immediately jotted down a note to ask her about her son David. I wondered how he is handling everything. He has been right alongside her through all of this. He has to have some type of trauma from all of this. I knew from my own personal experiences that sometimes when adults are dealing with things the children are overlooked. I felt somewhat traumatized just from reading it all, I can only imagine how it must have felt to be going through it.

I sent Valerie an email confirming receipt of her email and reminding her to schedule our next session at her convenience.

Although I was exhausted, I decided to treat myself to a glass of wine before bed. I needed to calm my nerves.

Chapter 15

Unlike yesterday when I arrived at work early today, I barely made it inside the building before the official start of my work day. To say that I was not feeling very motivated would be an understatement. Honestly, if I did not have Kara on my schedule today, I would have called off.

On my way into work this morning I realized that I had never confirmed with Curtis about my schedule for tonight to speak to Pastor Flee. As soon as I put my things down in my office, I sent him a quick text confirming for tonight. He responded right away with a thumb's up emoji.

My schedule was full today. I had a group session to sit in as the alternate therapist this morning for two hours. Then another client who was preparing to leave the clinic, so that would be an easy hour. I just needed to go over the exit plan and make sure there were support services lined up for outpatient care. Kara was my first appointment after the lunch hour, and I ended my day with a meeting with Bill to review my progress on our project.

I headed to the break room to make my tea before heading over to the group session. On my way there I saw Bill, but I did not go out of my way to acknowledge him. I was not ready to continue my discussion with him quite yet.

The group session was uneventful, but I did get to observe Kara again and I still felt there was more than an addiction issue going on with her. My next client, Antonio, was waiting for me when I returned to my office from the group session. He was extremely excited to be leaving soon and he came prepared with all of his outpatient information. He had actually done most of my work for me. I felt good about his progress and recovery. I think he just fell into the wrong crowd and made some bad choices. He really did not seem to have any underlying issues which drove him to become an addict. Since he was so well prepared, we ended a few minutes early. I told Antonio to schedule our last session for the following week and he would be released next Friday.

Since I had a few extra minutes, I decided to leave the building for lunch today. I rarely did that, but today I was not in the mood to run into Bill and I had not brought lunch with me. I grabbed my purse and headed to the parking lot to my car. Since I arrived later than usual today, I had to park around the side of the building. As I walked past all the other cars towards my ten-year-old Metallic green Honda Accord, I thought I must not be living right. I never noticed before today how many Mercedes, BMWs and Lexus there were in this lot.

I decided to stay at Panera and eat my sandwich and salad. The least amount of time I spent at the clinic right now the better. I thought about what Robin said about Pastor Flee. I smiled and shook my head. I honestly would not put it past Toni to try to set me up with the pastor. I did not really get that type of vibe from him though. I honestly thought that Curtis seemed to be more interested. I guess time will tell. I finished my lunch and made it back to the office with a few minutes to spare before Kara's session. I went over to my desk to put my purse away and I noticed a note on my desk. It was from Bill and it read, '*Sorry that I missed you Joy. I need to follow up with you about our conversation from yesterday. Please stop by when you get a chance. Bill*'

I did not have time to go to his office before Kara arrived, so I decided to call him.

"Joy, I really wanted to talk in person."

"Yes, I saw your note, but I thought I would give you a quick call because I am expecting Kara any minute for our session."

"You have plenty of time, Joy. Come down to my office now please."

I was instantly annoyed but obviously there was something going on, so I hung up the phone, grabbed my planner, and went to Bill's office. He was standing at the door waiting for me when I arrived. He smiled but I did not.

"Okay, I see that you are still upset."

"What is going on Bill?"

"First of all, Kara is not meeting with you today."

"Okay, you care to enlighten me on why?"

"She is meeting with another therapist as we speak."

"Another therapist? Why?"

"I need someone else to evaluate her to determine if she needs additional services or not."

I stood up and started pacing and said, "You are telling me that my professional judgment is being questioned?"

"No, now calm down, Joy. This is the only way I could get corporate to consider what you are asking."

I backed down just a little bit. "Bill, are you serious?"

"Unfortunately yes."

I sat back down and shook my head. "Please explain to me what the big deal is? They are not paying for it. Her insurance, or whoever is footing her bill, pays for it. What is their issue?"

"Joy, there are some things you really do not want to know about this new organization and how things are run."

"No, Bill you are wrong. I do want to know. In fact, I need to know."

He seemed shocked by me stating that I needed to know. "Joy, why do you need to know. What does that mean? What is going on with you lately?"

My blood was beginning to boil. I was not sure where to begin. I put my head down for a moment to collect my thoughts. Although Bill and I had a great relationship and I usually felt comfortable being open and honest with him, something inside of me was cautioning me right now to hold back.

"Bill, it is important to me that I understand the values of the company I am working for. This is more than a job to me. This is my career. I do not like to waste time and if I cannot manage my clients' care to the best of my ability, I feel as though I am wasting my time as well as theirs."

"I get it Joy; I really do but listen to me. You are so close to being able to leave and retain your full benefits. Just ride this out until you have your years of service in. You're going to be working with me more on the administrative side anyway. Making waves is not the way to go with this right now."

He was pleading with me. I could see it in his eyes. I felt bad for Bill. Somewhere along the way he had lost himself in the system. I stood up. "Can you just let me know the results of the other therapist's evaluation of Kara please?" As I walked to the door and opened it, he said, "Of course, Joy. I will personally bring the report to you and we can review it together and come up with a plan of action."

I nodded my head. "Thanks Bill." I walked out of his office. My next move was to pull my benefits documentation and research my options. I knew that I could not stay here if it meant I had to provide less than adequate care and treatment to my clients. I wish I could just ride the bench while waiting for my benefits eligibility date, but I simply could not see myself being able to do that. I heard that little voice in my head reminding me about the sermon where the pastor said, 'God makes you uncomfortable when He is about to make some changes in your life'. I had no clue what changes lie ahead, but I felt a shifting in the atmosphere. It seemed as if I slept walked through the remainder of my day. I met with my clients in the afternoon as scheduled, but I honestly could not recall anything we discussed. I almost forgot about my scheduled meeting with Pastor Flee until my phone rang at 6:00. I let it ring a couple of times before I answered to clear my mind.

"Hello."

"Hello Joy, this is Pastor Flee. How are you today?"

"Hello, Pastor, I am doing well and you?"

"I am blessed beyond measure."

"I am glad to hear that. Is it just the two of us talking tonight?"

"Oh, yes just you and I tonight."

I raised my eyebrow as I thought about Robin's thoughts about his motive. "Oh okay, well, how can I help you pastor?" I asked, trying to move the conversation along as quickly as possible.

"Well Joy, we have a real problem in our church. It is not just a problem for our church, per se, but it is a cultural thing. There is this stigma in the black community, and especially in our churches, about not seeking treatment for mental health issues."

"Yes sir, I am very aware. It is something we therapists talk about often in our conferences. Trying to break down those barriers within certain cultures."

"I am so glad to hear that you are aware of these challenges."

"Yes, I am, but I am still not sure I understand how I can help."

"I have this idea about having a therapist, you actually, do a series of workshops here at the church. Initially to the church leadership, the associate pastors' deacons etc. Eventually we can expand it to the entire congregation and ultimately the community."

As he talked, I became more and more interested. "Why me?"

He chuckled. "I had no choice."

Now I laughed. "What do you mean?"

"Your sister in law, Toni, is on the advisory committee and when we began discussing this topic, she was adamant that she knew the perfect therapist for this project."

"I see, well you do know that I live in Virginia, right?"

"Ah, yes I am aware that you currently reside in Virginia."

I noticed the emphasis he placed on the word 'currently'. I was intrigued, so I let that go.

"What is your timeframe for starting the workshops? Are you bringing in any other additional therapists?"

"Actually, Joy, I would leave all of that up to you. If you choose to accept this challenge, I will leave the timeline and planning up to you. You would have to present your recommendations to me and the committee, but it would be your baby."

"Well, I am definitely interested in discussing this further with you. I am going to need a little time to think everything over."

"Of course, take whatever time you need. If you give me your email address, I can send you the budget and salary information to you tomorrow."

"Ok wait, there is already a budget, and this is a paid position?"

"Yes, this is something that was in the works before I became pastor. There was a fairly large donation made a few years ago by the family of one of our members whose young daughter took her life. It was a real shock and tragedy, of course, and the family wanted to do something to ensure no other young people suffer in silence."

"Wow, I had no idea that had happened. Yes, Pastor, I am interested in seeing all the details. I will review it and get back to you within a week. Is that good?"

"Yes, that is fine. Once you receive the email if you have any questions, do not hesitate to email me or give me a call."

"Thanks Pastor. Can I ask you a question?"

"Of course you can."

"How do you know Curtis?"

He laughed. "Curtis and I go way back. We worked together for many years at the church I transferred from. I understand that the two of you went to school together."

"Yes, we both went to Penn State. He was a year ahead of me though."

"Curtis is a very spiritually solid man. No matter how much I try to convince him to preach, he just will not consider it."

"Yes, I am a little surprised that you are not considering him for this position."

"We did discuss it briefly, but it was a little more than he was willing to do right now. He has some challenges he is dealing with."

"Oh, I see. Well, send me the details and I will review everything and get back to you."

"Thanks so much Joy, it was a pleasure talking to you."

"You're welcome, Pastor Flee." After disconnecting the call, I jumped up and started yelling and screaming, 'Thank you Lord. I know this was all you'.

*****

I was busy the remainder of the week researching my benefits options at work, avoiding Bill as much as possible and doing my best to remain professional with my clients. Late in the day on Friday, Bill finally followed up with me about Kara. He came into my office unannounced, "Hey Joy, do you have a minute?"

"Sure, Bill, come on in."

He stepped inside my office and closed the door. He walked over to the couch and sat down. "Joy, I wanted to follow up with you about Kara before the weekend. The other therapist has completed their evaluation. I have reviewed their notes and yours as well."

He paused and I said, "And what did the other therapist say?"

"I would rather not get into the details right now, but I will say that there does appear to be some additional issues with Kara outside of her addiction. With that said, the direction at this point is to continue to assess what we can provide her here to address the addiction and then as a part of her outplacement services transition we will recommend the additional services that we suggest that she receive."

I could not believe my ears. I looked at Bill in disbelief, but I knew any further discussion was pointless. I already knew that my time here was short. I could also sense that Bill expected me to fight and I wanted to surprise him. "I am glad that my concerns were validated, and I will continue as you suggested. I will treat Kara's addiction issues and incorporate the other services into her outpatient plan."

Bill looked shocked and relieved and maybe a little afraid as well. He slowly got up from the couch and made his way to the door. "Uh, okay then. I am glad that we were able to resolve that. You can resume your sessions with Kara next week."

"Thanks again Bill. I will get her added back onto my schedule before I leave today. Have a great weekend."

"Thanks, you too." I watched him walk out of the door, and I could tell he was still trying to assess my mood and possibly was a little surprised that I gave up so easily. Bill did not know I was planning my transition. After receiving the email from Pastor Flee the other day and reading his proposal, budget, and considering all the possibilities, I knew my days at the clinic were numbered. I had also done a little research into my options and I discovered I could reduce my hours and still receive my full benefits package. I plan to write up a proposal to Bill in the coming weeks. I am not going to knee jerk react to anything. I plan to move with slow and deliberate intent to maximize my success as I transition into my next season.

I had big plans for this weekend. I was going to follow up with Pastor Flee and talk to both Toni and Robin about transitioning from my current job at the clinic. Before leaving for the day I made sure to get Kara on my schedule for the following week. My plan for her was to get her out of the clinic as soon as possible since she really does not have an addiction problem. I will be focusing my energy on lining up all of the other resources that I know that she needs.

As I drove home, I thought about Bill. We used to be so close and I was counting on him still being more than my boss, but a friend. I wanted to make my transition as smooth as possible, but I would need his help with allowing me flexibility in my schedule to accomplish that.

Chapter 16

The weekend flew by and it was already Monday afternoon and I was on my way home after a very productive day at work. I met with Kara and we have a plan to get her released within the next two weeks. She is doing well in her group sessions and I am confident that we can wrap up our individual sessions by then. Next, I have to start working on getting all the other services lined up and in her outpatient plan.

I have a session scheduled with Valerie tonight. I had reviewed her latest email again last evening and made my notes for our discussion. After that I planned to work on my proposal for Bill. I mapped out everything over the weekend but in order for me to move forward I need Bill to agree to my terms. I had followed up with Pastor Flee letting him know that I am interested but needed a little time to work out the details with my current employer. He was pleased that I was on board and told me to take whatever time I needed.

I logged in for my session with Valerie a little early. She was always very punctual, so I did not want to be late. Once Valerie joined, we both greeted each other and then we got started.

"Valerie, I got your email explaining everything that occurred when you were taken to the hospital. I can understand why it would be difficult to trust people after what happened."

"Yes, I feel like being able to trust again is going to be my biggest challenge."

"Is there anything you would like to discuss with me now about your email?"

"I just keep thinking back to when I was in the car with Paula. I really thought she was sincere about wanting to help David. Instead, I later found out she was putting him in the middle of what she thought were the steps needed to be taken with me and that was not her decision. David let me know shortly after I got home from the hospital that she had reached out to him. He was so distraught about what he was being asked to do he did not even talk with Celeste about it. I was furious Paula asked David to pretend he was the one that needed a psychiatric appointment and told him he needed to get me to sign papers to commit myself which I refused to do. I was also angry that Paula had been in touch with one of my friends and together they decided to have me involuntary committed before they discussed anything with my family."

"Yes, I agree that was a real betrayal of trust on her part. It is really a shame that David had to go through all of that. Okay, let's move on. How everything has been going since we last talked?"

"Well just this past weekend I fell and broke my wrist, so I have a cast now for about eight weeks. It is hard for me to type so I probably will be taking a break from sending emails."

"Oh, my goodness. What happened?"

"David's prom was over the weekend. I was in a rush to get to where they were getting their prom pictures taken. I missed a step walking into the house and fell on the cement hard. I cracked my phone case and immediately was in severe pain. I did not see anyone else around, so I got up quickly and tried to pretend nothing happened. As soon as I walked into the house, I saw David. He gave me a big hug and handed me his phone to take pictures with too. I went out back with the other parents and was so thankful to be included since David seemed apprehensive earlier given our family situation Seth put us in. I was all ready to start taking pictures and then realized I could not move my wrist. Another parent took several pictures from my phone and David's to help me out."

"Oh my. That sounds terrible."

"It was and as soon as we were finished taking pictures and David realized I was hurt, he insisted I go have it checked out. He introduced me to his date's parents, and they offered to take me to the hospital since it was going to be hard for me to drive myself there. I was embarrassed since it was my first time meeting them, but I was very appreciative."

"That was really nice of them to offer you a ride. Did they wait with you to give you a ride home too?"

"No, I reached out to Celeste and her husband dropped her off at the hospital so she could drive my car. I was able to get in and out of the hospital pretty fast. Celeste and I made it to the prom walk just in time to see David and his date go past with their whole group. David looked so handsome in his black suit with his silver tie and vest even though I thought his wavy blonde hair was way too long, but that seems to be the style now. His date's floor length white dress was gorgeous and had sequins on it with hints of silver."

"Wow, that is amazing that you were able to be seen so quickly at the hospital and still made it."

"Yes, it was and when I went to check in at the hospital, they asked me if my emergency contacts were the same since they had them listed as Seth and Paula. I was baffled to why my records would show this and immediately had my emergency contacts updated to Celeste and my Mom. The registration clerk commented that it was such a shame about what happened to Seth. I had seen on social media that people thought he was innocent and felt bad for him. I was really starting to get sick of it and told her I was not with him anymore. Someone else in the waiting area asked what had happened and kept asking me questions. Being in a small town everyone has to see if they know each other and they mentioned that their kid was the same year as mine. They then started in on how they met Seth and again I stated I was not with him anymore. People just do not seem to know when to mind their own business. It is so difficult with everyone knowing who I am and feeling like they are judging me for leaving him."

Valerie began sobbing uncontrollably. I wanted to let her get it all out and waited until she was calmer to give her my feedback.

"That all sounds pretty frustrating. You have every right to feel whatever you are feeling Valerie. You do not owe anyone any explanations, remember that okay?"

"Yes, I will try, but honestly it is hard sometimes."

"I am sure it is hard. Just hang in there. You are handling things very well at least from my perspective. Anyway, let's move on. How is work going?"

Valerie sighed deeply and I could tell she was trying not to start crying again. "Due to budget cuts, I was told I was being moved to Lila's team. Ever since she moved to a new group she had been reaching out and trying to get me to join her. I was very hesitant and told her I thought it would probably more than I could take on. She told me it was a pretty intense program with back to back meetings all day. Now I had no choice but hopefully since I made some changes to my medicine maybe I will have an easier time adjusting."

"I thought the last time we met you told me you went off all your medication. Did something change?"

"I was starting to have a bit of a rough time emotionally. When I met with the doctor for my follow up appointment, I agreed to taking something as needed for anxiety. I can usually tell when I am starting to get overwhelmed and it has been working pretty well so far."

"I'm glad to hear that is working out well for you. Were you still having a hard time with driving places before you ended up in a cast?"

"Driving to places I am familiar with like by Scott's school has been fine. Trying to get anywhere I haven't been before is stressful for me. Recently my friend Trish came to visit, and I met her for breakfast at Perkins. She was in town for an event for her church and we decided to meet about halfway close to my work. Even with my GPS I felt I needed to print out directions and use the navigation on my phone. I was feeling a little anxious that I might make a wrong turn, but at least now I have medicine if I feel that way again. I guess that day I was not feeling great emotionally either. Before I met her, I had gotten a call from Seth and he was pretty upset with me. He wanted to know why I was not going to our nephew's confirmation. I knew that there would be a ton of people at church and I just did not feel it was something I could handle. I had let my sister in law Deb know already and she was very understanding. When I left to meet Trish I was still shaken up from my conversation with Seth."

"It sounds like it is good for you to have the medicine for now in case you need it. Have you been reaching out to friends if you need support?"

"I find it helpful to talk with Celeste since she also has really good suggestions. I also am in touch with Darla frequently since she previously had a long relationship too so she can relate to some of what I am going through. I do talk with my family pretty frequently. I try my best to keep them up to date with how I am doing, and they have been incredibly supportive. Fran set up my Facebook account for me since that was something I always wanted to do. Hopefully, it will be nice to reconnect with people although I really do not want to share with a lot of posts."

"Have you had to see Seth face to face?"

"I did allow him to come over to the house so he could see David leave for the prom. I understood how important that was for him even though I really did not want him at the house with me, but Celeste came over as well. It was a little awkward, but it was an important day. Seth called me shortly after he left and to tell me another article would be hitting the news."

"Did he tell you what the news story was going to be about this time?"

"He did not get into specifics, but it just hit today actually."

"I have been meaning to ask you. How are your sons handling everything? I was especially concerned about David after reading your last email. That entire hospital admission scenario had to be a lot for him to deal with."

"It has been pretty difficult on them both. While I was in the hospital David did spend quite a bit of time at his best friend's house which I think helped since he is pretty comfortable there. I know change is hard for Scott, so even though he understands why I have made the decision to file for divorce he is disappointed with the fact that his parents are no longer together. I feel they both should be meeting with someone to talk about what our family has experienced, but right now they have both chosen to just confide in their closest friends. I also have had some good conversations with each of them so that we can help each other get through this."

"With your cast I guess emailing is going to be tough. I'd be open to giving you my cell so that you could send me messages using voice to text if you'd like?"

"That would be great. Thanks!"

After my session with Valerie, I decided to warm up something for dinner. While in the kitchen my phone rang. I did not recognize the number, but I answered it.

"Hello,"

"Hello Joy, this is Curtis."

I smiled as I thought, 'Well this is a pleasant surprise'. "Hi Curtis. How are you?"

"I am doing well. Did I catch you at a bad time?"

"No, I am just warming up some leftovers for dinner. I just finished with one of my online clients."

"Oh, okay, well I know you are a busy woman so I will not take up much of your time. I just wanted to follow up with you about two things. First, I am happy to hear you are interested in the pastor's proposal."

"Yes, I am extremely interested and excited about the possibilities. Although maybe I should think more about it since I heard that you turned him down."

"Oh no, please do not reconsider. It is a wonderful opportunity and if I were in the position to dedicate more time to it, I would certainly have taken him up on his offer. I just have a lot going on right now with my daughter."

"You have a daughter? How old is she?"

"Yes, I have two children, a son who is a senior in high school and my daughter is 13."

"Oh yes, that is a tough age, that is for sure."

"Yes, it is and doing it alone makes it even harder."

"I see and where is your daughter's mother?"

"My wife passed away a couple of years ago from ovarian cancer."

"Oh, I am so sorry to hear that Curtis. That has to be rough on you and your kids. I can certainly relate. I lost my mother when I was a teenager."

"Really? I did not know that."

"Yes, I did, and it was rough for me. My father was not in my life at all. I only had my older brother; he was married to Toni. Unfortunately, he died a couple of years later after my mom. I felt like an orphan. Toni was the only family I had."

"My daughter is struggling with the loss of her mom and with us moving to Harrisburg. She is having a hard time making new friends here and her schoolwork is also suffering. Anyway, I did not call to dump all of my troubles on you."

"I do not consider this dumping on me, but okay. So what was your second reason for calling?"

"Well, that is actually a tougher conversation. It is about Miles. He wants to talk to you."

"Oh, I see. I am not sure how I feel about that right now."

"I figured you would say that. Since you and I last spoke about him I have had a chance to talk to him and he filled me in on everything."

"And yet you are still lobbying for me to talk to him?" Maybe Curtis was not so nice after all.

"I just think that you both deserve that final conversation to get closure is all I am saying. Trust me I am not on either side."

"Honestly, I have given Miles and what happened between us too much energy and power over my life for way too long. I am finally in a place where I feel like I know what lies ahead for me. I am in a positive space right now. I do not want any negativity creeping in to mess everything up."

"I understand but let me ask you a question."

"Okay sure."

"Are you planning to move back to Harrisburg as a part of taking on Pastor Flee's assignment?"

"I am considering it why?"

"Then you should know that Miles is also back living in the area."

"Seriously? Ugh."

"Yes, that is why I think the two of you should talk and I wanted to make sure you were aware of that so you would not be surprised."

"He is back in Harrisburg? Why?"

"He recently took a position at the high school he attended. He said that school meant a lot to him and he always wanted to return there. Now he is the director of their counseling services department."

"Well, good for him. Are his wife and child or children with him?"

"Joy, I am not giving you all that information. You need to talk to him. Listen I will give you his number. He gave me permission to do that. You think about it and call him if and when you are ready."

"Okay, Curtis, that is fair."

I walked into my office to jot down Miles' number. After I wrote the number down and confirmed it with Curtis, I said, "Curtis, if you need any help with your daughter, please do not hesitate to reach out to me. If there is anything I can do, I will. I also can refer you to someone that I know, she is actually the therapist I worked with after Miles and I broke up. We are the best of friends now."

"Thanks so much Joy. I might just have to take you up on that offer."

"You are welcome Curtis. Have a good night."

"Good night, Joy."

I felt bad about Curtis' daughter and losing her mom. I could certainly relate. It must be hard for him raising a teenage daughter alone. I am not sure how that would have worked for Darien if he had not been with Toni. A young girl needs a woman around to help her through tough times. I was curious about his conversation with Miles and if they were rekindling their friendship also.

I was in such a good mood about the possibilities that lie ahead that I decided not to give the Miles situation any energy tonight. I planned to eat my dinner and work on my proposal for Bill in peace. Miles will be dealt with later. Curtis was full of surprises. He isn't at all like I expected him to be.

Chapter 17

I could not believe that June was here already. I have been so busy putting my plans in place to leave the clinic the month of May flew by.

I was pleased that Bill accepted my proposal with little to no fuss. Of course, he does not want me to leave the clinic, but he at least agreed to my request to change my schedule to accommodate my frequent trips to Pennsylvania. Since my face to face interactions with clients has decreased, I have more flexibility and can do some of my work remotely. Starting this week I have adjusted my schedule at the clinic to work the minimum required 30 hours between Sunday and Wednesday every other week. This will allow me to travel to Pennsylvania Wednesday afternoon through Sunday. I will be going to Harrisburg this week and meeting with Pastor Flee to get things started for this project which I am very excited about.

I have not been back to Pennsylvania since my visit to talk to Toni. My trip later this week will include a sit-down discussion with Miles. After many weeks of debate, I finally decided to contact him. It was a brief phone conversation. Just long enough for me to plan to meet with him while I am in town this week. I actually have an ulterior motive for wanting to connect with him. Based on what Curtis told me about his position as the head of counseling services, I may be able to include him as a speaker for one of my workshops.

That is if I am able to stand the sight of him once we have our long overdue talk.

He sounded the same when we spoke. I was pleasantly surprised that hearing his voice did not invoke the emotions I expected. I have continued my weekly EAP sessions and have been able to work through a lot of my emotions about Miles and many other things I had not dealt with over the years. I would like to think my sessions have helped me be more at peace with everything. Honestly though I have been so focused on my new project I have not allowed my emotions to reach the surface. Not a great thing but in this case useful for me right now. I feel good about this project and the possibilities it can open up for me. I believe I have found my purpose. Now that I am on the road to recovery from all of my past pain the thought of returning to my hometown is not as scary as it was before.

The timeline I gave Pastor Flee has me starting the workshops in late September. I have the summer to develop the content and recruit my team. I need to continue my hours at the clinic until next spring in order to get my full benefits. That means I have some time to get my house ready to sell and I will plan to crash with Toni or Robin for now. They are both more than happy with me considering moving back. I have removed my name from the list of therapists accepting new clients with my online company. Right now my only online client is Valerie and I am committed to working with her until she feels she no longer needs me.

Speaking of Valerie, I am scheduled to touch base with her soon. She has been unable to email me since she is still in the cast, but she has been sending me text messages here and there by using voice to text. She has good and bad days which is normal for anyone who has gone through what she has. Overall I do feel as though she is making great progress. Her most recent text was about her husband Seth sitting next to her at senior night for David's track team. Valerie was able to move away from him in between events and managed to find some friends to sit with but the entire situation was very annoying for her understandably.

"Hi Valerie. It has been a while since we met. How are you doing with the cast?"

"I am doing a lot better, thanks. I am not in as much pain and have a soft cast that is removable. It is still hard to type but at least it makes it easier to shower."

"How is work going?"

"It is pretty stressful being on a new team, but I still have the anxiety medication to take if I start to feel anxious. It has been challenge keeping up with things since my ability to type was diminished. I am still trying to get up to speed with everything I need to do, and Lila also made me her backup. She did not give me any notice ahead of time she was going to a conference and I had to do both of our jobs last week. She has quite a bit of time scheduled off coming up that I will have to cover but I am hoping to fit in a visit to my family soon since it is getting easier for me to drive."

I was becoming concerned about Valerie's job and the amount of additional stress it was putting on her. Whenever we talk about it, she seems agitated and pretty overwhelmed. She really needs a break. Taking medicine because of a job is not good. I was really starting to think it was important for her to find something new, but she said she was looking so maybe that will work out for her.

"Hopefully, you can work something out with Lila. I'm sure that would be nice for you to see your family."

"It really would, since my parents cannot travel and I have only talked to them on the phone the past few months."

"Have things calmed down at all with all the graduation activities? When I saw your text about senior night for track, I couldn't believe Seth is still trying to make it appear as though you guys are still together."

"It has still been a pretty busy time. We just had David's graduation party this past weekend. Seth and I did a combined one since he told me it was a dumb idea to each have our own. It really has been difficult to see him at all the events the past few weeks. I was very annoyed the night I texted you. Seth got really mad about that and told me about it when he called about the next event which was senior awards night. I made it clear that I did not plan on sitting with him and he told me how ridiculous I was being."

Valerie started sobbing and grabbed a tissue. I allowed some time for her to compose herself first and then I said, "It sounds like Seth is making things pretty difficult for you."

"He really is, and it seems he wants it to appear we are still together. I have no interest in working things out with him. For the graduation party, I used most of the same list from Scott's party two years ago since I really was not sure who to invite. I bought myself a new long crimson colored casual dress and went to salon to get my hair washed and styled before the party. I think some people came more out of curiosity to see if we would both be there. There were a few people that Seth worked with that came and Seth told me that I needed to make sure to go talk to them. I was friendly to everyone but did not like that he was acting like it was a political event or that he thought it was acceptable to tell me what I should be doing."

I could see that Valerie was getting a little upset, but she took a few sips of water and continued.

"I helped pack up as much as I could when the party was done but Seth got really angry when I said I was leaving. My friend Trish and her husband were coming over to my house once I got back so we could catch up. I have known her since we played T-ball together and it was really nice for them to make the trip for the party. I also wanted to let them know how things were going with the divorce process so far."

"Hopefully, Seth isn't giving you too much trouble on that although it sounds like he does not want to move on."

Valerie now took a few deep breathes before she responded. I can tell that she is learning how to handle her emotions a little better although feeling frustration and anger is understandable based on all that she has been through.

"I am getting extremely frustrated that Seth's attorney seems to be taking way too long to get back on things. It turns out Seth told him there is no rush and I will change my mind. I made it clear to my attorney that what Seth told his attorney is not accurate and definitely something I want to move forward with as quickly as possible. We have already put out an agreement and they put together a counter to it so it seems we are getting close. Just yesterday there was finally an email from Seth's attorney offering for all of us to meet so I asked my attorney to set that up. I really just want to move on and get this done."

"I'm sure you do. Do you want to talk a little now about the email you sent when you were admitted to the hospital or when you were there?" I could see that Valerie was a little worked up, but I thought I would see if we could get through a few questions.

"I guess that is fine. I did just get a Facebook message the other day from Lauren who was in the hospital with me. I was a little shocked at first that she was able to locate me since we were not supposed to share personal information such as our last name in the hospital it was possible that people could still have known who I was. I have not responded to Lauren yet, but I might when I feel ready. I am curious to see how she is doing since she headed to drug rehab when she left the hospital. Being in the hospital was really hard for me but at least I got to go home when I left. It was still an extremely traumatic experience for me when I was admitted. I tried to put what happened in an email because it takes a lot to piece it all together."

"I completely understand how you feel. We do not have to spend too much time talking about it. I certainly do not want to make you uncomfortable. I will say that things that are uncomfortable are usually the things we need to deal with."

'Okay I understand. Do you have any specific questions for me?"

"Yes, I know that you have told me that it was difficult for you to remember everything about the hospital. Can you tell me why being admitted is difficult for you to talk about even now?"

"There were people that thought they knew what was best for me and to not be honest about their plans was an act of betrayal. While everything was happening it felt like I was watching a movie, not like something that was actually happening to me. It all went so fast and next thing I knew I was on the psych ward and the nurses were trying to get me to take medicine. I did not trust anyone at that point and was afraid of taking anything. I tried to lock myself in the bathroom and screamed at the top of my lungs that I wanted a priest because I felt there was nothing left to live for. Eventually the nurse got me to come out of the bathroom and then I was held down so I could get an injection that knocked me out for hours. I felt like I was being put down like a dog and there was nothing I could do to get out of the situation I was in. I remained in the hospital for two weeks and while I got some rest nothing can make up for the trauma I endured by that experience. I should have been able to be there for my kids at a time when they needed me most and comfortable in my own home with friends close by like Celeste."

Now the tears really started coming. I let Valerie cry it out since it is really an important part of her healing. Once she began to compose herself, I continued. "Yes, I completely understand. It was a horrible experience Valerie and remember that you are allowed to have whatever emotions you feel."

After she calmed down a bit she said, "I guess sometimes it just seems like nobody can really relate to my feelings."

"Yes, well that is sort of true since they did not experience what you did it would be hard for them to understand. You have to realize that limitation also. Everyone is not going to be able to put themselves in your shoes for what you are going through with Seth or the situation surrounding your commitment to the psychiatric ward. Valerie, the most important thing is that you process your feelings in a healthy way so that you can move forward. Does that make sense?"

"Yes, it does, and you are right, I have to realize and accept that most people will never understand my feelings about everything."

"Tell me how have things been with Paula since your release?" I noticed Valerie shift in her chair a bit and take a few deep breaths. Clearly this was a touchy subject for her.

"I saw her at senior night for winter track directly after I was home from the hospital and we barely said hello to each other. I try to avoid seeing her by always closing the garage door as soon as I get home and not opening it until I leave. There have been a few times I have seen Paula pulling in her driveway the same time I pulled into mine and she does not acknowledge me. The whole thing makes it feel like she knew that there was something wrong with the actions she took. I feel really uncomfortable living next to her."

"I agree, there probably is some guilt there on her part. What do you think you will do long term? Are you considering moving?"

"I do think that I will want to move eventually but that seems to be such a huge task to take on. We have been in our house since right before David was born. With both boys being away at college soon it will be on me to probably pack and move everything. I am also not sure where I would want to live. I moved away from my family in DC when Seth and I got married so it might be an option to go back there or possibly move by UVA. It also depends on my job since I need to go into the office occasionally. It is really a lot to still work out and consider."

"We are just about out of time for tonight. You are making great progress Valerie. Even though some things are still difficult to talk about, I see you making progress overall.

My schedule has changed again. I am not working with any other online clients right now so my schedule should be wide open. Feel free to book another session whenever you are ready to chat again or you can text me as well."

"Ok thanks Joy, I really appreciate it. I will get on your schedule when I am ready. Take care."

Chapter 18

I left work and got on the road as scheduled. My trip was uneventful. There was very little traffic and there was beautiful scenery along 29 North and 64 as usual. I planned to stay with Robin again. I wanted to run some of my ideas past her before my meeting with Pastor Flee tomorrow afternoon at 4 pm. Prior to that, I would be meeting Miles for lunch for our talk. Robin expressed some concerns initially about having the business meeting directly after my lunch meeting with Miles. I planned to talk to her about that also tonight.

I knew Robin was booked until 9 tonight, so I decided to stop by my favorite sub shop to get a salad and a slice of pizza for dinner. I also got something for Robin. I pulled up to Robin's house a little before 9. She told me where to find the key and I let myself in. I got my bags settled in the guest room. I decided to wait for Robin to eat my food. I figured we could both sit in the kitchen, eat, and talk. While I waited for Robin, I texted Toni to let her know that I had arrived safely. She and I were planning to get together on Friday evening for dinner.

Robin arrived about 20 minutes after me. I was sitting in the living room waiting for her. She walked in and I said,

"Hey girl, oh, you look tired. Long day?" She kicked her shoes off, threw her bag on the chair, plopped down on the sofa and said, "Oh my goodness yes, today was a day. All of my clients were in rare form." We both laughed.

"Is it a full moon or something tonight?" I asked.

"It has to be."

"Are you hungry? I stopped by Naples and got salads and some pizza."

"You are my savior, girl. I am starving. I barely ate lunch today."

I stood up and said, "I'm hungry too. Want to go sit in the kitchen so we can both eat and talk?"

"Yes, that will be perfect. You go ahead and get everything set up. I am going to the restroom quick." As I walked to the restroom, I thought to myself how Joy was in a really good mood which was a little unexpected. I really thought that she would be a little more nervous or anxious about meeting with Miles tomorrow. I guess maybe her EAP therapy has done her some good and she has worked through things.

Ten minutes later Robin and I were both seated at the table digging into our salads. I put the pizza in the toaster oven to warm up a bit. The timer went off and Robin got up to retrieve the pizza. She brought the plate over, sat it down in between us and said, "Do you want to talk business first or shall we tackle the Miles conversation?"

I laughed. "Honestly, it does not matter to me. They are sort of both business related."

Robin made a face and said, "Miles? Business? Please explain." I couldn't wait to hear this explanation.

"I am not sure I can explain it, but I am interested in what he is doing professionally. I am curious to see if I might be able to utilize Miles in some way for my project."

Robin put her fork down and said, "You would really consider working with him?"

I hunched my shoulders. "Maybe, it depends on how our talk goes tomorrow."

"Wow, Joy I must say that you have come a long way in a short period of time. I am curious about how you feel you were able to do that?"

I laughed and said, "Is this therapist Robin or friend Robin?"

She smiled. "Okay, yes, that was very therapist like, but seriously, as your friend, I want to know."

I thought for a minute and finally said, "I cannot say that it was one thing in particular. I think there were a few things that have happened over the past few months, almost like the perfect storm."

Robin nodded as she continued to eat her food. In between bites she asked, "What were those things? Do you recall?"

"I think it started the last time I was here. Seeing Miles and the way I reacted, that really bothered me. Also the sermon Pastor Flee gave that day was powerful and impactful. My client Valerie has really made me think long and hard about my personal life. I also had an eye-opening experience at the clinic that made me realize I do not belong there. Last but not least, this opportunity with Pastor Flee is the icing on the cake."

"That all sounds wonderful, it really does, but you have spent the past fifteen years carrying a lot of pain and anger towards Miles. Don't you think some of that might come back tomorrow when you see him?"

"When I talked to him on the phone, I was surprised at how calm I was. Hearing his voice did not invoke much emotion at all."

"I agree that is surprising, but I just hope that you are not suppressing or masking your feelings."

"I understand why you are saying that. I have been extremely focused on this project with Pastor Flee. I do not believe I have been doing that, but it is possible. I guess we will see how things go tomorrow."

"Have you thought about your expectations?"

"Of course. I expect him to show up with a bunch of excuses and he will tell me how he has thought about me every day for the past fifteen years." I rolled my eyes and Robin busted up laughing.

"Joy, I think you have been watching too much television."

"Come on now, Robin. You know he is going to say something like that."

She hunched her shoulders and said, "Yes, it is possible. I remember you telling me how he was relentless with his attempts to contact you by phone and email."

"That went on for months."

"You were not curious about what he might say?"

"No, honestly I was not. I felt as though there was nothing he could say to erase the pain I felt. Especially after the STD diagnosis."

"I can understand that. Well if you need anything after you meet him tomorrow, just text me. I will check my phone in between clients."

"Thanks Robin, but I think I will be fine."

"I think so too. You really sound like you are in a good place right now."

"I really feel like I am finally headed in the right direction. Can we talk about the project?"

"Of course."

"Since our last conversation I have had this epiphany about it."

"Really? What's that?"

"I truly believe that the timing of this project and my clients Kara and even Valerie are no coincidence."

"I am not sure that I am following you. The project with the pastor is about bringing more awareness to the church community about the benefits of mental health services correct?"

"Yes, that is the beginning of it, but I believe it is supposed to be so much more than that. I am preparing for the workshops the pastor wants done but I am also looking beyond that to what else can be accomplished. You want to know why I am leaving the clinic?"

"You mentioned to me that you felt that was not the clientele you were meant to serve."

"Exactly, nothing against addicts because they need help but just not from me. My focus is now shifting to teenagers and young adults. I feel that is an untapped and underserved demographic. I can relate to them because I was them. I want to find the people dealing with fresh trauma, not finding them ten or twenty years later when it has manifest itself into a substance use or gambling addiction."

Robin was nodding her head. "I understand completely, and I love it Joy. I do believe that you are onto something."

Robin and I finished eating and cleaned up the kitchen. We ended up back in the living room where she filled me in on her latest dating shenanigans. She is seeing some guy from Baltimore. Robin never dates anyone local. She feels it is not a good idea because of her line of work. I am in no position to argue since I have not dated anyone since Miles.

We also talked about Pastor Flee and her prediction that he is looking for a wife. I have spoken with him several times and I really did not pick up on anything. I guess time will tell. I filled her in on my in-depth conversation with Curtis about his background, losing his wife, and the challenges with his daughter. I would really like to work with her, but I have not figured out a way to broach the subject with him. If I happen to run into him during this trip, I might mention it to him to see what he thinks.

After splitting a bottle of wine with Robin and an hour-long old-school dance party we were both exhausted and decided to turn in for the evening. After getting into bed, I checked my phone and realized that I had missed a couple of text messages. One from Curtis. His message read,

Heard from Miles. Just wanted to let you know that I am available to talk if you need to after your lunch appointment. Also try to remember to keep an open mind. Forgiveness is the final form of love.

I read his last line over and over again. Obviously, he knew what Miles' excuse was. I was not giving it anymore energy today. That was an issue for tomorrow. I typed a quick response which read, *Thanks Curtis. I appreciate your kind words and friendly reminders.*

I also had a text from Valerie which read, *I'm nervous and anxious. I just got confirmation today of a meeting with Seth's attorney tomorrow afternoon. Fingers crossed we can agree on everything and move the divorce process forward.*

I responded, *Valerie I am sure everything will be fine and remember to take your medicine if you really feel anxious. Hopefully, you have someone to go with you for moral support. Text me tomorrow and let me know how everything went.*

I placed my phone on my charger and went to sleep.

*****

In the car on my way to Café Fresco to meet Miles. My morning was uneventful. I slept in and then I spent some time reviewing my presentation for my meeting with Pastor Flee this afternoon. For about an hour before leaving, I just sat in Robin's living room and allowed myself to think about everything I could remember about me and Miles. I purposely focused on the happy times. I wanted to remember those first. Then I moved on to recalling the pain he caused me, and I tried to remember all of the questions I have always had in my mind. For many years the only thing I wanted to say to him was 'Why?'. Today the why was not important to me at all. At this point does it really matter? We have both moved on from it. I decided to just let him have the floor to say whatever he feels he needs to say. I guess I am in such a positive place right now that I am focused on moving forward. Looking back no longer appeals to me.

Finally it was time to head to the restaurant, so I stopped in the restroom and checked myself out in the mirror. I turned my head side to side and assessed my face. I thought I looked basically the same. Maybe a few pounds heavier but still just about the same. The major difference would be my hair. In college I typically had my hair in braids or twists. I rarely go anywhere besides work so these days I simply throw my hair up in a ponytail. Today I decided to be a little fancy and made it into a tight bun. My sleeveless fuchsia blouse looked great against my chestnut colored skin. I thought to myself if Miles hasn't missed me he will after he sees me today.

As I pulled into the parking lot, I noticed there was seating outside on their patio. It was a beautiful day and I hoped he would agree to sitting outside. I found a space, parked, and turned to grab my purse from the passenger seat. When I turned back towards my door to open it I noticed him. Immediately I felt flushed as blood rushed to my face. My palms were sweaty. Miles was walking towards my car. I have no idea how he recognized me; it has been over 15 years. I managed to open my door and get out of the car before he made his way over. He approached me with a wide smile and said,

"Joy Dickerson, wow look at you, you look exactly the same." I blushed and felt a little lightheaded. All of a sudden there were so many thoughts running through my mind.

"Hello, Miles. How did you know what I would be driving?"

He motioned for me to start walking and I did, and he answered, "First of all, I arrived about fifteen minutes ago. I wanted to make sure that I arrived before you did. Second Curtis may have given me a little clue about what kind of car you drive."

I chuckled. "Oh, I see. I will deal with Curtis later."

Miles laughed and I was reminded about his gorgeous smile. He really looked exactly the same. Maybe 10 pounds heavier at best and there were no other signs of aging apparent from my quick look at him. He looked great and I tried my best not to stare or smile too much.

"Would you like a table inside or out?" He asked.

"I would love to sit outside and enjoy this gorgeous day."

He held the door and motioned for me to enter. I walked up to the counter and looked over the menu. I loved their seafood pizza, but it was very garlicky and much heavier than I wanted right now. I decided on a salad. I gave my order and stepped aside for Miles to give his order. He already told me when we spoke on the phone that he was buying me lunch so there was no awkwardness about who was paying. After paying and getting our drinks we walked outside and selected a table. Once we were seated Miles said, "Joy, it is really good to see you. I am so glad you decided to meet me."

I sipped on my water and did not respond.

"Okay, I see that you are not going to make this easy on me, are you?"

I put my cup down and said, "Miles, I am really not trying to be difficult. I just want you to say whatever you need to say."

"Okay that is fair. I requested this meeting so I will say what I need to say to you. There are so many things I could say, but honestly I am trying so hard to avoid all the clichés."

I smiled. "Yes, please. Just give it to me straight Miles. After all this time why did you want to see me? What do you need to tell me?" I was so mad as soon as those questions left my lips. I promised myself I was going to let him lead this discussion.

"Joy first let me start off with a simple I am sorry. I know that seems so trivial based on everything that happened, but I have to start there. My life has been a series of decisions that have not always turned out the best for me." The waitress brought our food, so Miles stopped talking while she presented everything to us. When she walked away, he said, "May I pray?"

"Yes of course."

"Heavenly father I ask that you come into this space, a meeting between two old friends and bless our time together. Please allow open hearts and minds and Lord please bless the food that has been prepared for the nourishment of our bodies. In Jesus name Amen."

"Amen."

"Where was I?" he asked.

"Something about bad decisions."

"Ah, yes. Let me just get straight to the point. I can only imagine what you think, but here is the truth. The young lady you saw at graduation was someone I met at a party one time when I went home to New York. I barely knew her name until she tracked me down through mutual friends to tell me that she was pregnant, and I was the father. I honestly did not even remember sleeping with her Joy, but that party was a wild one. She said the baby was mine and I believed her. You know how I felt about how my father treated my mother. I was not going to do that to the mother of my child. Yes, I was dead wrong for not coming clean to you about everything. I planned to, but each time I just could not bring myself to do it. I knew how hurt and devastated you would be. Okay here is the cliché part that I cannot avoid. Joy she did not mean anything to me, not at first. Like I said we met at a party once. She says we slept together, and she was pregnant." He paused and waited for me to respond.

I simply said, "Please continue."

"It was the summer before our senior year. I went home at the end of Spring semester for the Memorial Day weekend and I attended the party. I came back to school and right before the Fall session began, she contacted me and told me. You and I were both so focused on senior year we were not seeing a lot of each other. That made it easy for me to avoid the tough conversation we should have had. As for graduation day, I had no idea she was planning to come. Although I planned to be there for my son my relationship with her was not a romantic one, at least not at that point." He stopped again to take a sip of his water then he asked, "Do you have anything to say? Any questions?"

I thought for a moment. "So, you just have the one child?"

He shook his head. "No, Joy I actually do not have any children."

I put my fork down. "I am sorry, but I am very confused. Please explain."

"To make a long story short, the child was not mine. I never married and do not have any children."

"Wow, that is very different than I imagined."

He scoffed. "Yeah, quite different than what I imagined as well. I can give you as much information as you would like but I know our time here today is short. I do want to address another item with you."

"What is that Miles?"

"Joy, I tried to reach you for several months after graduation. You never accepted my calls. I needed to tell you something important."

I interrupted him. "Yeah, I found out a few months later. There is no need to say it out loud right now." I said as I looked around the restaurant.

He understood and said, "Joy that part worried me the most all these years. I knew I was your first and the thought of me giving you something really tore me up inside."

This part of the conversation hit a nerve. This was the tough part. I could get over the heartbreak, but I could never not have herpes. I was beginning to get upset. I could feel my blood pressure rising and I felt my heart beating out of my chest. I did have many questions and although I did not think I needed them now, I wanted answers. "The child was not yours so does that mean you were sleeping around with multiple women?"

"No Joy, not when you and I were together. Before we met, I was a little on the sexually promiscuous side. I must have gotten it then because Sheila did not have it either. From the first time that you and I became a couple I never slept with anyone else until after graduation. I was faithful to you, Joy."

Tears began to form in my eyes, and I got up from the table. "I'll be right back." As I walked towards the restroom, I took deep breaths to regain my composure. I was not having a meltdown here in this restaurant today. I promised myself I would not allow him to take me back to my place of pain. Once inside the restroom I went into a stall, closed my eyes, and willed the pain I was feeling away. I was determined to handle this myself. I was not calling Robin or anyone else. I felt silly again for being so consumed by feelings about things that happened so long ago. I wondered to myself how in the world Valerie was able to work through all of her trauma in such a short period of time. I suppose that I am living proof that time does not heal all wounds.

As I watched Joy walk away, 'I couldn't help but feel her pain. I knew every tear that she shed was all my fault. I really loved Joy back then, hell, I probably still do. She looked amazing. Wouldn't it be nice if we could just pick up right where we left off? Well maybe not exactly there, but maybe she would give me a second chance?'

After five minutes or so, I had regained my composure. I exited the stall and splashed some water on my face. I rejoined Miles and he looked genuinely concerned and asked, "Are you okay, Joy?"

I tried to smile and said, "Not really, but I will be."

He hung his head for a moment. "I am so sorry Joy."

"I know you are, and I am too. Listen I severely underestimated how this meeting was going to turn out. I think you and I have a lot more we need to discuss, but it cannot happen here today. I have an appointment I need to get to, and I am sure that you need to get back to work."

"Yes, you are right. I do need to head back soon. How long are you in town for?"

"I am leaving on Sunday. I am not sure when I will have time again before I leave. It all depends on how my meeting this afternoon goes. Maybe we can talk on the phone?"

"I think that might be better for me as well. Why don't you give me a call when you have time so we can finish our conversation?"

"Ok great, I will try to call you later tonight once I get settled after my appointment."

Miles had finished eating while I was in the restroom, so he stood up to leave. I had barely touched my food, but I was not hungry anyway. I also stood up and he said, "You are not going to finish your salad?"

"No, I am really not that hungry and I need to get going myself."

He motioned for me to walk ahead of him and he walked me to my car.

"It was really great seeing you Joy, and I look forward to your call." As I turned to walk to my car my heart was beating out of my chest. I finally got to explain my situation to Joy. Somehow, I thought I would feel quite different than I felt right now. Even though she knew the truth I was still alone and so was she'.

I decided to drive back to Robin's house to freshen up before my meeting with Pastor Flee. As I drove, I thought about everything Miles told me, and I had so many questions. I definitely needed more answers.

I quickly freshened up my face and changed my blouse before driving over to the church. When I arrived his secretary told me he was running a little behind schedule and asked me to wait in the foyer. While I waited, I took out my phone and checked my emails.

I had an email from Valerie which I read immediately.

Joy,

Today was quite an emotional day. I went to my attorney's office to meet with Seth and his attorney. Celeste went with me for support and it was really nice to have her there. She was not in the conference room with us but in a separate area I went to when the attorneys were making updates to the agreement. The breaks were good so I could take some deep breaths and calm down.

We went back and forth so many times and my attorney said it did not seem they were going to settle. I told my attorney when we started that I was willing to take what they offered initially if I had to, but I was not leaving without it being done. I also made the point several times to Seth's attorney that it was going to get done today and tried to keep them there. I had heard about so many divorces dragging on and I really did not want that. I had thought about the details for what it might take to get this done for many years, so I was determined that we needed to settle on a final agreement now.

The last point Seth was really stuck on was the fact that he really did not want me to sell the house we had raised our family in. I knew it was not his decision on what I would do with it since he had agreed I would get the house, but I could tell he was getting close to giving in. I told him that my whole life was shattered over the past few months from what he did. It was a lot for me to take in so I did not think I would not be moving right away. He asked for a moment with his attorney and when they came back in, we finally had an agreement. When we all went to leave the room his attorney shook my hand and then Seth put out his hand to me like we had just wrapped up a sale. It was really an awkward moment, and I was thinking maybe he really did not understand what had just happened.

I am relieved to have gotten through this and just figured I would let you know

Valerie

The email from Valerie was exactly what I needed today. She is a strong woman and she inspires me to keep moving forward. She knows what she wants, and she presses through the painful stuff. That is what I need to do.

I responded with a quick note.

Valerie,

Today is the beginning of the rest of your life. Make the most of it.

Joy

When Pastor Flee was ready for me, I walked into his office with a renewed sense of purpose. I was surprised it was just the Pastor and I meeting. I thought the committee would also be seeing my presentation. Just as I was getting a little nervous his secretary came into his office and sat down. Pastor Flee said, "My secretary is here to take notes for me. You can begin whenever you are ready." I reached into my bag and handed her a packet which included copies of the information in my presentation. I began and got through everything in about thirty minutes. Pastor Flee was impressed. He would not stop smiling and thanking me. Even his assistant seemed to be impressed. He asked me to attend his staff meeting tomorrow afternoon and do a trimmed down version of the presentation for them.

As I drove back to Robin's house, I was pleased with the direction I was headed in. I thought about my note to Valerie earlier and I felt that message applied to me as well. I felt like today was the beginning of the rest of my life. I certainly planned to make the most of it.

Chapter 19

Once I got back to Robin's house, I sent her a quick text just giving her the thumbs up. I should have sent it earlier because I knew she was worried. She had clients until 7 tonight, so I should have a little time to myself to process everything that happened today.

I was pleased with how the meeting went with Pastor Flee and was excited that he wanted me to attend his staff meeting tomorrow. Thankfully, it was in the afternoon, so I had plenty of time to go back through my presentation and trim it down a bit as he requested.

Before Robin got home, I wanted to call Miles so we could finish our talk. I wanted and needed more answers before talking to Robin. After thinking about everything some more it just seemed a little too clean of a story to me. If he was truly innocent why hadn't he tried harder to contact me? Yes, he called, emailed etc., but he never just showed up and demanded to see me. I checked the time and it was a little after 5 so I took a chance and dialed his number. He answered on the third ring, "Hello."

"Hi Miles, its Joy. Did I catch you at a bad time?"

"No you did not. I just walked in the door."

"Okay great. I have some free time now before my friend Robin gets home, so I thought maybe we could finish our talk."

"Yes, I would like that."

"Well we left off with you explaining to me about Sheila, is that her name?"

"Yes, Sheila was her name."

"Was?"

"Yes, Sheila died over ten years ago in a car accident. That is actually how I found out that I was not the father. After she died, her family immediately came to get Malik. I did not understand why they were taking my son and her sister blurted out I was not his real father anyway. Ultimately we did a DNA test and I was not his father."

His voice cracked a bit and I said, "I am very sorry, are you okay?"

He cleared his throat. "Yes, this part is just tough for me, but I owe you answers, and I plan to give them to you. Anyway, after Sheila told me she was pregnant, and the baby was mine we did not immediately enter into a relationship. I was by her side during the pregnancy and afterwards just to co-parent with her. On graduation day she showed up with the baby unannounced. I figured you saw her kiss me and there was too much to try to explain right then and there."

"When did you find out about your STD status?"

"Ironically, it was right before graduation. The weeks leading up to graduation were incredibly stressful for me. I knew that I had to come clean with you about Sheila and the baby. I had an outbreak and went to the doctor. They diagnosed me and I planned to talk to you about it after graduation."

"I see and all those calls, voice mails, and emails were your attempt to tell me about the STD?"

"Yes, well, no. I wanted to explain everything to you, but the most important thing was to tell you about that."

"I see, so when did the situation with Sheila become a relationship?"

"After graduation it just sort of happened since we were together more and taking care of Malik. We never got married which is one of the reasons why I was not able to retain custody of him. He was barely five years old when his mom died. Sheila knew I was not the father. Malik's father was an old boyfriend of hers who had ended up in jail. Initially it seemed as if he might be in jail for a long period of time. He ended up being released after only a few years on a technicality with his case. He knew Malik was his, fought for custody, and won."

"Wow, Miles that is terrible. You have been through a lot. After Sheila though did you not date or find anyone?"

"No, not really, nothing serious. Honestly, I was so traumatized by the entire situation with Sheila. I literally shut down for almost a year. I was in a very dark place. I ended up seeking therapy and eventually worked my way through it and got my career back on track."

"I spent many years hating you."

"I know and I am so sorry Joy." I shook my head and closed my eyes tight to try to keep the tears from flowing.

After a minute of silence Miles finally said, "Joy, are you still there?"

I took a deep breath. "Yes, I am still here. This is really rough Miles. We are both now in our late thirties, never married and no children. Do you remember how we talked about getting married and having children together?"

He chuckled nervously and said, "I do remember that very well. Why didn't you get married and have children Joy?"

"I was stuck Miles. I was devastated by your betrayal. Then just when I began to fight my way back from that I discovered I had herpes. I felt as though I was being punished by God for having premarital sex. You remember I wanted to wait?"

"Yes, I remember, and I know I pressured you. You have no idea how sorry I am for that. I think that was part of my guilt also. How could I tell you that I slept with someone else and she had my baby when you gave me your virginity in hopes we would one day be married and have children of our own?"

"I threw myself into my career and never stopped until very recently."

"You never considered getting married or having kids?"

"No, not at all. Like I said before I was devastated and honestly, I felt that nobody would want to be with me because of the STD."

"There are so many things that I wish that I could go back and change but what is done is done. I have no choice but to move forward." I knew he was right but hearing his nonchalant attitude about it made me a little angry.

"Yes, I guess that is true for both of us. Things are happening for me though."

"Yes, Curtis told me about your project, and it sounds wonderful. I wish I could participate."

I planned to have a conversation with Curtis about sharing my business with Miles. "Actually, you could. I planned to talk to you about it."

"I already have a job that I really enjoy so far."

"This would not be a full-time position." I heard Robin come in, so I said, "Miles, my friend just got home, and I have not seen her since last night. Can we talk later or tomorrow? I would like to share more with you about the proposal and see what you think about being a part of it."

"Yeah sure, just give me a call when you have time."

"Okay great, I will be in touch."

I hung up the phone and went out to greet Robin in the kitchen. She brought food home from Tokyo Diner and I was starving. She and I sat at the table and shared hibachi salmon while I filled her in on my day. Gave her the entire Miles story. She could not believe it. She told me how well she felt I was handling everything. I did not feel anger anymore or hurt. I just felt sad. I was sad for Miles and how things turned out for him and I was sad for myself that I allowed so much time to pass me by. I believe that God places us where we need to be. There was a reason that I ended up in Virginia. Maybe it was to eventually meet Kara and get her life on the right path. Maybe I was supposed to meet Valerie to realize that I was stuck and needed to move forward.

After hanging out with Robin for several hours we both went to our rooms for the evening. I decided to log onto my laptop and check my email messages. I saw one from Bill which caught my attention, so I clicked on it right away.

Joy,

I am forwarding this email to you from Kara's mother. I know you are off, but I thought you would want to see this.

Bill

I scrolled down to see the attached email message.

To Whom It May Concern,

I am writing this message to express my sincere gratitude for one of your therapists. Her name is Joy; I am not sure of her last name. She was my daughter's therapist during a recent stay in your facility. My daughter has struggled for many years with a variety of issues. Most recently she was in your facility to address her drug addiction. Although Kara has struggled with drugs for many years now, I have never felt anyone has dealt with the root cause. When we admitted her to your facility it was our hope we might finally have found a place that could address all of Kara's needs. Words cannot express how thankful I am that Kara was assigned to Joy and that she saw the bigger picture. The transition plan she created for Kara has been wonderful. I finally feel as though Kara is getting the services she needs. I do hope that this message finds its way to the correct person and Joy is also made aware of how thankful we all are.

Sincerely,

Tricia Wilson

After reading the email I felt such a sense of accomplishment. I knew I was on the right track. I resisted the urge to send Bill a smart response. I would deal with him when I got back to work next week.

Next there was an email from Valerie. When I opened it there was a picture and just a short note that said, *This is from Senior Night for winter track which was two days after I was released from the hospital. My heart breaks for my son. Look at me. I look like a zombie. My eyes look so vacant. This is what he will forever remember about this night.*

I focused in on the picture and she did look somewhat like a zombie. It was terribly similar to how she looked during our first session. Although I understood her point, I felt like her son was probably just so happy to have her back home with him.

Valerie,

Although this picture is hard for you to look at do me a favor and take a look at yourself now in the mirror. See how far you've come in such a short period of time? That's progress. Keep moving forward.

Joy

*****

My day went as planned. I was up early and reworked the presentation for Pastor Flee's staff meeting. Everyone was very receptive to my ideas. Curtis was in attendance and gave me his nod of approval. I felt as though he was assessing my mood as well during the meeting. After the meeting was over, he followed me into the hallway. He was trying his best not to pry but I knew what he wanted to know. I told him I was fine and appreciated his support, but there was no cause for concern. Just as I was about to walk away, I remembered I wanted to ask him about his daughter.

"Curtis, how is your daughter?" He smiled.

"She is doing okay all things considered." I moved a little closer to him so that our conversation could be more private.

"If there is anything I can do just let me know. Remember I have been where she is so I might be able to reach her." He nodded and said,

"I really appreciate that Joy and I might take you up on that offer."

I smiled. "It would be my pleasure." As I walked to my car, I thought about how each time I spoke with Curtis he became more and more interesting to me.

Once I got to my car, I decided to text Miles to see if he might be available for lunch tomorrow. Now that I knew I had the blessing from Pastor Flee and his staff, I was ready to get moving and I needed to secure my resources. September would be here before I knew it.

I had already made plans with Toni to go to her house after my meeting at the church since she lived right around the corner. When I arrived Toni was still in the kitchen cooking. Denise let me in and was more than happy to entertain me until Toni was ready. Denise was your typical teenager, prone to mood swings, but today she was bubbly and full of energy. She was going over to a friend's house for a sleepover so Toni and I would be alone for dinner. Denise filled me in on all the latest happenings in her world.

Just as Denise was leaving Toni appeared and announced our dinner was ready. I hugged Denise and said my goodbyes in case I missed her on Sunday before I left to go back to Virginia. Toni made my favorite dish which was seafood casserole. We sat in the kitchen since it was just us instead of the formal dining room. We ate and talked mostly about my project with the pastor and I did fill her in on my lunch meeting with Miles. I did not share all the details, but I just said that we talked, and I was at peace with everything. That led us into a more in-depth conversation about Pastor Flee's project. After we finished eating, we went into the family room and Toni gave me more background on how this all came to pass.

Toni shared things with me about her childhood I never knew. She explained to me that her mother struggled with addiction and she has been in and out of therapy since she was a teenager. Her position was that therapy saved her life. She was extremely passionate about this initiative with Pastor Flee because mental health issues and addressing them in a professional manner is somewhat of a taboo subject in many black churches.

The more Toni shared with me about how this project was created the more I realized everything was coming together the way it was supposed to. All of these women were being strategically placed in my life recently, Valerie, Kara, Curtis' daughter, and the young lady who committed suicide. My purpose was becoming clearer and clearer as each day passed. Through the pain of those others I have been able to find my way to healing and my purpose.

I was in the correct field, but I was not serving the correct demographic. I wanted to find a way to reach them while they are going through or healing from the initial trauma. To help them heal before it manifests itself as other disorders, drugs, gambling, sex, or other addictions.

I decided to stay with Toni overnight. Robin was going to meet her friend and I was not interested in being in her house alone tonight.

****

The following morning I slept in a bit. I awoke to the sounds of Toni singing downstairs in the kitchen. I got up and went to the bathroom to freshen up before heading downstairs. Toni being the hostess that she is already had everything laid out for me. Toni had everything I needed except for a change of clothes. I was able to wash my face and brush my teeth. My cell phone was dead since I did not have my charger with me. I did not even bother to ask Toni for one since there was no one I needed to get in contact with. Of course Toni had made breakfast, so I ate a quick bite before heading back to Robin's house to shower and change.

Once I got back to Robin's house and plugged in my phone, I began to receive notifications of missed phone calls, voice mails and text messages. I quickly scanned them and there was nothing urgent. Miles confirmed the time for our lunch meeting and Curtis wanted to talk to me about his daughter. As I scrolled down further, I saw a short message from Valerie which simply said, *Yesterday was a challenge, but today is going to be much better.* I smiled and responded to her,

That's the spirit, keep that positive attitude.

I decided to call Curtis. I dialed his number and he answered, "Hello."

"Hello Curtis, this is Joy returning your call."

"Oh yes, thanks Joy for getting back to me. I was wondering if you were free for lunch today?"

"Actually I'm not. I am meeting Miles for lunch today."

"Oh, I see."

"Curtis, it is not a date or anything like that. I am meeting with him to talk to him about how he might be able to assist me with the project." Why was I explaining myself to him anyway? He wasn't my man, I thought to myself.

"Oh, I see. Well I was hoping I could introduce you to my daughter. I decided to take you up on your offer."

"I would love to. Can I possibly come to your house either before or after I meet with Miles to meet her?"

"What time are you meeting Miles?"

"We're supposed to meet between 12:30 and 1:00. I actually need to follow up with him to confirm the time and location. Where do you live?"

"I'm off Progress Ave near the church."

"Okay, well, why don't I come by after my lunch meeting with Miles? That way I can stay as long as I need to and not be rushed."

"That is perfect."

Curtis gave me his address and I told him I would text him when I was on my way. As soon as I ended the call with him, I texted Miles for us to meet at 12:30 at the Peachtree restaurant on Progress Ave.

I showered, changed, and busied myself reviewing my notes from the meetings this week and made some notes for my conversation with Miles. I also took time to put an entry in my journal expressing my gratitude for the opportunity with Pastor Flee and also that I have been able to reconnect with Miles to get the closure I needed to allow myself to heal. Things certainly seemed to be moving in the right direction in all aspects of my life.

Chapter 20

My new schedule at the clinic and my travel back and forth to Harrisburg was in full swing now. It was July and less than two months from the project kick off. I was in constant contact with Miles and Curtis. They were both actively participating with the project. Things went well with Shannon, Curtis' daughter. She is a lovely young lady. After our initial meeting she and I talk on the phone and text frequently. She feels that I can understand her. She knows that I am also a therapist, but I am not playing that role for her right now. During my last visit I sort of got the feeling that she is trying to make a connection between her father and me. Curtis is a nice man, but I am still working through my healing process. A relationship is not on my to do list right now.

Miles and I are also getting along very well, and we have both kept things very professional. This is real life, not a movie, so I do not expect us to rekindle anything. We are both therapists and know we are healing, and it really is not a good idea to get into a relationship during this process let alone with the person you are healing from. Right now my focus is getting everything ready for September. After that, I will be open to dating again.

Things at the clinic are status quo. Even though the email came from Kara's mom praising and thanking me for my transition plan, Bill is not interested in pressing the issue with corporate for changing their policies. I do appreciate him working with me and my schedule. I have continued to work with him to assist with more policy issues and documentation to lessen my case load. Bill has been appreciative and allows me the flexibility I need. He and I have been working together more closely and our relationship although is not back to the way it was, has improved.

I just arrived home from the clinic and was preparing for my session with Valerie. I went into my office and pulled up her last email to review it again.

I logged in about five minutes early and waited for Valerie to join.

"Hi Valerie. I was surprised to have gotten an email from you. I hope it was not too hard for you to type the email with your cast."

"I am done with the cast now, although I still had it when I typed that. It took me some time, but I really wanted to get that last message to you. I am so glad to be done with it although it will take some time to get my full strength back."

I could hear the excitement in Valerie's voice which was really nice to hear. She seemed pretty relaxed so hopefully things are starting to go a little better overall.

"I'm sure it is a relief getting out of the cast and finally getting to an agreement with Seth on the terms of the divorce. Have you heard from Seth since then?"

"He actually called me shortly after the meeting and wanted to see if I wanted to meet him for dinner that night."

"No, way. Did he really?"

"I could not believe he even thought that would be a possibility. He is interested in keeping in touch and continuing a friendship, but I really do not want that. I have been civil towards him mostly because of the kids but also just to get through everything so I can start to move on with my life."

"I understand how you feel and what you want but it seems that Seth has a different view on your relationship. It is going to take him a little more time to accept things will never be the way they were. I am sure that has to be tough on you though."

"Yes, it is very difficult."

"Well Valerie you know what you want so you just have to stay the course and continue to draw the lines and set the boundaries with Seth. Have you had to see him in person?"

"I did run into him at his attorney's office last Friday."

"Oh, really? Why did you need to go there?"

"Well, even though we had come to an agreement already the final papers had to be drawn up and signed. When the papers were ready Seth called to let me know and asked when I could get there. Seth arrived shortly after I did so we ended up going into the conference room together. The papers were still being printed so I was stuck in the room with him alone for a few minutes. I suspected that Seth would try to get there around the same time as me. I also knew him well enough to know that he would make comments about how I looked."

"Why did you think that? How did you look?"

"I had not bothered to straighten my hair since I was headed to the salon later. Of course he had to say how the humidity must have gotten to my hair and he liked the color my toes were painted like I cared what he thought. He told me he knew I was headed to my hair appointment soon since he had talked with Scott. After the person notarizing everything was finished, he asked them if we were still married. She made a comment back to him that it would be official when we get it back from the judge, but it was pretty much done. I did not know why he felt the need to say something like that."

"That could have been more for you than him. He wanted to make sure you understood in hopes maybe you would reconsider. Is that the last time you have seen him?"

Valerie let out a deep sigh.

"I should not have to worry about running into Seth as much in a few weeks since my boys are headed to college."

"Well that is good things should settle down soon. How do you feel about them leaving?"

She did not respond immediately. I noticed tears streaming down her cheeks. I am sure this will be a tough transition since it is a hard thing for most moms when their youngest heads off to college not to mention everything else Valerie has endured.

"Scott will only be a few hours away at UVA and I am up there quite a bit so I will get to see him. David is going to Florida State which will be about 11 hours away. Getting kids settled into college for the first time can be a lot of work. Scott and David want to take a road trip when he moves in. We are also going to take some time to vacation together which I am looking forward to. It is really going to be different to be on my own and I am sure I will miss them terribly."

I noticed the tears continued to flow but I was not concerned because it is really good for her to process her emotions.

"Yes, it is going to be quite an adjustment for you. Do you have any ideas on how you might handle the change?"

"I have started attending a divorce support group through my church to help me deal with everything I have been going through and it has been pretty helpful. I will have to start figuring out what I like to do with my spare time although I don't have too much of that right now because of my job."

"Yes, tell me how work is going?" I could see this was going to be a sore subject as Valerie seemed to tense up a bit.

"I have been having to put in pretty long hours with the new team I am on and traveled for a release planning session two weeks ago. It has really been hard to get much of a break."

"Transitioning to a new team can be challenging along with everything else you have going on. You just have to be careful not to allow yourself to get overwhelmed or burnt out especially now that the boys are both going to be gone. You cannot work around the clock."

"Yes, I am going to have to really work on that."

"Did you get to travel and see your family?"

"I spent some time at my parents over the holiday and while I was there, I met Darla for dinner. I also got to spend some time with Fran. It was really nice to see my family and have time with them. The following weekend I went to the Festival at UVA although I had to work more than I would have liked to. I planned on having a long weekend to relax but it has been difficult getting Lila to agree on when I can take off due to her vacation schedule."

I could still sense that Valerie was having anxiety and frustration with her job and I hoped that she could get more of a break to relax. At least she was getting out and interacting with people instead of staying home.

"That's good that you were able to get to the festival. Did you enjoy yourself? Did you go alone?"

"I met up with a friend for dinner and drinks Friday and then did some shopping on Saturday before I had work to do. Even though I was not with Seth anymore I could tell I am probably not ready to start dating anyone."

"I'm glad you got to spend some time with friends and family. It seems that the past few weeks have been pretty busy for you but overall you seem to be doing well."

"Thanks. Work has been stressful but at least I have time off soon to get David moved into school. I have had a nice time so far this summer and I am overall feeling a lot better."

"Well, Valerie we are about out of time for our session, but you can send me an email if anything comes up before we meet next."

"Sounds good. Thanks!"

After ending my session with Valerie I went into the kitchen to fix something to eat. As I sat down and began scrolling through my social media my phone rang, it was Curtis.

"Hey Curtis, what's going on?"

"Did I catch you at a bad time?"

"Not really. I just finished an online session with a client, and I was sitting here eating a bite. Everything okay?"

"Yes, I think so, but I do need to talk to you about something." He sounded serious. I put my fork down and sat up in the chair.

"Okay Curtis what is going on?"

"First of all I want to thank you again for helping with Shannon."

"Yes, of course. I have enjoyed talking to and spending time with her also."

"May I ask you a question about that and please be honest."

"Sure and honesty is all I give."

"Has she mentioned anything to you about you and I getting together?"

"Do you mean like dating?"

"Yes, has she mentioned anything to you?"

"Not directly but I have been getting that feeling recently. Did she say something to you?"

"No she did not directly to me, but she has been talking about it to other people and it made its way back to me."

"I see, well it is natural for her to want you to be happy, but we do have to be careful with how to handle this since she is making progress. I do not want to push her away."

"Yes, I agree. So what do you think we should do?"

"Why don't the three of us have lunch the next time I am in town?"

"We can both casually bring up how much we enjoy being friends or something like that."

"So it has never occurred to you that maybe we could go on a real date?"

"Actually it had not and please do not take this the wrong way Curtis. I am just not interested in anyone right now. I am focused on this project and getting it off the ground. I have been hurting for a very long time. Reconnecting with Miles is finally allowing me to work through the healing process. Now is just not the time."

"So that is not a hard no then?" he said chucking.

I smiled. "Curtis you are a great guy, really you are, but right now it's a no."

"You said right now. I can take that."

I laughed. "Okay but seriously we should get together and talk to Shannon together. I want to make sure that she is going to be okay."

"I agree. Let me know your schedule and I will make sure that we are available."

"Sounds good Curtis. Take care."

"You too Joy."

I smiled as I thought about my conversation with Curtis. I was becoming more and more interested in getting to know him better. I did have concerns about his relationship with Miles and the possibility of there being a conflict if I did decide to pursue a relationship with Curtis.

Chapter 21

Joy,

I wanted to let you know I did decide to respond back to Lauren, the woman I shared a room with when I was in the hospital. In her message to me she asked if I had my burning party to get rid of Seth's stuff. It's really difficult for me to remember a lot of the details of my time there due to being so heavily medicated. I have no idea what I may have said to her to make her ask me that question. I was very hesitant to respond to her since I was not sure what to expect. I tried to not give too much information since it is still tough for me to connect with people and determine who I can trust. I let her know I was doing well and had finalized my divorce. She told me she was home from rehab and had stayed clean. She was expecting another child but had not wanted more since she already had four children. I told her to stay strong and she will keep moving close to all she wants to accomplish. It did feel good to touch base with Lauren and I will be there for her if she decides to reach out to me again. After my experience in the psych ward I can really empathize with people that end up there due to unfortunate situations. Not everyone fits the definition of crazy as most people would think.

I know that we haven't really talked in detail about my hospital stay but I think I'm finally ready. When I first got to the psychiatric floor I kept pacing back and forth trying to escape, but I was being blocked by security guards and nurses. I was hoping to find a way out and thought I heard Fran's voice shouting in the distance, so I was trying to get to where it was coming from. A few hours later I finally got to my room. I was still very distraught about being committed and I was considered combative. I would not willingly submit to being medicated and finally I was held down and given an injection that knocked me out for hours. When I woke up, I felt disoriented and it took me a minute to realize where I was. I remember looking over and seeing an empty bed next to mine. I didn't want to be alone so I thought about who could come stay with me. The medication caused me to feel as if I was in a fog. My thoughts were all over the place and sometimes random things came to mind. Like I remember thinking about what Paula had said about my friend Jill and that she had similar problems to me. I told Jill when I talked to her later, she should come get help too and join me so I would have company. I really had lost my sense of reality and did not understand what was going on.

After a few days I realized I had to go along with everything in order to get out. I convinced myself I was put in the hospital to be protected from everyone trying to find out what was going on and I really did not belong there. With my new attitude about my situation I decided to venture out and interact with other patients. It was really scary a first since you really had no idea what anyone was in there for. There was one guy that seemed pretty normal. By normal I mean he didn't appear to be as spaced out as most of the other patients. He had just gotten there the day before I did and was working on a puzzle. I guess since we were both somewhat new, we were not as heavily medicated so we started chatting. He did not feel he belonged there and said his family thought he was a little stressed. I thought I could relate to how he was feeling given how I ended up there.

When we had free time were encouraged to exercise by tracking our laps and could get a water bottle if we met our weekly goal. We both seemed to be motivated to get in our laps and he would give me a high five each time he passed by.

Of course there were many restrictions on the floor related to visiting hours and phone calls. It was tough to catch a moment when one of the two phones were not in use since we had to share with everyone else on the floor. Fran was in charge of who could come see me until the staff felt I was doing better. I was then allowed to have whoever I wanted to come during visiting hours except those Fran had specifically excluded. There were only two people allowed at a time, so I created a schedule as I reached out to friends by phone. I like to be organized and this helped give me times to look forward to since when visiting hours went by without someone it was really lonely. I was limited to only a total of 10 minutes per hour on the phone for incoming and outgoing calls. I was not permitted to have my cell phone, so I built my own phone list. Celeste and David would retrieve numbers for me from home. I had so many people I wanted to get in touch with, so it took a lot of planning.

After being reprimanded a few times about being on the phone too much I had a friend bring a stopwatch so I could keep track of exactly how long I was on. Although Deb was not allowed to visit even though she worked at the hospital we would talk on the phone. I asked her to bring me pencils since I noticed at the nurse's station the bucket was always running low. I did not get to use the ones she sent since we had to use only the small ones without erasers. When I was first on the floor, I was listing my thoughts about everyone and trying to determine who I could trust. I really don't know what else I was writing, but it was a way I was getting through my emotions. Deb also sent a giant chocolate chip cookie which she knew was my favorite. For about the first week in the hospital I did not have makeup with me and did not think much of it until I saw another patient putting it on in the hallway with a mirror one of the nurses gave her. Jill brought me some next time she came to visit, and it helped me feel a little better. One of the best visits was when my friend Trish surprised me by driving from several hours away to see me. I was glad that she was able to get in considering the limitations on the number of visitors.

We were allowed to wear our clothes from home but with some modifications. There were a few of my pants that I still am not sure where the ties went since they had to be taken out which bring back the memories of being committed. I know I should probably just get rid of them, but I just can't for some reason. It still doesn't seem real what happened and maybe I just keep them, so I know that it was not all just a bad dream. David did come a few times to visit me which was nice, but it also broke my heart considering how hard it must have been for him. One of the visits he came with Celeste and she brought the mail for me to go through. I had to keep up with paying bills since Seth was still not around. Seeing the huge pile of mail caused me to feel anxious and lightheaded that I felt I might pass out. It was at times like this when I was reminded of the mess Seth left me with to handle that I become angry. David helped by writing out the checks and I figured it was a good lesson for him to learn anyway. I shared as I talked with my parents and close friends that all I wanted to do was go home, but it seemed like there was no way to leave. They did not feel I should be there either, but no one seemed to know what to do and they seemed genuinely concerned. I took comfort in knowing that the people closest to me didn't feel I needed to be there.

Aside from visiting hours which everyone looked forward to, like most everyone else Art became one of my favorite *activities. Which is really odd, since I've never been much of a craft person. In the middle of all this chaos and uncertainty in my life I found comfort and relaxation in coloring pictures with pencils. It was also during this time that we got to pick songs to listen to and have some regular soda which we did not get to have with our meals. I had several friends bring in Swedish fish along with other treats I shared. There was some down time throughout the day, so we did get to know each other since most rooms had multiple patients in them. It was hard to see people come and go while not knowing how long it would be before I could go home. I also saw there were some that had it a lot harder than me. Their next steps included group homes, rehabilitation centers or a more secluded psychiatric center for continued treatment. I remember feeling grateful that once I was released, I could return to my own home.*

The last night I was on the psych floor was probably the most frightening. There were several new patients and one of them seemed pretty dangerous. I am not sure what he was there for, but when I was in the TV room he talked about being banned from several states. He walked into one of the girl's rooms which caused a big alarm and lockdown. She came into the hall crying hysterically and was so scared. This was in addition to the other incident I wrote you about before when the nurse got hurt by a patient who tried to leave. Most of the time I was able to get a good night sleep mostly because of the medicine I would take but that night it was really hard to fall asleep. I said a prayer before I went to sleep hoping to get to go home.

The next day when I met with the team handling my case, they decided I could finally go home. I had to be at a certain level with my labs and was finally there. I was in tears because I was so overjoyed that I was going to get to leave finally. I was told I had to meet with my psychiatrist regarding my medication and if I missed the appointment, I would end up back there. I heard it loud and clear and they made me feel someone would hunt me down, so I made sure Celeste knew about it when she picked me up. The last thing I wanted to do was go back to the hospital. I could not wait to be back home and be in my own bed.

It is painful to talk about what I went through which is why I figured it was best to share this in an email to you. I might not be able to talk about it during our sessions, but it did help for me to write it down.

Valerie

It had been a couple of weeks since my last session with Valerie when I received her email. It stopped me dead in my tracks. I felt her pain and sense of betrayal in every word. It angered me and made me sad also. I had to fight the urge to reach out to her. I wanted to request a session with her, but that was not my place. She was in control of that. I had felt for a while that she had been putting off the hospital stuff because it was too painful, and I now see that not only was I right, but it was much worse than I imagined.

I was currently in Pennsylvania for the weekend. I had a great meeting last evening with my team of presenters which includes Robin, Toni, Curtis, Miles, and Sylvia, who is a colleague of Robin's, and she is also Shannon's therapist now. Robin was currently away visiting her friend and I am preparing for my lunch date with Curtis and Shannon. We decided on Red Robin, it is one of Shannon's favorite places. Curtis and I talked briefly after the meeting yesterday about our approach with Shannon. I suggested I take the lead and he agreed.

Just as I was about to walk out of the door my cell phone rang. I grabbed my phone from my purse and saw it was Miles calling. I answered, "Hey Miles, what's going on?"

"Oh, nothing I was just seeing if you had lunch plans today."

"Yes, actually I do. I am headed out the door now to meet Curtis and Shannon for lunch."

"Okay, well I will let you go to your date." He emphasized the word date I am sure on purpose, but I was not falling into his trap today.

"Maybe next time give me a little more notice?" I suggested.

"Yes, now that I know I have competition I will have to make sure I get on your schedule first. In fact, can I get on your calendar for lunch the next time you are in town on Saturday?"

I laughed. "We will see about that Miles. You take care, I will talk to you later."

I smiled and shook my head as I walked to my car. I thought to myself maybe I need to have one of these 'We are not dating conversations.' with Miles also.

As I pulled into the parking lot at the restaurant, I saw Curtis standing outside by the front door. I did not see Shannon and wondered where she was. Curtis saw me pull in and walked over to my car to open the door for me. As I got out, I said,

"Hey Curtis, good to see you. Where is Shannon?"

"She is inside, using the restroom."

"Oh, okay well is there a wait for a table?"

"No, they said they would seat us as soon as you arrived."

As we approached the front door it opened. Shannon came out and rushed into my arms for a hug. I hugged her tightly and pulled away and said, "Well hello Shannon it is great to see you too my dear."

She laughed. "I have been waiting for this all week."

I turned and looked at Curtis and we both smiled at each other as we all walked inside together. The hostess took us to our table, and we all began looking at the menu. When the waitress arrived, we all placed our orders without delay. Shannon seemed to be very giddy today, I had not actually seen her like this before. I decided to start the conversation.

"Shannon, you seem to be in a great mood. Seems like you had a great week this week huh?"

She smiled. "My week was okay, but this is the best part."

I noticed Curtis shift in his seat a little. I got the feeling that he severely underplayed her excitement about him and I being a couple. I knew I needed to tread lightly, but we needed to hit this head on.

"Oh really? Why is this the best part?"

She laughed. "Because you are here with us of course."

"I see and me being here with you makes you happy?"

"Of course it does Joy, because you are my friend."

I nodded my head. "Yes that is right, I am your friend."

Shannon frowned a bit. "Well you are my Daddy's friend too."

"Yes, your father and I are friends. We used to go to college together."

"Yes, I remember you told me that."

"I am very happy you enjoy my company and friendship so much Shannon but tell me how is school and everything else going for you?"

"School is okay, and I am enjoying my sessions with Ms. Sylvia also. She is really nice, and she understands my feelings, but not like you do. She understands grief, but not because she lost her mom when she was young like you and I did."

"Yes, that is true. As a therapist I am sure she does understand, but it is different when you have experienced the same thing as the other person. However, as a therapist we are not supposed to share our personal stories with our clients."

"Oh really? Why is that?"

"It just is not healthy for either person." Curtis chimed in.

"As therapists we are trained to listen more than we talk. We want the client to share with us their thoughts and feelings."

Shannon nodded and said, "I guess that makes sense."

"I can share things with you because you and I are friends, you are not my client."

"Okay, I understand. But sometimes is it hard to separate your friends from your clients?"

I laughed. "Yes, it can be difficult sometimes, especially if you have worked with a client for a long time."

"You have known my father for a long time huh?"

"Yes, but not really. We went to college together, but he was a year ahead of me and I really only knew him because he was friends with my boyfriend."

"Do you still have a boyfriend?"

"No, I do not, but I like it that way."

"Why is that? Do you like women, Joy?"

I laughed, "No, dear, I am not interested in dating women."

"Why don't you have a husband or a boyfriend then?"

"I guess I have just been so busy with my career I have not taken the time out for that."

"Well, don't you want to be married?"

I shrugged my shoulders. "Honestly, right now I am not sure. When I was younger, I thought about it."

"I want to get married one day and have children."

Curtis jumped in. "That is great Shannon but not anytime soon okay?" We all laughed.

"Yes, Daddy, I know I cannot date anytime soon either, but you can."

Curtis looked at me and said, "Yes I know I can honey, but honestly, I am not interested in dating right now."

"Why not?"

"I am not ready."

"Mom would not be mad, Daddy. She told me she wanted you to be happy again."

Curtis smiled. "I know dear she told me the same thing." I sensed that Curtis wanted some help.

"Shannon people grieve differently and on their own timeline. You have to remember that. Your father is not ready to consider the possibility of dating again right now."

"That is okay especially since you are not ready to date anyone right now either."

"Shannon your father and I are just friends dear. We are not interested in each other."

"Says who? That is not what I heard him telling his friend on the phone last week."

Boom there it was. As my mom used to say out of the mouths of babes the truth came out.

Curtis looked as if he had just seen a ghost. He tried to recover quickly but stammered his words, "Shannon, wha what are you…?"

She interrupted. "Daddy I heard you on the phone talking to one of your friends about Joy."

I felt things were getting out of control so I decided to jump in to handle the immediate crisis with Shannon, but Curtis and I would talk in private later.

"Okay, listen Shannon honey, I am not sure what you heard, and it really does not matter right now. Your father and I are just friends. Although we have known of each other for a long time, we really just met. He and I are working together on a project for the church and I enjoy my talks with you. Can we just leave it like that for now?"

She nodded her head. "Yes, I understand, but I just want you to know before my mom died, she told me not to let my father be alone too long. She wanted him to be happy again. At first I could not imagine my father being with another woman until I met you Joy."

I smiled and reached over to place my hand on hers. "Shannon I am so very honored you think that highly of me. It really means a lot to me but as I said, there is so much more involved in a relationship that leads to marriage. The most important thing is the two people getting married are the ones who decide that not anyone else."

She laughed. "Yeah, I get it and I am sorry if I made either of you uncomfortable. You are both very important to me, so it just seemed a natural fit."

Curtis finally said, "Shannon, I am perfectly capable of finding my own partner when the time is right. I found your mother, didn't I?"

Shannon smiled and before she could respond the waitress showed up with our food. Curtis said the blessing and we all began to eat in silence. I was starving and this western BBQ bacon burger was exactly what I needed. We all ordered burgers and the waitress had to refill our basket of fries multiple times.

Things turned out well. We were able to finish our meal and I really enjoyed myself. After everything that was said I decided not to bring up Shannon's comment about him talking about me to someone. It was not important. If he brought it up, then we could discuss it. I just wanted to enjoy the things that bring me joy and work towards making things better for as many people as I could reach.

Chapter 22

With the workshop being a little less than a month away, my schedule was very hectic. I kept to my every other week trips to Pennsylvania, but I found I needed more frequent interaction with my team, so we were doing phone and video conferences in the evenings a few times during the week. I had just finished a video session with Toni, Curtis, and Miles when I received an email from Valerie. We had not talked since early July and we were not scheduled again for another week or two. I grabbed my water bottle and took a sip before reading her email.

> *Joy,*
>
> *It has been a pretty rough week for me so I figured I would send you an email before our next session. Last week I used vacation time to get David moved into school. It was really nice having time with him and Scott. I did not realize though how much all that has happened has really affected them both. They talked about how David was treated by Paula and how Scott was not informed of what was going on since he was away at college when I was admitted to the hospital. Hearing all of this from my kids really affected me and I broke down and sobbed afterwards.*
>
> *I knew I was having a rough day yesterday since I could tell it was affecting me emotionally, so I decided to use sick time and take the afternoon off. I did inform Lila I was not feeling well, and she pressed me for more information.*

Since I still consider her a friend, I did let her know a little about what was going on. I also told her later I did not know if I would feel better today or not and she started talking about company policy for time off. This was the first time I had used any sick time since I had been back to work from when I was in the hospital. I did work today, and she mentioned to me I should consider taking medical leave, but I really did not feel I was at that point. I also let our manager know my decision on that as well when I talked with her.

I think Paula may have gotten the code to my house when she told me the police needed it the day she took me to the hospital to get to David. It is really hard sometimes to replay what happened that day since it was so traumatic. There are times I get pretty upset, but I am trying my best to keep things together for me and my kids and I need my job. I am keeping up with what I need to for work and have not gotten feedback there have been any problems. I am feeling a little better now and will try to take it easy this weekend. I will let you know if I need to schedule a session sooner, but for now I am good with the time we have scheduled.

Valerie

After reading Valerie's email I was angry. There were so many things I wished I could say to her, but it was not appropriate for me to do so. I stood up and began pacing back and forth in my office, talking to myself.

I really think Valerie continuing to live in that house is not a good idea. The constant memories of her life there, even though there were happy memories will still be difficult. I do hope she realizes moving is the best thing for her in order for her to move forward with her life.

Oh my goodness. Wait a minute. Am I talking about Valerie or myself?

I went back over to my desk and sat down. I pulled up my company's website and searched for their locations in Pennsylvania. Why hadn't I thought of this before? I could transfer to another facility in order to finish getting my time in to qualify for benefits. I did not have to wait until next year to move. I could move now. I just needed to find a facility with an opening. I spent the rest of the evening researching my options and also sent an email to a realtor about my house. It was time for me to make a move. I had spent enough time hiding out in Virginia. I needed to return home and get on with my life.

*****

The week flew by and I just got back from Pennsylvania. I ended up taking a vacation day today so I could participate in a church activity yesterday which was promoting the workshop. I have my session with Valerie tonight, and tomorrow Bill and I are scheduled to talk about me transferring to another facility. I found a few openings but wanted his input before making any decisions. I did finally have a conversation with him about his recent behavior and he immediately apologized to me. He assured me that he meant no harm by any of his comments. I'm not so sure that is true since he then shared with me that he had broken up with his long-term girlfriend about six months ago. Either way, I made it clear to him I was not interested.

I also met with the realtor last week before my trip. She did a walk through and gave me a small list of suggested improvements to make my house more appealing. Of course she swears it is a sellers' market right now and is encouraging me to get everything done as soon as possible to get it listed. I had a few appointments this coming week to get estimates from contractors on the work.

I made great time driving back in the middle of the day and had plenty of time before my session with Valerie, so I made the most of it by beginning to take inventory of things in my house that I wanted to keep versus those things I could part with. I became so engrossed in my inventory I was almost late for my session with Valerie. I heard the reminder and I rushed into my office and logged on.

"Hi Valerie. I got your email. Sorry you seemed to be having a rough time. How are things going now? How is work going?"

She burst into tears immediately and grabbed a tissue but did not cry for too long. She was able to regain her composure fairly quickly and finally responded to me.

"I was struggling but things are getting a little better. I spent some time making sure I had followed up on everything after vacation and feel like I am back on track. It is still a lot of hours so hopefully that gets better at some point. I have decided to sell my house in Chatham and sent an email to Seth since he wanted the option of buying it first."

"Did you tell your kids you have decided to sell the house?" She still appeared to be pretty emotional as she continued to dab her eyes as she spoke.

"I let them know and they understood. They seem to have mixed feelings since that is where they grew up, but they are also bothered by living next to Paula."

"Have you seen her at all?"

"I haven't but last Friday when I got back from Hallmark movie night with a friend, I saw several cars next door. When I sat in my living room trying to relax, I could hear Paula's family in the yard. I started to wonder what they thought about my family not that it really matters. When I come in my house the first thing I do is lock the door from my house to the garage."

Valerie seemed like she was trying to hold back from getting too upset again so I said, "It sounds like you are not very comfortable there anymore."

"The house and especially the garage door just have bad memories for me since that is where Seth went out when he left the night he told me about the allegations against him and where Paula came in when she took me to the hospital."

"Yes, that is very understandable. Has Seth been in contact with you?"

"He called last Friday and said he had good news to share. The grand jury was not moving forward with the case against him. He was going to let the kids know and the story would probably be in the local paper the next day. I really did not know what to say him, so I got off the phone as quickly as I could. I am relieved that our family will not have to deal with the media hype of a trial, but there are so many unknowns. I am just trying to focus on moving forward the best I can."

"That sounds like a good plan. How else are you doing overall?"

"Most of the time I am doing ok, but I have some rough patches here and there. My high school reunion is coming up soon, so I decided I wanted to try and get in shape. I reached out to someone I know that was starting some personal fitness sessions. I thought that would be much better than going to a gym. He is also a retired boxer and he mentioned I might enjoy learning how to punch. It sounded like a good idea, so I gave it a try. I had a session with him this past Saturday and it was great. Boxing was definitely quite a workout and it seemed to help me gain some confidence back."

"That sounds great Valerie. Any other new activities?"

"I have really not gone out too much since it can be hard to face people in public. I decided since I felt better after my boxing session to go to an Italian festival that evening with some friends and had a really nice time. I knew people were probably going to be talking about Seth since the article ended up on the front page that day. I thought it was more important to have a good time then to worry about what might be said about Seth. I figured I did not know if I would be around much more since I had made the decision I was moving. It really ended up being a wonderful evening seeing so many people that I will miss."

"It sounds like you are doing pretty well."

"I am, but I struggled a bit it was difficult earlier this week when the follow up story ran about the grand jury findings. The article included details from the witnesses about the night of the incident that were very disturbing. I really don't like to talk about it because I can just picture everything that happened even though I was not there." She hesitated for a moment then continued, "With all of these new details being made public it made me feel very self-conscious facing people knowing what was out there for people to read. Yesterday there was an all employee meeting in the office. I was eating lunch with one of my co-workers she told me she saw everything in the paper and wanted to make sure I was ok. I thanked her for being so thoughtful and tried to change the subject since I really did not want to have anyone else overhear what we were talking about.

During our employee meeting I ended up asking a question about next year's benefits that I think was on a lot of people's minds since our VP said he would discuss it further if asked. In the past I would not have had the confidence to ask a question in front of such a large group. I am starting to feel stronger after everything I have experienced and fought through."

"That is great that you are feeling more confident Valerie but let us talk a little about why this is difficult for you. Is it because you are afraid of others knowing the details?"

"One of my close friends after reading it asked me if Seth ever acted that way towards me. She felt really bad and wished there were something she could have done. The incident happened at our Richmond house and I could never step foot in that house again."

I could see how upsetting this was to Valerie. She grabbed another tissue and was trying to hold back her tears, but she just could not. I let her go for a minute and then said, "Valerie everything you are feeling is okay. You really do not have to try so hard to be so strong, especially here with me. I know you want to be strong for your kids, but here with me is your place to completely open and honest. Also it may not feel this way to you, but you have made a lot of great progress." She listened and took a few minutes to compose herself and I continued, Valerie you are showing your strength in so many ways. You just told me you felt confident to ask a tough question during your meeting at work. I think you will find your self-confidence will continue to grow in all aspects of your life. I believe you are slowly getting your voice back."

"Thanks. The same day that the follow up story came out I also got an email from my attorney that had the copy of the divorce decree from the judge, so everything is final. I immediately contacted my church to find out what I needed to do to start the annulment process. I know it sometimes takes years to finish and wanted to pursue that in case I meet someone in the future. That would be the only way I could get married in the Catholic church and even though I have not started dating it is something that is important to me."

"That is all really positive progress. It is great you are preparing for your future by planning ahead. Well Valerie, we are about out of time but feel free to send an email if anything comes up before our next session."

"Sounds good."

I resumed my inventory activity and really made some great progress. After about an hour I decided to take a break. I sat down on the sofa and my phone rang. It was Miles.

"Hello Miles." I answered.

"Hello Joy. You know why I am calling you right?"

I rolled my eyes, sighed, and said, "Yes, and I am sorry, but I had a client tonight and I have just been busy since I got in the door."

"I understand, but it does not take that long to send a text to say I made it safely. I was worried about you driving alone since I know you did not get much sleep last night."

"Yes, that is correct thanks to you and Curtis. Keeping me up half the night listening to old school music and reminiscing about college."

"Well, I had a ball."

I smiled. "I did too. It has been awhile since I have had fun like that."

"Do not take this the wrong way, but I could tell and you really should allow yourself to have some fun from time to time."

"No offense taken. You are right and trust me I plan to. Things are going to be very different for me in the next year."

"I am glad to hear you say that. Any idea what you are going to do after the project is over?"

"Yes, I have a few ideas, but nothing set in stone yet. Once things are a little more set, I will let you know."

"That sounds good. Alright well I am going to let you get back to whatever I interrupted. I just wanted to make sure you were home safe. I will be in touch in a few days with my updates for the workshop."

"Okay Miles sounds good. Take care."

Miles was right, we did have a good time last night hanging out at Robin's house. Listening to music and talking about old times. Robin enjoyed herself as well. She continues to keep score between Curtis and Miles. She feels that they are both jockeying for position to win my heart. I told her my heart is doing just fine although I am enjoying the attention from both of them. It has been so long since I have had any attention from a man.

Chapter 23

It felt as if I blinked and September was here. My workshop was just one day away. I decided to take some days off so I came to Harrisburg for the Labor Day weekend and I stayed through the week to ensure everything would be in place for this weekend's workshops.

I followed Bill's advice and applied at two locations, one in King of Prussia and the other in York. I had my initial interviews for both during my last trip in August. I got called for a second interview for the York location and had that interview yesterday. I am hoping I get the position in York.

I have continued to spend time with both Curtis and Miles. Since we are all working on this project, we have been spending time with the three of us together in person and virtually. Robin joked about us being on a three-person date. I guess I could see why she sees it that way because it was obvious to me both Curtis and Miles are interested in me, but they are both being respectful at least for now. I have a suspicion as soon as these workshops are over, they will both switch into full court press mode.

Every now and then I allow myself to think about it and if I had to choose today, I believe I would choose Curtis which is a little crazy for me, according to Robin. She does not consider me to be a risk taker. She thinks Miles is the safe choice, you know already been there and done that. Curtis is fresh and new, the unknown, which is honestly one of the reasons I am drawn to him a little more. I think it is also because of my affection for Shannon. She is such a wonderful young lady. I have always wanted children. I realize she is basically grown, but the likelihood of me having children at my age is pretty slim at this point. I feel if I tried again with Miles our inability to have children would one day be an issue for us both.

Toni knocked on the door of the conference room I was using as my makeshift office at the church and interrupted my daydream. She walked in and said, "What are you smiling about?"

I straightened myself in the chair. "Oh, nothing really. I am just extremely excited to see how well everything is coming together."

"Yes, I agree with you. Everything has come together very nicely. I was just coming in to give you the update on the numbers for the workshop registrations."

"Okay great, have a seat and let's review everything."

Toni and I reviewed everything one last time. I had to make a minor adjustment and swap two rooms around to accommodate the registration for one workshop which slightly over performed, but all in all we were in great shape.

*****

Later that night I was back at Robin's house and I decided to check my emails. There was one from Valerie. Although I have been busy with work and coordinating everything for the workshops, my communication with her remained fairly consistent. I believe she is making great progress.

Joy,

I just got back from visiting David at Florida State for family weekend. It was really great to see him, and Scott traveled with me. I also had a friend that lives close by come to the football game with us. I thought it was probably going to be somewhat of a rough day since it would have been my wedding anniversary. Afterwards me and my friend went out for a few drinks and were talking to some guys at the bar. It was really fun being out, and I am still trying to get used to the idea of possibly dating someday.

After I got back to the hotel Seth called me and wanted to talk about the football game he went to earlier that day. He then went on to say how he would always love me. I told him he really should not be saying things like that since we are not together anymore. It does seem he is struggling with the fact we are divorced, but I am trying to move on with my life.

Seth decided he is not buying the house, so I have spent the last two weeks getting it ready to put on the market. This week is going to be pretty hectic. The photographer is scheduled to come on Thursday. I have already met with the realtor, so all the rest of the information is ready to go.

I know I mentioned my first boxing session the last time we met, and I have been going at least twice a week since then. I am really enjoying it and going to start researching to see about getting certified as a personal trainer. I think it is an amazing workout and confidence builder so I could help other women.

Valerie

Valerie's email made me smile. I was happy for her and the progress she is making. I was pleased that she decided to sell her house. I know that is going to be tough for her but living next door to Paula was not healthy for her for so many reasons. I sent her a response.

Valerie,

Thanks for updating me on how everything is going. I was happy to hear you are getting out with friends and at least considering the possibility of dating in the future. Great progress on the house but remember big changes can bring on anxiety and stress so just be mindful of that as you continue to move forward with all of these major life changes. Looking forward to talking to you soon.

Joy

Robin walked in the door just as I was finishing up the email to Valerie.

"Hey Robin. How was your visit?" She smiled.

"It was nice but too short." She made a pouty face and I laughed.

"Yes, I know it is all my fault because you had to come back for the workshop tomorrow."

"Yes, it is your fault, but as soon as I am finished tomorrow, I am heading back to his house."

"Wow, maybe you should consider moving?"

"Oh no, I am not uprooting my life and business for any man."

"Come on, Robin. Eventually you will have to make some changes."

"Maybe eventually, but I am not there yet."

"Well it is your life, but all I can tell you is I have never seen you happier than the past few months."

"Okay, that is enough now. Please stop it. You are going to make me cry."

"Please don't. Let's change the subject. Sit down and let me fill you in on a few minor changes for tomorrow." Robin sat down and said, "Wait before you start. What did you eat?"

"Actually I have not eaten anything."

"You want to order salads from Naples?"

"Yeah sure." She reached for her phone and placed our order.

While we waited for our food to arrive, we talked and I brought her up to speed on the changes for her session.

"Since we had a few more people enroll, we changed the room you will be in to accommodate everyone."

"Well, that sounds great. Tell me Joy what are the next steps after the workshops tomorrow?"

"Our plan is to start with the leaders of the church. Initially Pastor Flee only wanted the deacons and associate pastors, but I convinced him to expand the group to include all positions of leadership within the church. It is required for the deacons, but only strongly suggested for the other ministry leaders."

"Okay that makes sense, but after we train them on the importance of mental health and how it can coexist with spiritual counseling then what?"

"After the church leadership is trained and onboard, we will move on and have workshops for the congregation. I will continue to work closely with church leadership to provide guidance as a mental health professional. I'll also work to identify when members should possibly seek professional help. Obviously, we cannot make someone do that, but the point is to raise awareness at all levels including leadership on how to recognize there is an issue and members themselves understanding that although prayer is very powerful sometimes we need a little more help."

"Where do you see yourself in the future? I know you are planning to leave the clinic."

"I do plan to continue working with the church also, even though at some point I realize the money will run out. That is why my long-term plan is to start my own practice."

"Where do you plan to find your clients? You cannot have mine." She joked and I laughed.

"Your clients are safe, Robin. I want to focus my efforts more on young people, teenagers and maybe college aged. I have been inspired by what Miles is doing at his school and I would like to figure out a way to set up a similar program in the public schools."

"That sounds like a great idea, Joy."

Robin and I continued to talk about my plans for the future. I pressed to get her to tell me more about her friend, but she would not budge. Once our food arrived, we found a movie and watched it and ate our food. I went to bed as soon as the movie was over. I wanted to be well rested for tomorrow.

Chapter 24

My cell phone rang just as I walked through the door from work. I've been back in Virginia for a few weeks. I cannot believe it is October already.

"Hello, Robin. I just walked in the door."

"Oh okay, sorry, but I just have not talked to you in a while. I wanted to touch base."

"Yeah, it's fine. I have some time before my session tonight."

"You're still seeing clients? I thought you gave that up a while ago?"

"I stopped accepting new clients, but I kept the ones I had. I am down to my final client and she is doing very well. We typically only have video sessions once a month now, but we email and text on a regular basis. I suspect soon she will terminate her services."

"Well, that is good she is doing well. So what has been going on with you? When are you coming back this way?"

"It has been a bit of an adjustment for me being back here full time for the past few weeks. But I needed this time to get my house together to list."

"How is that going? Is everything ready yet?"

"Almost, in fact, the contractor should have finished today and with any luck I can get the house listed by the end of the week." I walked into the kitchen to check the progress. Everything looked complete and there was an invoice on the kitchen table.

"Yes, I just checked, and it appears everything is finished so I am going to contact my agent to let her know so we can get this ball rolling."

"What else has been going on? Any update on the job yet?"

"Great news on the job. I was offered the position in York that I wanted. They are allowing me to have a flexible start date since it is a new position and I am relocating."

"That is awesome news. Why didn't you call me and tell me?"

"I don't know. They called to make the offer, I took a few days to consider it, and I just accepted it the other day."

"So when can I expect my roommate back?"

"Oh, so you miss me huh?"

"I guess I got used to you being here."

"That is funny, especially since you never seemed to be there when I was there anyway." She laughed and said,

"Yeah that is true, but things are back to normal now."

"Wait! What happened?"

"Same as always but listen I do not want to talk about that right now. I would much rather hear what is going on with your love life."

I scoffed. "What love life?"

"You know that little love triangle you have been a part of for the past few months."

"I told you that was all work related. I still talk to both of them from time to time, but it is not every day like before."

"You sound a little disappointed."

"Maybe, a little bit, but not really. I was not sure I wanted anything more to come of it anyway. I just enjoyed working with them brainstorming and putting together the presentations for the project."

"Okay, Joy this is me. You can be real with me. Stop being coy and tell me how you really feel."

"I'm being serious, I really wasn't expecting anything to happen with either one of them. Yes, I have enjoyed getting to know Curtis more and I have enjoyed spending time with Miles as well but there's just something there that gives me pause with Miles."

Well, I will leave that alone for now, but please do not fall back to only being focused on work again. I really enjoyed seeing you having a good time with Curtis and Miles. How is Shannon doing?"

"I hear you and I won't, but with this move and job change I am not sure that now is the time to start anything new anyway. Shannon is fine. She and I still talk every day."

"Joy, I am going to leave it alone like I said, but I have heard it is not the right time excuse for a long time now, I am just saying. Let us change the subject. Have you thought about where you want to live?"

"I have thought about it but have not decided yet. I was hoping to maybe come up one weekend and maybe start looking."

"Well, my weekends are free again so I can tag along if you would like."

"Yes, that sounds good. Well listen I need to run since it is almost time for my session. I will be in touch once I have a date set for my next visit. It has to be soon because November is right around the corner."

"Okay, well just let me know. Take care dear."

"You too, bye."

After ending the call with Robin, I went into my office and sent an email to my realtor to let her know all repairs were finished, and I was ready to go. I prayed the house sold quickly. I would love to get settled back in Pennsylvania before winter set in if possible.

Still a few minutes before my scheduled time with Valerie, so I went to the kitchen to grab a bottle of water and some nuts to snack on. I returned to my office, logged on and waited for Valerie to join. She was right on time as usual.

"Hi Valerie. How are you doing? It seemed from your email you have been keeping pretty busy."

"I really have been. My reunion was fun, and I connected with a few more people on Facebook after that from high school. I was supposed to travel directly after that for work, but I had to cancel. Scott ended up in the hospital, but he is ok now. I tried to run the planning session the best I could remotely, but Lila was making it really difficult. Since I was not there in person she told the team not to contact me even though I was available. I felt bad I could not be there and the person that had picked up to lead the sessions really appreciated any help I could give her."

"I am glad Scott is okay now. It sounds like work continues to be a challenge for you."

"It seems it is not really a good team for me to be on. I have been getting dumped on a lot by Lila, and I tried to push back a bit. I also did not appreciate how she treated me before when she suggested I take a leave from work. I have been upfront with Lila about how I feel things are going and also talked with our manager. Hopefully I can see if there is another team eventually to move to, but I am trying to get through it the best I can."

"That sounds like a good plan for now but continue to take your pulse on a regular basis about the amount of work stress you have. Any stress is not good for you right now with everything else you have going on. Have you been able to find some things to do for yourself?"

"I reconnected with a friend that has a son at UVA. We met up and went to a field hockey game and dinner which was great. Also, my junior prom date reached out to me and we have been talking quite a bit. He puts me in a good mood, and it has been fun catching up. I have been going to all the home UVA football games which has been great. I saw one of Brandon's fraternity brothers at a UVA game and we exchanged numbers. It got me thinking maybe I could try and reach out to Brandon somehow, but I really do not know what I would say after not being in touch for so long. For now I am just having a good time catching up with friends, but maybe soon I might be ready to pursue some type of a relationship."

"It really seems like you are making a lot of progress Valerie. Just remember to take your time with things. Especially as we move into the holiday season. This will be the first holidays without your husband. That is bound to be tough on you and the boys. We are out of time for today, but feel free to reach out if you need to let me know anything before our next session. If you think we need longer times again let me know."

"I will. I think I am probably just going to need another session or two and then might take a break for a while. It has been very helpful being able to connect with you via text and email outside of our formal sessions. Through our conversations I feel that I have learned how to handle things much better. I am able to work through a lot on my own and am also getting pretty comfortable talking with just a few of my closest friends."

"That works for me. Thanks for the heads up."

After my session ended with Valerie I decided to go upstairs and start going through my closet to pick which clothes to keep and which ones to donate. Before heading upstairs, I poured myself a glass of wine. I turned on some music and started dancing, singing, and going through my clothes. An hour later there were piles everywhere. My wine glass was empty, and I just finished a Whitney Houston concert when my phone rang. I had to dig it out from under a pile of clothes to answer it. I was pleasantly surprised to see it was Curtis.

"Hello, Curtis. Long time no talk."

"Hello, Joy. It has not been that long, but I am happy to hear you missed me."

I blushed but said, "I did not say I missed you, I simply said it has been a while since we talked."

"Okay, I know what I heard." He said with a laugh.

"Anyway how have you been?" I asked.

"I have been good. No complaints at all really. I must admit it has been a little strange not having our nightly check-in the past few weeks."

"I know, right? I was just talking to Robin earlier, and I told her the same thing. It has been strange having all this free time in the evening."

"So what have you been doing to fill the void?"

"I have been just doing stuff around the house. I am in the process of putting it up for sale. There were some minor repairs needed, so I have been focusing on that."

"How is that going? Everything taken care of?"

"Yes, actually, the contractor finished everything today while I was at work."

"That is great news. So when are you coming back to visit?"

"Nothing is set in stone yet, but probably in the next couple of weeks."

"I would like to take you to dinner while you are in town." I hesitated for a moment and thought about how I should respond.

"Okay yeah, sure, I should be able to accommodate that request."

He laughed and said, "Great you can fit me into your schedule?"

"Of course, especially since you are giving me such advance notice."

"Just let me know when you decide when you are coming, and I will make the necessary arrangements."

"Okay, Curtis, but nothing fancy please. Just dinner."

"Yes ma'am. Now that we got the important stuff out of the way tell me what is next?"

"I was just explaining everything to Robin earlier. I really need to get an email out to everyone. Anyway, we plan to start the next round of workshops for the congregation mid-November. We will offer sessions during the day, the evenings and weekend times. Once I get the schedule nailed down, I will email you all so you can let me know which sessions you can cover."

"Okay, that sounds great. I can tell you the church leadership thoroughly enjoyed the sessions. They have not stopped talking about it and you, of course."

"I'm very pleased that everyone enjoyed it and I also enjoyed being able to work with everyone. Well Curtis, it has been nice talking to you, but I need to get off this phone. I was in the middle of a clothes project and I need to get back to it so I can get to bed sometime soon."

"It has been nice talking to you too, and I look forward to hearing when you decide when you are coming to town."

"I will be in touch, good night." I smiled as I ended the call with Curtis. I was a little surprised at how nice it was hearing from him. I'm also looking forward to having dinner with him.

"Good night, Joy." After ending the call with Joy I smiled as I thought about the possibility of going on a real date with her. She was an amazing woman. Shannon has really become attached to her and Stanley approves of her as well. My only concern is if she still has feelings for Miles. I suppose time will tell.

"

Chapter 25

I am on my way to Pennsylvania to attend an orientation for my new job. It turns out I need to start sooner than initially thought, but I am going to be able to work remotely most of the time until my house sells. I am going to be performing clinical review which means I will be mostly reviewing the therapists case notes and confirming their recommended treatment meets the standard of care based on the diagnosis of the patient. I am pleased they are allowing me to work remotely. I need to get three days of orientation completed before the holidays. It coincides with me needing to be in Pennsylvania for the phase 2 workshops also.

It also works out well with my realtor being able to show the house and not having to worry about me being there. I packed to stay for three weeks. It looks like I am actually moving now. I have never been able to pack light. I decided to just plan on staying through the Thanksgiving holiday. The rest of this week I will be in orientation, next week we will begin the phase 2 workshops and then the following week is Thanksgiving. I have no clue what I am doing for the holiday this year, but at least I will not be spending it alone as I have in years past.

On Friday I am having dinner with Curtis and I am excited, well maybe a little nervous. Lately I have been allowing myself to consider the possibility of something more between us. Since the workshops in September, Miles has faded into the background. I rarely hear from him, which

I am fine with. He does attend the meetings and responded to my emails about phase 2.

My thoughts were interrupted by my cell phone ringing.

"Hey, Robin. I am about an hour away."

"Okay I was getting worried and wanted to check on you. I thought you would be here when I got home."

"Yeah me too, but I got stuck at the office in a meeting with Bill a little longer than I anticipated."

"Is he still giving you a hard time?"

"No, I think he is finally in the acceptance phase."

We both laughed and she said, "Good because no matter what he says or does you are coming back to Pennsylvania now."

"No, Bill has actually been quite helpful with getting things set up for me at my new job. He has vouched for me and convinced them to allow me to work remotely until my house sells. Oh, that reminds me. Are you going to be able to go house hunting with me this weekend?"

"Yeah, sure, that is no problem. I have no plans."

"I'm sorry. I was hopeful you and your friend would work things out."

"Nope, not a chance. That ship has sailed."

"Are you ever going to tell me what happened?"

"Nah, probably not."

I scoffed. "You are so wrong. How can you always be all up in my business, but never want to divulge any juicy tidbits about your life to me?"

"Take notes my child. You will learn these skills one day." We both laughed.

"I cannot stand you sometimes, but I will always love you."

"I know you will, you cannot help yourself."

"Girl get off my phone. I will see you soon."

"Wait, it is late? Did you eat yet?"

"No, I did not, and I really do not want to stop."

"Do not worry about it. I will have something ready for you when you get here. Just take your time and drive safely."

"Thanks, Robin. I'll see you soon."

I ended the call and smiled thinking about how close Robin and I had become. She was like the aunt I never had. I always had a great amount of respect for her, not just because she was older than me, but because of how she always made me feel so important. I cannot recall when we actually crossed over from being therapist and client to being friends, but I never felt any different. Even as her client she always made me feel as though my problems were hers also and we were going to figure it out together. I wondered if my clients felt that way about me. I hoped they did, because I really did care about them. It was not just a job for me. I genuinely wanted to help people deal with their issues and live a more fulfilling life. Valerie has certainly become more comfortable with me. I receive emails and text messages from her often. She keeps me updated on people she has reconnected with on social media and also people from the hospital like Lauren, the young woman who went to rehab. She recently had a panic attack and texted me about it because she was put on a performance place on her new team at work. I didn't say this to her, but I honestly do not feel that is the best place for her to be right now. I believe she is also realizing this and has begun to look for other employment.

Just last week I received a letter at the clinic from Kara. She is doing well, and she wanted to thank me personally for pushing for her to get additional testing and services. She has ended up living in a facility that provides her with all of the support she needs to care for herself and her son. Kara's issue was not the drugs; they were a symptom of the bigger problems she had. She becomes easily overwhelmed and thus turned to drugs. She has intellectual disabilities. What I do not understand is how a person gets all the way through school and well into their twenties with no one noticing they need help. I am glad she is finally getting what she needs.

By the time I arrived at Robin's, she had my dinner ready for me on the kitchen table. I was grateful because I was starving and exhausted. We chit chatted while I ate my salad and then we both retired to our respective rooms. I could not go straight to bed since I had just eaten, so I decided to soak in the tub to relax a little bit.

I drew my bath and settled into the tub and had some soft music playing from my phone. I closed my eyes and began to relax in my own thoughts. It did not last five minutes before my music was interrupted by an incoming call. I grabbed my towel to dry my hands, picked up my phone and answered,

"Hello, Curtis."

"Hey, Joy, did I catch you at a bad time?"

"Well, yes and no. I was just relaxing a little bit before bed."

"Okay sorry to have interrupted, but I wanted to make sure you made it safely."

"Oh, yes I am sorry. I completely forgot you knew I was coming in town tonight."

"I guess our conversations are forgettable huh?" He laughed.

"No, I just have had a lot on my mind. Hey while I have you. Have you spoken to Miles lately?"

"Not in the past couple of days why? Everything okay?"

"I was just curious. I did not know if you two kept in touch much since we've stopped working on the workshops together."

"Well our relationship is not really one where I would call him on a regular basis or anything. Our lives are very different. He doesn't have children. My contact with him has primarily been through our work with you these past several months."

"I understand, but I really wanted to know how much he shared with you about what happened between me and him."

"I'm not sure exactly what you mean Joy. Before he spoke with you, he told me about what happened with the other girl and how you found out about it on graduation day."

"So that is all? He did not mention anything else?"

"No, he didn't. Joy what is this about? You are scaring me a bit."

I thought for a moment about how to approach this very delicate subject with Curtis. It was obvious to me that we were both interested in one another, so it was a conversation that we needed to have. I feel it needed to be sooner rather than later. "Curtis, I need to tell you something that is very personal. I am sharing this with you because I feel that you are someone that is becoming a special part of my life. You're a friend and I trust that you will keep this just between us."

"Okay Joy, seriously you are really starting to freak me out."

"I'm sorry Curtis just bear with me. Once I get this out, I think you will understand. Curtis, I have herpes. I contracted it back when I was in college and I was only with Miles." As soon as the words left my lips I began to cry. This was my worse fear, finding someone and them possibly rejecting me because of my STD status.

"Wow, okay. This is not at all what I expected, but Joy, it's okay. It's not a death sentence for you or us. I really appreciate your honesty."

"Thank you, Curtis, I really appreciate you being so understanding and kind. I have dreaded having this conversation for a while." It is amazing the sense of peace I feel now. I still have herpes, but I feel free. I have spoken my truth to someone who I care about and who appears to also care for me.

"You're welcome Joy. You are a wonderful woman. I am looking forward to us continuing to get to know each other better and explore what the future brings for us both." I was a little surprised at how what Joy told me did not really affect me. I can't lie I would have never thought I would be so open and accepting of being with someone with a positive STD status, but for some reason it really doesn't matter to me at all.

I continued to cry, but my tears were now tears of joy. Curtis and I continued to talk for a little while longer, but we changed the subject and began talking about Shannon and Stanley before I suggested that we get off the phone. I was still in the tub and the water was ice cold.

The following morning I awoke when I heard Robin leaving. It was a good thing because I forgot to charge my phone. My phone was dead, and I needed to use my GPS to find my way to my orientation. I plugged my phone in to charge a little bit while I dressed for work and made a quick bite to eat. I headed out the door with my charger to continue charging my phone as I drove. I had several text messages from Curtis, but I did not have a chance to read any of them. I was focused on getting to orientation on time.

*****

I was so glad orientation was over, and I was headed back to Robin's house for the weekend. The past three days were a little more grueling than I expected them to be. I no longer had the perception all administrative jobs were a piece of cake. This one was going to require my full attention until I got the hang of it.

I was supposed to be having dinner with Curtis tonight, but we had to postpone due to something coming up with his son. I did not press for details because I was exhausted from orientation. I planned to spend the evening with Robin. I wanted to fill her in on my conversation with Curtis last night.

Robin and I ordered pizza and wings and sat in the living room eating, talking, and laughing for hours on Friday night. We did have a serious discussion about Curtis and Miles, and she helped me to see their perspectives. Me and Curtis made plans to meet for lunch on Saturday. I also decided that I needed to talk to Miles to clear the air with him about everything I was feeling. I also felt he deserved to hear it directly from me about me and Curtis. Robin also felt that I should let him know that I told Curtis about me having the STD.

Chapter 26

As I drove to meet Curtis for lunch at the Underdog, I thought about our conversation the other night. I was very nervous seeing him in person after sharing something so personal with him. Robin helped me to see how Curtis may view Miles as competition. I need to assure Curtis that I do not have any lingering feeling for Miles so that he feels comfortable with us continuing to pursue a relationship. Since all three of us are friends I suppose things from the past need to be settled and dealt with before forging ahead into the future.

As I approached the restaurant, I did not see any available parking spots. I loved their food, but parking was always an issue. I circled around to the back and fortunately caught someone just as they were pulling out. I parked and scanned the lot to see if I noticed Curtis' car and I did not. As I walked in, I noticed Curtis seated at a table towards the back of the restaurant. He saw me and stood up and motioned for me to join him. As I approached, he smiled and reached for a hug. I gave him a quick hug and sat down as he said,

"It is so good to see you, Joy."

I smiled and said, "It's good to see you too."

He picked up the menu and began looking over it. Meanwhile, I already had my order memorized. I always got the exact same thing, sweet and tangy wings, all drums, extra crispy and loaded waffle fries. After a few minutes, the waitress showed up and took our orders. After she left Curtis reached across the table and took my hand in his and said, "Joy, I know it was very difficult for you to share that with me and I want you to know that it really is not an issue for me."

"Curtis, I really appreciate your understanding and I want you to know that enjoy our friendship and I realize maybe it could blossom into something more. With that said, I do not feel we are there yet. I need you to slow down a bit, okay?" He nodded so I continued, "It has been a very long time since I have been in a relationship and I want to take my time. I am in the middle of several big life changes right now. A new job, selling my house, relocating just to name the big ones. I am not sure I am ready to add a new romantic relationship onto that list."

He interrupted, "Can I say something now?" I smiled.

"Yes of course."

"Joy, I am fine with everything you have said. Yes, I do like you and I would like to see where things could go, but I am in no rush either. Honestly until I reconnected with you, I had not even considered trying to date again. I felt I was still grieving my wife and helping Shannon deal with the loss as well."

"Then we both agree now probably is not the best time to get into anything serious right?" He nodded.

"Yes, I agree and in addition to that I think at some point if we decide to pursue a relationship, we both need to have separate conversations with Miles." I nodded in agreement.

"Absolutely I agree with you on that. It is somewhat of a sticky situation since we were all friends before and obviously my prior relationship with Miles could make things weird or awkward. I do plan to talk to him sooner rather than later though. I feel as though he deserves to know what I shared with you since it may also impact him. I also want him to know that I am not interested in rekindling a romantic relationship with him.

"Ok great, so we are both interested in seeing where things can go but we are going to take our time getting there?"

"Yes, I believe you summed that up perfectly." We both laughed. I continued, "For the record, I do not handle jealousy well. It is a major turn off for me. If we are ever in an intimate relationship you should be secure in my commitment to you and never have to feel jealous." He smiled.

"I like that. That is deep and I can certainly handle that. In the future, possibly." We both laughed and then the waitress showed up with our food.

"The waitress arrived with our food. Curtis took my hand and blessed the food. I felt such a sense of peace when I was in his presence.

By the time I got back to Robin's house she was waiting at the door for me. We had planned to go house hunting. She had picked out a few neighborhoods and some open houses for us already. As we drove, I updated her on my lunch conversation with Curtis. I felt it went well and he seemed to be genuine with how he felt about things. Time will tell.

*****

Miles surprised me and showed up at church on Sunday. We were planning to meet for lunch after service anyway. We sat together and afterwards I had a brief conversation with Toni and the pastor then we were on our way to lunch. We drove separately and met up at the restaurant. Miles being the gentleman he is waited for me to arrive and opened my car door for me. He looked okay, but like maybe he had lost a few pounds.

Once we were seated and had placed our orders I began, "So Miles I thought it was time for us to have a serious discussion about our relationship."

"Okay Joy let's do it. What do you need to say?"

"I'm serious Miles. I've appreciated your assistance with the workshops over the past few months and I have enjoyed getting to know you better. With that said I wanted to let you know that Curtis and I are exploring a relationship."

"Joy, first of all, I am not surprised about you and Curtis and second, you do not owe me any explanations."

"I know, Miles, but as a friend I felt you should know. I hope the three of us are able to continue working together on the workshops in the future. I do not want things to be awkward. There's something else. I told him about my STD status."

"That's fine, Joy. I can't apologize to you enough about that."

"Yeah, I know, but unfortunately sorry isn't enough to fix this."

"Yes, I know that is true and believe me every day since the day I found out and until the day I die, it will haunt me." I finally realized that I needed to forgive myself. I have been holding on to this guilt for far too long.

Now I felt a little bad for being so hard on him. I do not believe that he willingly or carelessly infected me but still it's a very serious thing. I could tell that it really bothered him though. "I know, Miles, and that is why I wanted us to have this conversation so that we can both move on past this. There is no reason for you to continue to walk around carrying that guilt and for me to carry the shame. What is done is done. We both need to move on and accept it."

He nodded in agreement and simply said, "Thanks, Joy." The waitress appeared with our food. We both ordered the stuffed shrimp. Miles reached across the table for my hand and blessed the food.

Miles and I finished our meal and then we shifted to discussing the next phase and beyond. He was already committed to facilitating a few workshops for me next week, but he was interested in what was next.

"As for what is next. That is to be determined after the new year. I have some ideas but after these sessions we have coming up that will be it until after the new year."

After lunch as I drove to Robin's, I thought about all of the tough conversations I had this past weekend. Even though they were tough they were necessary, and I believe they all ended up with everyone feeling better, at least I hoped so.

The next week was a blur. I spent the entire week at the church during the day and some evenings. I worked my job remotely and I sat in on as many workshops as I could. My team did an excellent job, so I felt comfortable leaving them to facilitate without me. The final workshop was held Sunday afternoon after church. We had all planned to attend the final one and meet briefly afterwards. We all stayed in the conference room after the attendees left. I addressed them all, "First of all I want to thank you all from the bottom of my heart. I put the call to action out and you all delivered. I know I can be tough to work with sometimes, but you all came through and did not disappoint."

Pastor Flee walked in and said, "I agree 100% with everything that Joy said, except the part about her being difficult to work with. I cannot confirm or deny that statement." We all laughed. He went on to say, "I appreciate you all and I think the work you have done here will go a long way with our leadership and our congregation. I want you all to enjoy the holidays.

Pastor Flee said his goodbyes and we all hung around talking for a few more minutes. As we walked out together Robin asked, "Hey, what is everyone doing for Thanksgiving?" Everyone collectively said they had no real plans or just planned to stay at home.

Curtis said, "Why don't you all join me and my kids at our house?"

"Really? Are you sure Curtis?" I asked.

"I am down for that. My kids are not coming home this year." Robin said.

"Me too." said Miles.

"Okay then well I guess we are having Thanksgiving at Curtis' house. What can we help with?"

We all huddled together and made plans on who was bringing what and set the time.

I rode home with Robin. She was so excited about how well everything turned out and mentioned she had a great feeling about the possibilities with phase 3.

*****

Thanksgiving turned out very nice. We all had a great time. The food was delicious. The conversation was good. It felt like home with all my friends. We ate a little later, so I was able to swing by Toni's house earlier in the day and spend a little time with her and the kids. Of course she wanted me to be with them, but she said she understood I wanted to be with my friends.

I left on Saturday to head back to Virginia for at least a week or so. It was really up to me. I could continue working remotely and stay in Virginia if I wanted to, but I had gotten accustomed to being around Robin and I really enjoyed being in Pennsylvania the past few weeks. I was anxious to get my house sold so I could relocate. There were no offers yet on my house. I knew it was a tough time of year, but I remained prayerful the right person or family would come along.

I went into the office on Monday to finish clearing out my office. Bill was still on vacation from the Thanksgiving holiday, so I packed up my things and headed back home to finish my day from there. When I checked my emails after getting back to the house, I had received one from Valerie.

Joy,

I wanted to send you a quick note to touch base. I decided to take vacation time the week of Thanksgiving since both of my boys were going to be home from school. I had been saving up my days, but I have gotten pretty frustrated with work. Since I was put on an improvement plan as I shared with you before I cannot try to transfer to another team, and I feel like I am being watched like a hawk with everything I do. It really did not seem like there was a warning this was coming. Maybe I missed it somehow due to putting in so many hours. We have had a lot of issues with our vendor partner, so I have been working every weekend and also have to send management update reports every night.

I was really glad to have some time off and was not sure what to do about the holiday. Typically we would go to my parents, but since the boys wanted to split their time with me and Seth I decided not to travel. We ended up going to Celeste's house around lunchtime on Thanksgiving and then my kids went with Seth to his brother's house for dinner. It was strange being home by myself when they left, so I kept busy by starting to pull out items from the office closet to go through. I am really trying my best to get rid of as much as I can before the move since I do not have as much room in my Charlottesville home. My sister in law Deb sent food home with the boys for me which was really nice. I made sure to send her a text right away thanking her. She replied and said how different it was not having me there and hoped I was having a nice holiday. It is going to be an adjustment for all of us to move forward and I plan on doing my best to keep people in my life that mean a lot to me. I still struggle at times with trust because I tend to see the good in people, but that is not necessarily a bad thing. Sometimes it takes putting yourself out there regardless of what people think to truly find out more about a person and what they mean to you.

Every time I finish a boxing session it really lifts my spirits. I decided to do some online Black Friday shopping and ordered a punching bag set so I can work out at home *whenever I want. I did a little digging into what I would need to do for getting certified as a personal trainer for boxing and might start on that in my spare time. It is refreshing to have something new to work towards given how things have been with my job.*

Valerie

I smiled as I typed my response.

Valerie,

It is always good to hear from you. I continue to be concerned about the amount of stress your job situation is putting on you, but I know that you are considering your options. I know this holiday season is going to be different for you and your boys but stay close to your family and enjoy doing some of the things you haven't been able to enjoy for a long time. Hang in there and keep focused on your goals. I love the personal trainer idea. Go for it.

Joy

Chapter 27

I decided to return to Pennsylvania for the remainder of the year. I wanted to spend the holidays with my friends and family. After only being home a few days I realized how much I missed everyone. As I packed and prepared my house for the realtor, I decided to send Valerie an email letting her know I wanted to touch base briefly before Christmas and asked her to book a 15-minute session.

After everything was packed, I decided to drive past the clinic to say my final goodbye to Bill. Even though the past several months have been challenging for us we have worked together for over ten years and we worked well together. I felt I owed him a lot especially for his assistance with getting the new job. Unfortunately, he was in a meeting, so I decided to leave him a message to call me instead. As I walked out of the clinic, I felt such a sense of peace. Although I was a little nervous about what lie ahead, I knew putting the clinic behind me meant I was headed in the right direction.

*****

I had been back in Harrisburg for a week and loving every minute of it. I worked from home most days and Robin had allowed me to take over her home office space for my office. Curtis and I were talking and spending more time together, which Shannon loved. On nights when Robin worked late, I went over and had dinner with Curtis and Shannon, sometimes Stanley joined us if he was available.

Toni was happy to have me around and she and I met a few times for lunch. She was pressuring me to spend Christmas with her and the kids which is probably what I will end up doing. Robin's kids were planning to come with her grandkids for the holiday. Curtis and I had not discussed it, but I did not want to assume he wanted us to spend it together.

After my email to Valerie she responded, and we were scheduled to chat shortly. I wanted to see her and hear her voice to make sure she was handling everything well. Her continued work issues and moving were all major stressors. I logged in and waited for Valerie to join.

"Hi, Valerie. Thank you so much for agreeing to touch base with me. I saw your email about what happened since our last session. I wanted to make sure you and I talked before the holidays. Is work getting any better for you?"

"No, not really. I have found taking the anxiety medicine once in a while helps when I get upset. I really should not have to deal with that kind of stress with work, so I started looking for a new job."

"That sounds like a good idea. You have been struggling for a while now to find the right balance between work and your personal life. It also just does not seem as if your supervisor is will to work with you."

"I am trying to find something near Charlottesville so I can move there after I sell the Chatham house. There have been some buyers interested so hopefully it will not be too long now. I have gone through a lot in the house to get it ready and my kids will be back again soon for their winter break."

"I'm sure that it will be nice to have them home."

"I am looking forward to it. I really have missed having them around. It will also probably be our last time together in Chatham, so they will want some time with their friends. I am sure it will be hard on them once I move, but I do have to do what is best for me."

"Yes, Valerie, you are correct. It is time for you to start putting yourself first."

"I am trying to, but that is not always easy. I am still taking time a few days a week to do boxing even though I am pretty busy getting ready for my move."

. "I wanted to mention to you that I understand what you're going through right now with trying to sell your house and packing. I am also relocating."

"Oh really? Hopefully that is a good move for you. Packing is such a pain and is exhausting."

"Yes, I know and just remember it will not always be easy, but you are doing a great job. You have really come a long way and remember your boys are becoming adults. They are branching out and starting lives of their own. You have to be able to do the same thing."

"Yes, I know you are right. Thanks for telling me you think I have come a long way. It is nice to hear that. Sometimes I feel that way, but other times not so much. I am thinking maybe you and I touch base once more after the first of the year to see how things are going."

"That works for me. I really have enjoyed working with you. Have a great holiday with your family."

"Thanks you too."

After ending my session with Valerie I felt good. I really felt as though she has come a long way. I think she is much stronger now and will heal from all of this trauma and be fine on the other side of this. With that said, she may need more therapy at some point especially as she continues to work through her trauma.

*****

The days were short, and they passed quickly. Before I knew it, Christmas was just a few days away. I was helping Robin decorate her house and move things around to accommodate her family who were arriving the following day. Packed a few of my bags and planned to stay with Toni while Robin's family visited. We were putting the finishing touches on the tree when my phone rang. It was Curtis.

"Hey Curtis, how was your day?"

"It was great, and I am finished working until the new year. How about you?"

"Same here, well almost. I am going to finish up a few things from here tomorrow and then I am off until the new year as well."

"That is great, so what are we going to do?" I smiled and said,

"What do you mean?"

"Well we are both going to be off work and I would like to spend some time with you."

"I would like that as well. Maybe you can help me find somewhere to live."

"That is not exactly what I had in mind but yes I can do that." I laughed.

"So what did you have in mind?"

"I am not sure, but if you are open to it I can plan a couple of days for us, nothing fancy but some day trips. What do you think?" I thought for a moment then said,

"Okay I am game. You plan and I will be ready to go." The past couple of weeks have been great. I was feeling more and more comfortable with Curtis and I really enjoyed spending time with him.

"Great I will make some plans. One more thing. What are your plans for Christmas?"

"I'm actually going to Toni's house tomorrow for a few days. Robin's kids and grandkids are coming in for the holiday. I planned to spend it with Toni and the kids. You and I had not discussed it and I did not want to assume anything."

"It is fine. Honestly, I wanted to invite you over here, but I was not sure because the holidays have been rough for us, so I wanted our first Christmas together to be nice." I blushed and said,

"I understand and it is fine. I am sure if you wanted to Toni would not mind if you came over for dinner."

"That is a possibility but let me see what my son plans to do. I am sure Shannon would love to spend time with you, but it may have to be a decision made that day because of how her moods are at times."

"I will mention it to Toni and just let me know when you know if you are going to come or not."

"That sounds like a plan. I am going to let you go and will talk to you tomorrow."

"Okay, Curtis have a good night."

"Thanks, you too." I was very happy that Joy is open to allowing me to plan some special days for us. I am also excited about the possibility of us spending Christmas together this year.

I ended the call and Robin was staring at me grinning from ear to ear.

"What?"

"Oh Joy, I think you are in love."

"Oh please, Robin, stop it."

"Listen Joy, I know that look and it is definitely the look of love."

"I do not know about love, but I do enjoy Curtis' company and I am just trying to go with the flow to see what happens."

"Okay, we will see what happens." She said still smiling as she sashayed into the kitchen.

I thought about my conversation with Curtis and I was intrigued by what he might come up with for our day trips. Maybe Robin was right. I was a little fond of Curtis. Robin returned and said,

"Oh yeah, I meant to tell you I thought about what you and I talked about regarding Miles and I will invite him over to dinner."

"Oh that will be great, Robin. I know he does not have anyone, and he has been a little down lately. I thought since he and your son were around the same age it would be a good fit. Miles needs some friends."

"I spoke to Ray and he was open to it. I will contact Miles a little later and invite him over."

"Great, thanks Robin."

*****

I did not realize how much I missed spending Christmas with my family. For so many years I sat alone in my house in Virginia working or doing anything to forget about the fact that most everyone else was enjoying the holiday with their families. Toni invited me every year and I always found an excuse not to come. I did not want to drive alone because it was too far, too cold, or the weather was bad. After the day we had today I will never miss another holiday with my family on purpose. I received a text message from Valerie earlier and she too is having a wonderful holiday with her family this year. She also mentioned that she finally connected with Brandon and she seemed very happy about that as well.

Toni made a huge breakfast and we all ate until we were stuffed. We exchanged gifts and then I went to my room for a nap. When I woke up, I had a text message from Curtis telling me he was coming over for dinner. I jumped up and ran downstairs to let Toni know we were having guests after all. I helped Toni in the kitchen until it was time for me to get ready. Now that Curtis was coming it meant I had to dress to impress.

Curtis arrived right on time. I was so happy to see Shannon and his son Stanley both came with him. I introduced everyone and Darien and Denise entertained our guests while Toni and I finished getting everything ready. Once we were all set, we called everyone into the dining room. Curtis blessed the food and we ate, laughed, and had a great time. I smiled as I recalled the memory of Toni telling me the first day I she saw Curtis and I together in church that he was interested in me. Of course she was right.

As if he could read my mind he reached over and placed his hand on top of mine and said, "Thanks so much for inviting us. This is the best Christmas we have had in a long time."

I smiled. "You are welcome, and I agree this is the best Christmas I have had in a long time as well."

After dinner Curtis and I helped Toni in the kitchen even though she tried to refuse our help several times. The kids all watched Christmas specials in the family room. After we were finished in the kitchen Curtis, Toni and I joined the kids in the family room. Toni led us all as we began to sing Christmas carols together.

We were interrupted by my cell phone. I took my phone out of my pocket.

"It's Robin; I better answer it."

"Hey Robin."

"Joy, there has been an accident. You need to come to the hospital right away."

"Wait, Robin what happened? Are you okay?"

"Yes, I am fine, it's Miles. Just hurry."

"What hospital?"

"The trauma center."

"I am leaving now." I hung up the phone and started walking towards the door. Curtis was following close behind me.

"Joy what is wrong?"

"I have to get to the hospital now."

"What happened?"

"I am not sure, but Robin said there was an accident and I need to get there right away."

"Okay I will drive you there but who is hurt?"

"It's Miles."

"Miles? Okay which hospital?"

"The trauma center." Toni and the kids stood by listening to our entire exchange. Toni said,

"You guys go. The kids and I will be fine." Stanley chimed in,

"Dad, I can drive Shannon home if you want." Curtis thought for a minute and said,

"Yeah okay I will drive Joy's car. Here are my keys. Drive straight home and do not go anywhere else." Stanley nodded and took the keys from Curtis. We turned and left. Once we got in the car Curtis began asking more questions.

"Do you have any idea why Robin would have been with Miles?"

"Yes, Miles was having dinner with Robin and her family."

"Oh, I see. Did she say what kind of accident?"

"No, Curtis she did not say, just hurry to the trauma center." He sensed I was getting irritated and reached over and grabbed my hand. We rode in silence the remainder of the way to the hospital.

Chapter 28

Joy,

I just wanted to update you on how everything has been going for me over the holidays. The past few weeks I struggled to hold back my tears while I was at church. It is hard to see families together I have known for years because I start getting upset since I feel mine was ripped apart. I know things were not good with Seth for a long time and I am better being on my own, but it is still really hard to deal with.

I did not want to be home two days before Christmas since this is when we used to have our big party, so I decided I would go to my house in Charlottesville even if I was alone. A few days before that I thought about how it really has been nice getting back in touch with people thru Facebook and thought about Brandon since it looked like he lived close to Charlottesville. I sent him a connection request and then we started messaging each other. He was going to be around when I was getting into town and we decided to meet up as I mentioned in my text to you. I was definitely a little nervous since I did not know how things would go after not seeing him for so long, and I also had not been out with anyone over the past year since things ended with Seth. I decided I was just going to see how things went with Brandon and looked forward to catching up with him. He was always open and direct so I felt like I could tell him what I had been through. Brandon was very understanding so I hope we stay in touch at least as friends although I may be interested in exploring if there is more there since I found I was definitely still attracted to him.

Scott met up with me at our Charlottesville house the next day on Christmas Eve after he spent time with his dad and then we traveled together for the holiday. I was incredibly grateful Scott, David, and his girlfriend went to church with me on Christmas Day. We then went to my parents' house for dinner and I got to see my brother and his family. It was just so nice to have a relaxing holiday. Scott and I also took a short trip to see UVA play in a bowl game and had a great time. I did get to see Brandon for a few minutes when he stopped by where we were tailgating. We have been texting back and forth almost every day since we got together, so I guess I will just have to see where that goes. I am trying to relax and have fun even though it is in my nature to be a planner.

Valerie

After rereading the email I had received from Valerie just after New Year's I stood up and I paced back and forth as I tried to mentally prepare myself for my session with Valerie. I honestly felt as though she was handling the holidays very well all things considered. She has made great progress over the past few months but the first holiday season after a major family life change is always the most difficult.

The past two weeks have been tough. Up until two days ago I have been at the hospital around the clock watching over Miles. The doctors finally reduced his sedation enough for him to wake up. They finally feel he is out of the woods and now we can focus on the next phase, which is healing and rehabilitation. It was touch and go for the first couple of days.

We still really do not know exactly what happened, but Miles's car ended up running head on into a tree. The police did find skid marks from another vehicle, but they left the scene. When they arrived there was only Miles's car there. He had a broken leg, a few broken ribs, and a concussion. He also had internal bleeding. I shuddered as the image of his car flashed in my memory. I could not believe he survived it. His car was almost split into two pieces.

Robin's son Ray left her house about 10 minutes after Miles left. He came upon the accident scene, recognized Miles's car and called Robin right away. Robin and Toni have both been so supportive during this time taking turns sitting with me at the hospital. Curtis hung in there with me the first couple of days, but he has faded into the background now. I know he has to work, and I do too for that matter. I have yet to return to the office, but I am going to have to do that soon. I have been working from Robin's house this week and spending as much time as possible at the hospital with Miles. Robin says she understands especially since he does not have any family to support him, but she has cautioned me to consider how Curtis might feel. I understood Robin's concerns, but honestly this is very difficult for me. I would much rather be spending my time focusing on building my relationship with Curtis, but I know that Miles doesn't have anyone else. After my session with Valerie, I am going back to the hospital to talk to the doctors about his therapy and what comes next.

When Valerie scheduled her appointment for today, she let me know it would be her last session. I was truly going to miss talking with her and was looking forward to hearing her plans. I connected and was happy to see Valerie smiling.

"Hi Valerie. I saw this is the last appointment you have, and you feel you are good with that."

"I am. I have really appreciated everything you have done for me, Joy. Things have really been turning around well for me."

"That is great to hear. Did you have any luck with your job search?"

"Actually, I did. I had a second interview earlier this week at a company right by UVA and accepted the offer yesterday. I start in two weeks and already gave my notice. I am so excited to have a fresh start."

"That is wonderful. How about your house? I know sometimes it can be hard to sell a house around the holidays. I am actually doing that myself so I can relate."

"I accepted an offer on the house and the closing is later this month. I have scheduled the moving company to pick up everything from my house this Friday. The boys headed back to college and all their stuff is ready to go. I have gotten tremendous help from friends to get everything packed up. I am sure there will be stuff to go through and get rid of to truly make the place in Charlottesville my own."

I could see her start to tear up a bit since it seems leaving is starting to hit her, so I let her cry, but it was tears of joy.

"I am sure it will take you some time. I am really happy for you. It sounds like you have wonderful friends and it seems like everything is coming together. I saw your email about the holidays, and you mentioned reconnecting with Brandon. Have you seen him since then?"

"He helped me get some of my boxes to Charlottesville when he was passing by Chatham last weekend. We are actually going to a basketball game together when I get back there later this week."

"That sounds like fun."

"It should be, and I am just going to see where things go for now. I am looking forward to having a good time."

"I am so happy for you Valerie. I really feel we have made a great connection over the past year. Feel free to reach out anytime."

"Thanks Joy. I really appreciate that, and you have helped me tremendously. There is one other thing I wanted to mention. I am planning on picking up my medical records at the hospital when I come back for the house closing. I just think that will help give me closure to have the details of what happened."

"I see and I hope you get what you need from that. It may stir up some things and please do not hesitate to reach out to me if you need to talk. It truly has been a pleasure."

"Thanks Joy, and good luck with your move as well."

"See you, Valerie."

I really am going to miss her, but she seems to be in a good place and really has come out such a stronger person after her experiences. I truly feel that she has finally realized that the most important form of love is self-love. You absolutely need to learn how to love yourself before you can give or expect to receive love from anyone else. She also seems to have a good support system. I hope she reaches out someday, but that will be up to her. I hope that getting her medical records does not set her back in her healing process.

She may require some additional therapy after going through those. I also hope that she finds what she needs from her relationship with Brandon. Working with her over the past almost year has truly impacted my life. Sometimes when we are having trouble recognizing what we need to heal God has a way of putting it right in front of us.

As I prepared to leave to go to the hospital my cell phone rang. I grabbed it out of my purse and was pleasantly surprised to see it was Curtis calling.

"Hello, Curtis."

"Hi, Joy. Where are you?"

"I am at Robin's house right now but am getting ready to head back down to the hospital. Everything okay?"

"Ah, yeah, everything is fine. I was just hoping you and I could get some time to talk."

"Of course Curtis, we can talk anytime."

"It is just lately you have been so preoccupied with Miles and always at the hospital I feel like we are drifting apart."

I sighed and said, "I know what you mean and honestly I feel the same way. I am not sure what to do about it right now though. Miles does not have any family Curtis. I cannot abandon him."

"I understand and I would not want you to abandon him, but we were just starting to make some progress in our relationship."

"Yes, I know. I should have a better idea after the meeting with his doctors this afternoon about exactly what type of support he is going to need. Maybe I can call you back later after I talk to the doctors?"

"Okay, yes, that sounds good."

"I'll talk to you later."

After I ended the call with Curtis, I put my phone in my purse and immediately headed out the door. Toni was planning on meeting me there to be my support person. Before starting to drive I sent her a quick text letting her know I was running a few minutes late. She responded okay already here, be safe but hurry up.

"As I walked off the elevator, I heard machines beeping and people scurrying all over the place. I turned towards Miles' room and saw Toni covering her face headed towards me. I rushed to her.

"Toni, what's wrong?"

She was shaking her head and finally said, "Joy, I am sorry, but I cannot stay here. This is too much like Darien." She pushed her way past me towards the elevators and I followed behind her.

"Okay but what happened?"

She pressed the elevator button and turned to me. "He started having a seizure, so I called the nurse in and then his machines started beeping and more people came into the room. They told me to get out. I am not sure exactly what is happening Joy, but you need to get in there. I am going to go downstairs and wait down there. I just cannot be up here in the middle of all of this."

I gave her a quick hug as the elevator arrived and then turned and sprinted back towards Miles' room. His bed was gone, so I turned and went to the nurse's station. His nurse was not there but the other nurse told me to go to the waiting room and someone would come and talk to me as soon as they knew anything.

Several hours later I had fallen asleep on the waiting room sofa. I felt a gentle nudge and slowly opened my eyes. It was Mile's nurse.

"Ms. Dickerson. The doctor is ready to see you now." I sat up, gathered my things, and followed her to a small room beside the nurse's station. The doctor was already there waiting for us.

He motioned for me to sit down and the nurse closed the door behind us. He began, "Ms. Dickerson, Miles is stable again, but he gave us all quite a scare. He is having some swelling in his brain which caused the seizure your friend witnessed. We have put a small shunt in to help relieve the pressure. We are going to have to monitor him very closely over the next 24 hours."

"Okay, doctor, are there any other concerns?"

"As of right now our main concern is getting the swelling under control."

"I was planning to talk to you today about his prognosis. Any idea when he will leave here and what type of support he will need at home?"

"It is too early to say, but I would expect once he leaves here, he will need to go to a rehab facility initially. I do not see him being at home for another month or two."

"Oh I see; well thank you doctor so much for your time. Am I able to see him now?"

"I think it is best to let him rest. Why don't you go home and come back tomorrow? If there is any change, we will contact you."

"Thanks again doctor." I turned to the nurse. "Please make sure you call me if anything changes." She nodded as I left the room. I went downstairs to find Toni and she was exactly where she said she would be. When she saw me approaching, she stood up and then I noticed Curtis approaching also.

They both asked almost in unison, "How is he?"

"He's stable for now. They ended up putting a shunt in because his brain began to swell again."

Toni began shaking her head. "Joy, I am trying my best to be here for you, but this is too much for me. It is like I am reliving what happened with Darien all over again." She began to sob, and I hugged her.

"Toni, I understand, and it is okay. I really appreciate you trying to be here for me, but I know this is too much. It will be fine. I am actually about to leave now. The doctor suggested I let him rest for today and come back to visit him tomorrow."

Curtis chimed in, "Okay, that sounds like a great idea. You have both been spending a lot of time here and you need a break."

Toni gathered her things and we all walked out to the parking garage together. Toni seemed to have calmed down by the time we got to her car. I promised to keep her posted. Curtis and I watched as she drove off.

He then turned to me and said, "Joy, I want to follow you back to Robin's house because we need to talk."

I was too exhausted to argue. I simply nodded my head and walked towards my car.

Back to Robin's house Curtis and I decided to talk in my room to have more privacy. I was so emotionally and physically drained I just let him drive the conversation. At first, he just stared at me. Then he got up and began pacing back and forth. Finally he stopped right in front of me and said, "Joy, I have a lot to say and I want you to promise me to listen to everything before you respond to me okay?"

I nodded my head and he continued, "This may surprise you; I am in love with you. I want to be with you. This situation with Miles is a very difficult one. We are both close friends of his and he has absolutely no one else. I know in the past I have appeared to be very indifferent towards him, but I realize I need to be by your side with this." He paused for a moment, so I raised my hand and he said, "Yes Joy."

"Can I say something now?"

He smiled. "Yes of course."

"First of all I am not surprised you are in love with me because I am in love with you too. Second, I have to ask you are you sure about this because I fear Miles has a very long road to recovery ahead. If we are going to be in this together you have to stick it out with me until the finish line."

Curtis walked over to me, knelt down, and cupped my face with both of his hands.

"Did you say you loved me too?"

I smiled. "Yes, I did and yes, I do." He pulled me up into his arms and picked me up and swung me around.

I began giggling and screaming, "Curtis, put me down."

He put me down just as Robin knocked on the door.

"Come in."

She peaked her head through the cracked door.

"Is everything okay in here?"

Curtis smiled. "Everything is just fine, and Joy loves me too."

The END

Epilogue

Nine Months Later

I sat at my desk reading through my old journal entries and reflecting on the past year while I waited for Curtis to arrive. Today we were going to sign the lease for my new office space. So much has happened over the past nine months. It was hard to believe I have been back in Pennsylvania full time for that long already. The first six months were very grueling and stressful, but we all made it through. Miles is finally back home and back to work.

Somehow, I managed to sell my house in Virginia quickly and for a decent price. I was able to finish the necessary hours to qualify for benefits in June. The workshops have been a huge success and we are now offering monthly workshops at various churches in the community. My dream of opening my own counseling office is coming true. Things with Curtis are great. He really stuck to his word and was with me every step of the way as I supported Miles in his recovery. Our relationship is exactly what I need in my life. We have a good balance of mutual respect and love for one another. Even though my house has been sold I am still living with Robin officially. I spent several months at Miles' house, but for now I am going to stay here with Robin. Curtis convinced me not to buy anything right now. He just keeps telling me to wait and for now I am very comfortable with how things are.

It is hard for me to think about all the changes in my life over the past year without also thinking about Valerie.

Of all the clients I have worked with over the past year she was my favorite, the one who had the most impact on my life and I'd like to think that I also impacted hers. Although we are no longer professionally connected, I do hear from her occasionally through emails or text messages.

Valerie seems to be in a really good place in her life overall. Her new job allows her to finally have the work/life balance she needs. She is able to spend time focusing on herself and what she wants to do for the first time in a very long time. She has continued with boxing as a form of exercise and stress relief as well as walking. Shortly after we discontinued our sessions, she did resume in person therapy with someone else to continue working through her issues with post-traumatic stress disorder (PTSD).

She did pursue and finally get copies of her hospital records. She was determined to put together all the pieces of the puzzle as to how she ended up being committed. This has raised some additional questions about those close to her even though they had the best intentions. Valerie has continued doing research on her own and has uncovered that many of the symptoms encountered during trauma and extremely similar to what would be exhibited by a person with a bipolar diagnosis, but the treatment could be vastly different. She is still trying to find out more about options to help victims and their loved ones during traumatic experiences obtain the care which is customized to what each individual is looking for to help them best through their own situation. She fought but unfortunately was not able to get her commitment expunged. She is still a little unhappy about that for a variety of reasons, but one of them being that she has lost her right to own a gun for the rest of her life. She expressed to me that she has never actually touched a gun, but she does not like the idea of decisions being made for her that were outside of her control.

One major victory for Valerie was that she did file her paperwork for an annulment with the Catholic church and she received an affirmative decision in a little less than a year. Being able to marry again if that becomes a possibility in the church was particularly important to her. It also means that she is finally seen as no longer bonded with Seth in the eyes of the church. It seems she is understanding the concept of self-love and focusing on her own happiness. She is in a relationship with Brandon and he has been incredibly supportive. She tells me that he makes her smile and she is able to relax and put her guard down with him which is amazing.

Overall, she has realized that everyone really cared for her. They just did not know what to do when she was trying to work through her emotions of the trauma she experienced from Seth's betrayal.

I heard Curtis pull up outside. I grabbed my phone and sent him a quick text telling him I would be right out.

I gathered my things and headed out to meet Curtis. As I walked towards the car his smile widened and he got out to open my door for me. I leaned in for a quick kiss on his cheek before getting into the car. Life has a way of giving us exactly what we need when we need it. I believe I am living proof good things do eventually come to those who wait.

Discussion Questions

1. Which character, Valerie or Joy did you most connect with?

2. What feelings did this book evoke for you?

3. Which part of the book stood out to you most?

4. How do you feel about how the story was told?

5. How well did you feel Valerie handled the situation with her neighbor?

6. Do you feel that Valerie's sessions with Joy were helpful?

7. What are your thoughts on how Joy handled her issues while attempting to work with Valerie?

8. Do you think Valerie should have acted differently towards Seth?

9. Should Joy have given Miles a second chance instead of getting together with Curtis?

10. If you got the chance to ask the authors of this book one question, what would it be?

11. If you needed a therapist would you consider seeing Joy? Why or why not?

12. An overall thought on the book and the authors writing style.

Connect with Us

Terri D and Julie both want to say thank you for taking the time to read our book. We both hope you really enjoyed it and ask that you please leave us an honest review on Amazon.

We would love to hear from you, so please connect with us via our websites, Facebook, Instagram, or Twitter.

Terri D's information:

Website: www.authorterrid.com
Facebook: https://www.facebook.com/AuthorTerriD
Instagram: https://www.instagram.com/author_terri_d/
Twitter: https://twitter.com/AuthorTerriD

Julie's information:

Website: https://juliebellatrix.com/
Facebook: https://www.facebook.com/JulieBellatrix/
Instagram: https://www.instagram.com/juliebtdub/
Twitter: https://twitter.com/juliebellatrix

Closing Notes and References

Although this is a work of fiction, we discussed some very serious topics in this book.

If you, or someone you know, needs help with any of the topics listed below, we have included a few resources that may be able to assist you.

Trauma:

Traumatic Events: https://www.nimh.nih.gov/health/topics/coping-with-traumatic-events/index.shtml

PTSD: https://www.nimh.nih.gov/health/topics/post-traumatic-stress-disorder-ptsd/index.shtml

Therapy:

Therapy: https://www.nimh.nih.gov/health/topics/psychotherapies/index.shtml

Black Girl Therapy: https://therapyforblackgirls.com/

STDs:

Center for Disease Control and Prevention: https://www.cdc.gov/std/

Sexual Assault and Domestic Violence:

National Sexual Violence Resource Center: https://www.nsvrc.org/

National Center on Domestic and Sexual Violence: http://www.ncdsv.org/

National Resource Center on Domestic Violence: https://www.nrcdv.org/